The Book of the Baku

The Book of the Baku

R. L. Boyle

TITAN BOOKS

The Book of the Baku
Paperback edition ISBN: 9781789096606
E-book edition ISBN: 9781789096613

Published by Titan Books
A division of Titan Publishing Group Ltd
144 Southwark Street, London SE1 0UP
www.titanbooks.com

First Titan edition: June 2021
10 9 8 7 6 5 4 3 2 1

This is a work of fiction. All of the characters, organizations, and events portrayed in this novel are either products of the author's imagination or are used fictitiously.

A CIP catalogue record for this title is available from the British Library.
Printed and bound by CPI Group (UK) Ltd, Croydon, CR0 4YY.

The Book of the Baku

For Owen

NOW

Some stories are true that never happened.

ELIE WIESEL

Sean runs through the garden, his only thought to put as much distance as he can between himself and his pursuer. Rain pours down the back of his neck, and his torch slices the blackness as he pumps his arms, a rapid seesawing blade of light. He fights a path through the bracken, heedless of the way it scratches and tears at his skin, gritting his teeth against the pain in his swollen knee.

He slams into the door of the shed as he hears an abrasive grating. Without looking, he knows the stone cherubs have turned to watch him. He tries to slide the key into the lock, but his hand is shaking too much.

Snatching a glance over his shoulder, he sees the figure coast towards him, not twenty paces away now. It glides as smoothly as if it were moving on runners. Though the rain-thrashed garden is otherwise clear of mist, the figure rides upon a thick bank of fog that obscures it from the waist down.

With a sob Sean turns back to the door and uses both hands to guide the key home. The lock clicks open and he is inside. He slams the door behind him, locks it, then grabs the chair and wedges it beneath the door handle, before backing away.

He strains to hear over the muffled thump of his own heartbeat, his ragged breath, the rain drumming on the corrugated roof of the shed, the wind whisking the trees. He is trapped. Trapped by the thing waiting for him on the other side of the door.

Knock.

Knock.

Knock.

Sean's horror swells. He jumps back and bangs his hip against the edge of the desk, knocking the pages of Grandad's manuscript to the floor. His legs crumble like dry sand. Huddled on the ground in a puddle of scattered papers, he points the muzzle of his gun at the door.

He is soaked in sweat.

Shuddering.

He shakes his head slowly from side to side. This can't be happening. This can't be real.

A sudden burst of static erupts from the old radio on the desk. It fades, as though tuned by an invisible hand, to the voice of a male broadcaster.

'Has died in her 102nd year. Buckingham Palace said the end was peaceful, and the Queen was at her side. Members of the royal family—'

Sean's eyes trace the length of the cord, which lies on the floor like a dead snake. Plug pins pointing upwards towards the ceiling. Drawing electricity only from the air's malignant energy.

Knock.

Knock.

Knock.

Chills ripple over his skin. Breathing hard, he tightens his finger on the trigger, ignoring the sly whisper in his thoughts that says there is nothing he can do to protect himself.

'"She was," he said, "admired by all people, of all ages and backgrounds, revered within our borders and beyond." Parliament is to be recalled for MPs to pay their tributes next week. The Queen Mother's body will be—'

The broadcaster's voice sounds old-fashioned, laced with the elegance of a bygone era.

Knock.

Knock.

Knock.

'...who, at times, had seemed so indestructible, but whose life finally ebbed away at a quarter past three this afternoon. She died at her home close to the castle, where she'd been since the funeral of her younger daughter, Princess Margaret—'

The key pops out of the lock, lands with a dull *thunk* on the floor. Blowflies stream through the gap in the keyhole, the low drone of their beating wings accompanying the basal chord of Sean's own horror. They darken every surface, an undulating mass that makes the room pulse like a living thing.

The door handle begins to turn.

Sean's heart slams into his sternum. He wants to press his eyes closed and pretend he is somewhere else, somewhere bright and loud and warm, or just somewhere – *anywhere* – far away from here.

But he can't look away.

Can't move.

A tear tracks a path down his cheek, like the tip of an ice-cold finger. He stares at the door handle as it twists, knowing what stands on the other side, knowing what has come for him.

The Baku.

BEFORE

For as long as he can remember, Sean has been curious about his grandad, but he never expected to actually meet him.

Mr Collins, one of Creswick Hall's in-house psychotherapists, introduces them in a private room, then quickly makes himself scarce. Sean sits across from Grandad and studies his face over the two cups of tea that cool between them, seeking the family resemblance.

The old man doesn't really look like Mum, but Sean catches glimmers of her in his expression, jigsaw pieces that match two faces. The shape of his eyes, the rounded nose, the dimple in his left cheek. Sean sees Mum's face flickering beneath the surface of his skin, haunting him.

The old man's face is weather-beaten, wrinkles crease the skin around his blue eyes. White hair explodes from his head, Albert Einstein on a bad hair day. And he is tall – BFG tall – but with a curve to his shoulders that softens the severity of his otherwise imposing appearance. His grizzled eyebrows twitch and jerk with his every changing thought, like two fat caterpillars on steroids.

Sean likes his voice right away. Deep and low, it's the sort of voice you just can't imagine raised in anger, because it would pulverise your teeth and blow your socks clean off. The old man has charisma, even if he is about one hundred and seventy years old. A Gandalf-like twinkle animates his eyes, and he seems to fill the room with his presence.

Sean listens as Grandad tells him he has a house with a conservatory that will be perfect for his sketching, that he's bought him a wooden carving set so he can learn to sculpt. He hopes he has the right materials, but if there's anything he needs, all he has to do is let him know. He wasn't sure what to get because he'd never been much of an artist. An author, yes, but that was many years ago now. He knows Sean doesn't want to return to his old school so he has enrolled him at Allerton Mills, a local school with a great Ofsted report. He has even met with the headteacher, a lovely lady who knows all about his… circumstances. He has a library, too, did he mention that before?

He really does think Sean will get along just fine.

Everything is going to be alright.

Sean lets Grandad's velvet voice wrap around him, tucking him up against all the world.

But he does not say a word.

DAY 1

Grandad seems jittery when he comes to collect Sean from Creswick Hall, even though he has visited many times since their first meeting two months ago. He misplaces his car keys, only to discover after a great deal of searching that he's left them in the car's ignition all along, and he twice tells the story of how, that very morning, he found a pregnant hedgehog trapped in his garden fence. Sean feels a bolt of pity for the old man. It must be a shock at his age, taking on the care of a mute, partially-crippled thirteen-year-old boy. It would be strange if he *wasn't* feeling nervous.

He slings his suitcase in the car boot. He hasn't brought much with him: clothes, painkillers, his knee brace, acrylic paints and well-worn paintbrushes. The clay robin he sculpted for Mum. And the gun. He wants to get rid of it, but throwing it in the garbage doesn't seem like the right thing to do and he definitely can't leave it lying around. Its presence makes him feel nervous and grubby, but he tells himself if he keeps hold of it, at least it won't fall into the wrong hands.

He gets into the car beside Grandad. His feet dangle over the edge of the seat like a little kid's. He's going to be fourteen in just a few weeks, but he wouldn't look amiss in a class of ten-year-olds. It's embarrassing. His left foot hangs a full three inches further from the floor than the right. He abhors his deformity. It is always the first thing people notice about him, their eyes dragging down his body, lingering on the twists of his legs, as though they are all there is of him.

When Mum had asked the doctors why Sean had been born with arthrogryposis, the condition that twists his legs into the shape of hockey stick ends, they were unable to answer. Random mutations are rare, but not impossible. Even with no genetic link, such things could occur.

In other words, it was just bad luck.

Sean has lost count of the number of surgeries he has undergone to straighten and lengthen his left leg. Now, his knee looks as though it has been through a mangler, and his legs are so severely scarred the thought of wearing shorts makes him break out in a nervous sweat. He called an end to the operations last year, resigning himself to an eternal limp and a measure of daily pain to save himself from the agony of further procedures. Mum had tried to persuade him to carry on, but not for long and not with any real fervour. She, better than anyone, knew he'd had enough.

In the car, Grandad fills the silence with nervous chatter, but Sean barely hears him. Words are white noise to him, broadcast on a frequency he has learned to filter out. His thumb circles the scar on the back of his hand as Grandad drives.

They pass the outskirts of Dulwood, the estate Sean grew up on, and the sight of it makes his chest ache. When they stop at the traffic lights, he sees Arlo's little sister, Holly, skipping across the road in that funny way she has, every fourth step a shoe-scuffing shuffle. She's carrying a paper bag from The Codfather and Sean realises it's Fish-and-Chips Friday. Mel, Arlo's mum, never needed to ask Sean what he wanted – a battered sausage with chips. For Arlo, it was XL haddock with mushy peas and an oven bottom cake. Holly, on the other hand, insisted upon studying the menu in the shop, taking her time to decide, as though she were sampling food from a Michelin-star restaurant. When Arlo and Sean teased her, she would shower them with insults, her brilliant mind spinning out quick-witted vitriol that would have made even the hardest lads on the estate cringe and hide their faces in their hoodies.

The traffic lights change.

Grandad drives on.

Sean twists in his seat to watch Holly, but she has turned down her street and he can't see her anymore.

Less than fifteen minutes later, Grandad drives through the small village of Bockleside where he lives. It's a much nicer neighbourhood than Dulwood. The houses don't have bars across the windows for one thing, and instead of high-rise blocks of flats the properties are all detached, separated by fences and walls. Intercoms built into stone posts frame high iron gates. The roundabouts are planted with neat rows of flowers and there are splashes of colour everywhere. Sean thinks of Dulwood, where everything is grey and sad-looking and the only flowers people tended are the ones they've left by the lamppost outside Chubb's Keys, where Spaceboy was run over and killed by joyriders.

The teenagers walking home from school in this neighbourhood wear blazers and polished smiles. Sean can't see what they carry in their pockets, but he doubts they contain switch-blades or small bags of powder. He wonders if any of them are on first name terms with the local coppers, like he and his mates on Dulwood are.

They pass a large Tesco, and a park with huge wrought-iron gates. Sean's thoughts turn – as they have turned many times over the past few months – to how close Grandad's house is to his old estate. He wonders what happened between Mum and Grandad to make her cut him off the way she had. What could have been so terrible that she never visited him, never called?

If only Mum had stayed in touch with Grandad, things could've been so different. I could have been one of those lads, neat clothes, easy grin. What would Mum say if she could see me now? What did Grandad do to make her hate him so much?

Sean shakes the thought away.

Mum isn't here.

Stupid to even think of her now.

Grandad takes a left turn onto a private driveway. Gravel crunches beneath the car wheels. The grass fringing the drive is overgrown, the flowers are wild. The road ends in front of an imposing house, a towering edifice of age-blackened stone. Automatic sprinklers water the grass, ivy snakes the walls.

Sean follows Grandad down a narrow path that cuts through a manicured lawn to the front door. His eyes move everywhere, taking everything in. The natural scruffiness of the driveway with its overgrown weeds and wild flowers contrasts with the neat grass and tidy flower beds around Grandad's house. Sean wonders what this means, if it means anything at all. Perhaps the old man simply can't be bothered to tend the entire driveway, or perhaps he is a loner, deliberately cutting himself off from the rest of the world, unconcerned with the things that lie too far beyond his own front door.

Grandad slides a key into the lock of the front door. Built from solid oak, punched with black studs and enforced with cast-iron hinges, it looks more like the entrance to a castle than an ordinary house. A wooden sign reading *The Paddock* is mounted above it.

Sean tries not to gawp, but he feels like he has stepped into a time machine and been spat out in the seventies. He is stood in a hallway that is easily as big as the front room in his old flat. The carpet is patterned in green Aztec, a blur of shades that feel as though they are shifting beneath his feet, and the wallpaper is an ugly mush of geometric browns and oranges. A wide staircase sweeps up to the second floor.

Grandad hangs his keys on a rack above a side table. There are other keys on the hooks, but only one of them catches Sean's eye: a long, narrow key. The crenelated ridges of the age-blackened brass are like grimy teeth in a shattered grin. Looking at it makes Sean's stomach clench.

Grandad is talking to him, but the old man's words blur and dim under the thump of Sean's pulse. The key grows sharper, almost psychedelic in its clarity, while everything else in the hallway fades. He has to force himself to wrench his eyes from it.

'—haven't decorated a room for you yet, thought you might prefer to choose one yourself,' Grandad is saying. 'That way you can do it up however you want to. Oh, and before I forget, Miraede will be popping over tomorrow. I think she just wants to see that you've settled in alright. Anyway, why don't you look around and I'll go make us a cuppa.'

Words of gratitude waltz through Sean's thoughts in a perfectly ordered procession, but when he opens his mouth to frame them, they turn to wet cement in his throat. It is as though each unspoken sentence dries to create a thicker barrier for those behind it, and now his voice is blocked behind an impenetrable concrete wall.

The doctors and specialists explained his conversion disorder as '*a way of displaying psychological distress in a physical manner to deal with a trauma*'. The condition, they said, could manifest in different ways. Some sufferers lose their vision, some lose their hearing or their sense of smell, while others suffer paralysis.

Sean lost the ability to speak.

Grandad walks down the hall, leaving Sean alone in the hallway. The wall's ugly colours swirl around him, making him feel as though he is stood in a funhouse corridor. He opens the nearest door and walks into a vast dining room. Dust sheets are thrown over some of the furniture and Sean imagines the shapes beneath coming alive at night, dancing through the house beneath their blankets. He quickly closes the door and moves down the hall to the next room, which is just as empty and unlived in as the last.

What am I doing here? If I'd passed the old man on the street a few months ago, I wouldn't have looked at him twice. Maybe I did pass him on the street! It's not as though he lives that far from Dulwood.

The tightness in his chest slackens a notch when he steps into a library. Smaller than the other rooms, it is made cosy by a log fire and two green and orange checked sofas. The walls are lined with books and an oriental rug covers the wooden floorboards. Traces of life provide a comfort Sean had not realised he had been seeking until he found it: half a cup of cold tea on the table; a rumpled blanket tossed over the sofa; logs in a wicker basket beside the fireplace; a messy pile of paperwork beside a computer. Sean catches a glimpse of a patio through slits in the blinds.

He moves to the bookcases. There are crime novels, gardening books, classics, memoirs. He starts pulling random titles down, examining their covers, sometimes reading the blurbs. Those that intrigue him, he keeps stacked in one hand. Sean notices a few of the books have Grandad's name embossed on the front. *Elbert Blake*. He had forgotten Grandad used to be an author.

He trails a fingertip across the spines, tracing a line in the soft patina of dust. A sudden static shock makes him jump. He frowns, his eyes hesitating on the bookshelf. His fingertip tingles; the bones of his hand hum, like the tines of a struck tuning fork.

He pulls a book from the shelf.

It is a hardback entitled *The Baku: A Selection of Short Stories.* The front cover depicts a statue of a beast mounted on a plinth. The head of an elephant, merging at the neck with the body of a man. Its chin is dipped in a predatory pose and its wrinkled trunk, gnarled and scabrous, hangs between its nipples. Its elephant ears are latticed with capillaries, their thinning edges ripped and frayed. Curved yellow tusks protrude from its jaws, twin scythes stropped to a fine point. Its wide neck and shoulders are corded with thick veins that are engorged with dark blue blood. There is something insane inside the beast's eyes, something terrible and timeless.

On the inside cover, there is a list of the short stories in the collection. Sean flips the book over and reads the back of the jacket.

When fears escape the burning pit,
And evils you did not commit,
Torment your dreams and steal your peace,
Your innocence screams for release.
The horrors grow, as horrors do,
Each night they boil and swell in you.
You dared not close your eyes to rest,
Or give yourself to sleep's cruel test.
But sleepless nights will take their toll,
They whip your body, break your soul.
And in the end, despite your fight,
You tumble into endless night,
Where blood and tears clog your screams,
There's no escape from your dark dreams.
Slaked in sweat you thrash and shake,
Give anything to finally wake.
No more of this! You've reached your end,
The time has come to tell a friend.
Confide in me, Child, and you'll part
With that terror in your heart.
For there's a darkness deep in me,
That feeds on pain and misery.
Give it to me, relinquish dread,
And fall asleep in peace instead.

Sean feels a delicious thrill of anticipation. He has always found a strange comfort in horror stories, though Mum never approved of his proclivity towards darkness.

There's enough evil in the world, Sean. Why go looking for more of it in books?

Pushing thoughts of Mum from his mind, Sean walks out of the library, *The Baku* tucked into the inside pocket of his jacket, the rest of the books forgotten.

He stops on the staircase to study the photographs that line the wall. Even though Mum never used to talk about Grandad, she occasionally spoke about her own mother, Ocean Storm, who died of cancer when Mum was fourteen years old. Sean can tell from the slivers of Mum he sees in her face that the flame-haired woman in the pictures is her.

In one of the photographs a man stands behind Nanna Storm, his arms circling her waist. It takes a moment for Sean to realise the man is Grandad. His hair is dark, his face unlined, but it isn't his youth that makes Sean feel as though he is looking at a stranger; it is the way he is watching Nanna Storm, smiling in a way Sean has not yet seen. Like there is happiness trapped inside his bones. Nanna Storm is looking into the camera, laughing as a breeze whips threads of fiery hair across her eyes.

In the next photograph, Nanna Storm is holding a chunky toddler. Even though the child bears little resemblance to the woman she will become, Sean knows it is Mum. There are other photographs, too, cataloguing Mum's childhood: lying on a candy pink blanket as a baby, toothless and giggling at the camera; wearing a tulle tutu and a tiara, opening a present beneath a Christmas tree; in her school uniform, gap-toothed and grinning; posing for a professional photograph, Grandad looking slightly stiff, but Nanna Storm beaming unreservedly at the daughter wriggling in her arms. A perfect nuclear family, blissfully happy, unaware of what the future holds for them.

Sean swallows the knot in his throat and moves up the stairs.

The bedrooms are large and gloomy, possessed of the same neglected feeling as the empty rooms downstairs. Heavy brocade curtains are drawn across all the windows, thickening the darkness. Sean chooses a room at the back of the house with an en suite bathroom and a beautiful roll-top desk. There is a wardrobe in one corner, a set of drawers in the other. The bare, dusty light bulb throws out a bruised, sickly light, and even when Sean switches on the tassel lamp by the side of the bed, shadows dominate the room.

He tosses his suitcase onto the bed, opens it and takes out the box that contains his clay robin. He has covered it in bubble-wrap for safekeeping but now he carefully unwraps it and sets it on the window ledge. He takes the gun from his bag, puts it in the bottom drawer, then grabs handfuls of pants and socks from his suitcase and shoves them on top. The bullets, which he keeps in a plastic box, he tucks into the back of the wardrobe.

He leans over the desk and throws the curtains open. Dust swirls from the thick fabric, and when he squints into the sunlight he gasps in surprise.

Grandad's back garden looks like a photograph taken straight out of *Gardener's World*, but not one of those perfectly manicured ones where flowers grow in colour-coordinated squares. Grandad's garden is wild and anarchic and alive.

Half the size of a football pitch, the vast lawn is edged by sloped borders of flower beds that rise and fall like the waves of a windswept ocean. Climbing roses the size of cabbages drape the boundary wall. Blocks of hardy winter vegetables grow in neat rows. A kidney-bean-shaped pond in the middle of the lawn is surrounded by stone slabs, and the huge tree beside it bursts with red berries. A nest swing hangs from one of its thick branches, and beneath its sun-dappled shade there are a table and four chairs. A white-framed greenhouse is nestled in the bushes, near a seating area decorated with potted flowers. Bird baths are dotted around, and as Sean watches, two robins swoop down to jab their beaks at the offerings there.

His gaze wanders to a dilapidated shed in the opposite corner of the garden, half buried beneath overgrown brambles and tree branches.

His breath catches in his throat.

Perhaps it is simply because the building is such an eyesore, but he feels the sudden urge to close his eyes or turn away. He resists, tethered by curiosity. Branches and vines have withered across the shed's walls in a spindly embrace, lichen grows across the blackened windows, like rot over empty eye sockets. Five stone cherubs stand guard at the door, their lower bodies submerged in the tall grass. Their gentle faces smile beneficence, but Sean swears there is something shifty in their mildewing eyes. Something… not quite right.

The silence of the bedroom seems to thicken until it possesses a physical weight. Sean feels exposed. Watched. He spins round, sure there will be someone standing behind him. But, of course, there is no one there.

He takes a deep breath, expels it shakily. Telling himself he is being silly, he heads back downstairs.

'Ah, there you are, lad,' Grandad says, looking up when Sean enters the kitchen, which, with its Formica worktops and brown and cream floor lino, is as much of a homage to the seventies as the rest of the house. 'Come with me, there's something I want to show you.'

Grandad passes him a steaming cup of tea and leads him through the house, stopping in front of a locked door.

'I know from your old art teacher how much you love to sketch and paint,' he says, sliding a key into the lock. 'So I've set up a sort of workshop for you. This is your room now.'

He opens the door and Sean follows him into a spacious conservatory. Sunlight cascades through the sloped glass ceiling, exposed red-brick walls are laced with veins of creeping plants, and a stone lion trickles water into a basin below. A patio door set in a wall of glass leads into the garden. Flowers decorate every shelf and ledge, they hang in baskets from the walls. It's like Grandad scooped up a pocket full of summer before autumn could erode its colour.

Sean's gaze rests on the workbench. A large oak table is laden with art supplies and equipment. There are paints of every variety: oils, acrylics, watercolours, pastels. An exquisite wooden watercolour box, a set of sketching pens, canvasses, brushes and bottles of brush cleaner. Sponges and rollers. A stack of art books. A wooden carving set. Sketchpads. Modelling tools. An easel. Sculpting clay and a roll of armature wire.

'Your art teacher, Mr Donal—'

Mr Dolan.

'—told me that you'd only just started working at sculpture but that you showed great promise. I thought you might want to experiment with it, so that's why I got the clays and the armature wire.'

Sean knows from scrimping and saving for his own supplies that none of it has come cheap. The old man must have spent a fortune on him.

Sean moves to the table, picks up a book. *Michelangelo: The Works of Il Divino.* There are other books, too, about modern artists such as Georgia O'Keeffe and Francis Bacon, Salvador Dalí and Frida Kahlo.

'To be honest, I didn't really know what to get,' Grandad says, his eyes moving over the equipment uncertainly. 'Never been much of an artist myself, but the lady in the shop was very helpful. She said if there was anything you wanted to exchange then it wouldn't be a problem. I've kept all the receipts, so…'

Sean feels Grandad watching him, hears the hesitancy behind his words, the deliberate delicacy of his tone. His kindness loosens something inside Sean. Words of thanks catch in his throat. Grandad nods once, as though he understands. He drops his hand on his grandson's shoulder. The smallest gesture, packed with a world of unspoken words.

DAY 2

When Sean comes downstairs in the morning, Grandad takes him outside to show him the hedgehog he rescued.

As they walk down the path, Sean can't help but marvel at the garden's beauty. Bursts of colour explode against the greenery, wind chimes harmonise with the chirruping birds, foliage rustles beneath a lick of wind. The space works a sort of magic on Sean, makes it easier, somehow, to breathe around the ache in his chest.

They pass the huge, red-berried tree, and Sean notices a gold placard nailed to the trunk: *Ocean Storm 1955–2002*.

As they approach the crate by the wall in which the hedgehog is housed, Grandad presses his finger to his lips – an irony that is not lost on Sean – then crouches down in the tall fronds of grass. Sean kneels beside him and peers into the crate.

The hedgehog is curled in the corner, half buried beneath a heap of leaves and straw. Grandad has attached a water bottle to the side of the crate and left a small pile of what looks like scrambled eggs on a little plate.

'I think she's pregnant.' Grandad's whisper smokes on the cold air. 'Most hedgehogs have their hoglets in the summer months so they have time to bulk up for the winter. I'm afraid this litter will struggle to gain enough weight to survive hibernation. Still, there's a chance one or two of them might survive.'

Sean can tell from Grandad's tone that he does not believe they will. Perhaps he should feel bad for the unborn litter, sorry that the odds of surviving are stacked against them, but he doesn't.

Being vulnerable doesn't make them special; surviving is a struggle for everyone.

Sean is reading *The Baku* while eating his cereal when Grandad comes into the kitchen. The old man's eyebrows jerk up at the sight of the book and the colour drains from his face. Sean looks at him in alarm, but Grandad just presses his lips together and turns away. He sets his cup in the sink then sits at the table with Sean to work through the crossword in the newspaper.

Sean returns to his book. The first short story in the collection is called 'Luca'. Luca is a thirteen-year-old boy who struggles with insomnia and night terrors. For as long as he can remember, he has dreamt of the Mirror-Eyed Man, a tall, stooped and silent figure. Though Luca only ever sees the Mirror-Eyed Man's silhouette in profile, somehow he knows that he must never look into his eyes, that to do so would be to erase sanity and give himself over to horror and madness.

As soon as Luca falls asleep, the Mirror-Eyed Man is there, sliding into his dreams as though he is always waiting on the edge of sleep, anticipating the direction the boy's subconscious will take him. Sometimes, Luca dreams the Mirror-Eyed Man is sat on the edge of his bed or on the wing-backed chair in the hallway, sometimes he is stood in the corner of the kitchen or at the back of his classroom at school. But it is only when the old man lifts his head to look at Luca that the boy wakes up, sweat-soaked and screaming, moments from seeing what is reflected in that black-mirrored gaze.

Luca's mother has consulted doctors, sleep specialists, therapists and hypnotists, but still his nightmares persist. Nothing seems to help, until the day he visits the carnival with his mum and baby sister and sees the Baku, an ivory-carved statue of an elephant-man, which claims to eat the nightmares of children.

Lost in the story, Sean is barely aware of Grandad's presence, just as he is barely aware that his tea has grown cold and his cereal turned to gloopy mush. His spoon travels to the bowl less and less until even his breakfast is forgotten.

Luca stared at the Baku, clutching the sheet of paper upon which he had written his nightmare. Something about the statue made him hesitate to press the note into its mouth. He was reminded of the time he visited Madame Tussaud's. He had been staggered by how real the wax models had looked, stunned by the precision of detail that had gone into the crafting of each one. And yet, as perfectly as they had mirrored their living counterparts, he had not for a moment questioned whether they were alive. Their perfectly rendered eyes were empty, hollow in a way that betrayed the absence of soul.

The Baku is different. When Luca looks at it, he senses a dark sentience crackling within it. As he considers the statue, he cannot quite shake the conviction that it is considering him in return.

Yellowed by the passage of time, its ivory flesh is like ancient papyrus, wrinkled and coarse. Its thick trunk is accordioned, its small, black eyes sunk in shadow-swagged sockets. The cords in its muscles are like steel cables, scored by deep blue veins. Like a bust from classical antiquity, its arms are severed at the shoulder, but Luca can see enough of its muscled neck and broad chest to know if it did have a body, it would be that of a man.

A little girl shoves past him, startling him from his thoughts. She pushes her note into the statue's mouth. Something flickers inside the Baku's eyes and a chill rushes over Luca's skin.

'Luca, come on!' his mum snaps, Betsy squirming in her arms. 'We need to go, your sister's getting cranky.'

Luca nods and forces himself to take a step towards the Baku. He knows he is being ridiculous, but the thought of touching the statue is repellent. He is suddenly convinced that as soon as he puts his scrap of paper in the Baku's mouth, serrated fangs will clamp down on his flesh, severing his hand at the wrist.

But his mum is watching him, waiting. The dark pouches beneath her eyes remind him of last night, when she had rushed into his room and shaken him from sleep as he screamed and thrashed beneath his covers. Luca knows that he – not his baby sister – is the reason she looks so exhausted. Betsy is a brilliant sleeper. A dote. At four weeks old she was already sleeping through. Luca, on the other hand, cannot recall the last time he had a decent night's sleep. He is sick of hearing people tell him he will outgrow the nightmares with time. He wants to outgrow them now.

He lifts the scrap of paper to the Baku's mouth. Apprehension surges through him, but he feels for a hole beneath the Baku's lowered trunk in which to drop the note.

The walls of its mouth feel damp and soft. Warmth creeps over Luca's skin and the sweet smell of rot engulfs him. He shudders, tries to drop the note, but the paper just sits there on the Baku's tongue. Gritting his teeth together, he shoves the note further down the statue's throat, trying to ignore the resistance he meets, telling himself he is imagining the pained look in the Baku's eyes, imagining the choking sound emanating from the back of its throat, imagining the warm, cloying—

The sound of a ringing doorbell rips Sean from the story. Miraede. He had been so engrossed in his book he had forgotten she was visiting today.

Grandad goes to let her in, and Sean hears the murmur of conversation in the hallway, voices pitched low so he can't hear what they are saying. A few minutes later Grandad comes back into the kitchen.

'Miraede's waiting for you in the library,' he says. 'You go on through, lad, and I'll bring some drinks in soon.'

Miraede is sat by the window when Sean enters, and she smiles as he settles into the chair across from her.

'Hi, Sean.' He ignores her and looks out at the rain-streaked garden. 'Your grandad's house is lovely! I hope you're settling in well.'

One thing Sean has noticed since losing his voice is how discomforting people find long silences to be. As though the quiet is a ditch, hiding a monster they are terrified to see, and their words are the rubble they have to keep shovelling to keep it buried.

Miraede is not one of those people.

When Sean does not say anything, she just smiles.

Like she knows what face the monster wears and is not afraid to see it.

'Arlo has written you another letter.'

Miraede pulls an envelope from her bag and holds it out to Sean. When he doesn't take it, she sets it on the table between them. Sean recognises the handwriting on the front, almost as familiar as his own.

'He asked me to give it to you. Jake and Gracie have been asking after you, too.'

The scar on Sean's hand itches and he rubs his thumb over it in slow circles. His gaze sweeps over the garden and settles on the shed. He shivers, despite the thick jumper he is wearing.

Miraede follows his gaze to the shed. When she looks back at him, her face seems a little paler, her dark eyes troubled.

'Your friends miss you, Sean.' Her voice is soft, like the rose petals Grandad so lovingly tends, and just as pretty. 'You should write back to them, maybe invite them over here to visit. I'm sure your grandad wouldn't mind.'

Sean's thoughts spin back to when he lived on Dulwood. When everything was sweet. No, scrap that. Everything was crackerjack. He had a home, a *real* home, and he had friends. *Brilliant* friends. Life was normal, and though he did not know it at the time, normal was good. Normal was great.

'Sean?' Miraede is sitting forwards, her worried eyes on his face.

Admittedly, his old flat was a bit of a dump. The damp was so bad, the skirting boards were almost completely rotted away and the ceiling over his bed sagged with corroding plaster. The thin walls did little to keep out the cold, or stifle the sounds of the neighbours, who huddled, crablike, above and on either side of them. Conversations and arguments filtered through to Sean with no less clarity than they would through a cardboard box, and he regularly struggled to sleep through the maddening thump of someone's bass or the rhythmic pounding of the horny couple upstairs.

'Have you thought any more about the regression therapy I mentioned last time I saw you? It can be a useful way to help conditions such as yours. There was a patient I treated for conversion disorder not so long ago, a different presentation to yours, of course, but—'

Mum was only sixteen when she had Sean, and he wonders whether that was why they were so close. With little money to spare for the sorts of activities most kids could indulge in, Sean's mum had been forced to think of things they could do together on a budget. They would go for long bike rides, play board games while stuffing their faces with junk food, visit the museum in town. When he was little, she would come up with art projects for them to do, helping him weave paper into colourful patterns or using food colouring mixed with glue to paint. As he got older, Sean began to come up with more ambitious ideas, and then it was he helping Mum when she got stuck. Making ships in bottles, DIY lava lamps or patio chandeliers.

When she found out that he had been selected for the Future Creators course, she had increased her shifts at The Dog and Gun, despite the fact she already worked too much. She had always hated Dulwood and promised him over and over that he wouldn't live there forever.

'—can't protect yourself from pain this way, Sean,' Miraede is saying. 'You can't just unplug the socket and disconnect yourself from the world.'

Sean feels a scowl cramp his face. He stares at the shed, thinking that, in many ways, it is just the same as he is now: shadow-draped, remote, silent.

And full of secrets.

As soon as Miraede leaves, Sean throws Arlo's letter away unopened, then goes into the conservatory to finish reading the first short story in *The Baku*.

After feeding his note into the Baku's mouth, Luca enjoys a few nights of dreamless sleep, but all too briefly. Paranoia begins to nibble at his thoughts. He becomes increasingly agitated, convinced someone is watching him. He starts to catch glimpses of the Baku and the Mirror-Eyed Man, sensing them always hovering at the peripheries of his vision.

After a few weeks of this, the nightmares return, only they are far worse than any he endured before. So vivid, so *real*, that even upon waking, Luca cannot be sure he is not still dreaming. The two worlds of sleep and consciousness, always so clearly divided, have merged into one, so that there is no relief to be found in either. He begins to find crumpled notes beneath his pillow, each one detailing, in a child's immature handwriting, the dream from which he had just awoken. Luca knows, somehow, his note, his *nightmare* has roused the Baku. It no longer wants to sleep. It does not want his dream. It wants to purge.

Luca leaps from his bed, as though it has come alive beneath him. He spins round, crashing into his swivel chair, which rolls on its castors across the floor with an eerie squeak. His room smells ripe and foul, and even though he is laced in sweat his breath puffs in white clouds from his lips. He feels the Baku's presence, like a slick film against his skin.

He lifts his pillow, already knowing what he will find there. Even so, the sight of the rolled-up wad of paper elicits a choked sob from his lips. Stifling his revulsion, he reaches down and picks it up, smooths it out.

Name: Luca Russell
Age: 13
Nightmare: The Mirror-Eyed Man

Luca stares at the note that he fed into the Baku's mouth less than a week ago. The ink has smudged, the beast's saliva making it bleed across the paper, but the handwriting is unmistakably his own.

The Baku has given him his nightmare back.

A flicker of movement at the edge of Luca's vision makes his blood run cold. He is not alone.

The Mirror-Eyed Man is perched on the edge of his bed.

Even with the morning sun slanting through the blinds, Luca can only make out the edges of the old man's silhouette. He is sat with his hands on his lap, long fingers tapering over his knees. His body is a mass of writhing darkness, but Luca has an impression of a thin, cruel face, an instinct for the condensed evil that has sidled into his room.

Wake up wake up wake up wake up!

But he is *awake. He knows it, feels it in the visceral fear that floods his system and twists the course of every coherent thought towards blind panic. Finally, the Mirror-Eyed Man has found a way to unlock the door that separates nightmares from reality and it has come for him.*

The figure on the bed shifts, and as it does, Luca's paralysis breaks. He tears out of the room, slamming the door closed behind him. But when he starts to run down the stairs, the Mirror-Eyed Man is stood there, blocking his escape.

Luca takes a step back.

The Mirror-Eyed Man does not move. The curve of his spine and the long strands of hair that float round his neck give the impression of an elderly man, yet there is nothing frail about his towering height, about the featureless darkness that vibrates through his form. Luca has only ever seen him in profile before, the sharply jutting jawline, the flat slope of his brow, the hook of his nose, but now he can discern no shape or depth to his face at all.

Because the Mirror-Eyed Man is turning to look at him.

For a moment, Luca merely stands there, observing the slow twist of the Mirror-Eyed Man's face to his. Only when a slithering darkness ripples through the black glass of his eyes does Luca throw his hands in front of his face and stagger back. Leaning his shoulder against the wall, he slides down the hallway, which seems to elongate before him. If he can just make it to his mother's bedroom… If he can reach her in time… He tries to call out to her, but only a whispered cry escapes his lips.

Keeping his gaze lowered, Luca glances over his shoulder again. The landing is clear, the Mirror-Eyed Man has gone. But his heart continues to jackhammer in his chest, as though some primal instinct can still detect the unseen danger.

He turns back around.

The Mirror-Eyed Man is kneeling on the ground right in front of him. His jaw is wrenched wide, framing a soundless scream. Luca sees himself trapped in the mirrors of those terrible, infinite eyes, and the madness reflected back at him is a freight train slamming through him, obliterating his sanity.

He tumbles into howling darkness and Luca knows no more.

Sean closes the book and a shadow falls across the front cover. He looks out of the window, expecting to see dark thunderheads blotting out the sun, but the sky is a hard-boiled blue, unseasonably clear of clouds.

He flips to the front of the book, notices it was published in 2003. He thinks of the red-berried tree in the garden and the dates on the placard nailed into its trunk. *If Nanna Storm died in 2002, then Grandad wrote* The Baku *right after her death.*

Sean shivers, rubs his hands up and down his arms, which have suddenly erupted in goosebumps. Relieved to have finished the story, he snaps the book closed and drops it on the table.

BEFORE

The sensor lights in old Mrs Jones's back garden flicked on as Sean, Gracie, Arlo and Jake raced across it, but the windows of the house remained dark. Sean struggled to keep up with the others. He wished he had worn his knee brace, but he hadn't known, when he'd left home, he would be spending the evening climbing over fences and walls. That had been Arlo's idea. It would have only taken Sean fifteen minutes to go home and get it, but a lot could happen in fifteen minutes with Arlo, Gracie and Jake, and Sean didn't want to miss anything.

They had managed to garden-hop almost all the way to the bottom of the street, a new record. True, at number eight, Mr O'Leary's dog, Marine, had almost taken a mouthful of meat from Jake's backside, and Fat Gav at number twenty-two had thrown half a shattered brick at them, missing Arlo's skull by mere inches, but these close encounters only made the adventure more exciting.

It was almost midnight but the air was warm, the indigo sky awash with stars. The long summer was tantalisingly close, but for Sean it could not arrive quickly enough. Holidays abroad were a luxury he had never experienced, but then few kids on Dulwood had. Besides, he had Gracie, Arlo and Jake to hang out with, and together they never ran out of things to do over the school holidays. Now, as he raced through his neighbours' back gardens, he felt as though he had reached the peak of happiness. Life just didn't get any better than this.

They scrambled onto the bins at the edge of Mrs Jones's garden so they could peer over the fence into the next property, which belonged to Harvey Fallon. Harvey was a recluse with a chronic stammer, a guy who kept himself to himself but whose name seemed to be permanently welded to the lips of the local gossips. He was a psychopath, a pervert, a paedophile, a freak. Or so they all said. The allegations were slung his way as though they didn't matter even though, as far as Sean knew, not one shred of evidence existed to support any of them. Sean couldn't understand why young mums would cross the road with their prams on the rare occasions they saw Harvey walking towards them on the street, or why kids carrying baseball bats would knock on his door and try to goad him into coming outside.

'My turn to go first,' Sean whispered, his breath ragged from the run. His knee ached, and once again he found himself wishing he had gone back for his brace, but it was too late for that now.

Garden-hopping rules dictated that everyone had to take turns crossing a garden alone, and only once they had reached the middle of the lawn could anyone else join them. That solitary walk through someone else's back garden in the dead of night always cranked up the adrenaline, especially in the houses where the homeowners were ex-convicts or owned dogs. But Sean knew Harvey did not have any dogs, and he hardly ever left the house; crossing his garden would be a piece of cake.

Sean swung a leg over the fence, readying himself for the drop.

'Wait,' Arlo said, eying the house. 'This is too easy.'

'You're right,' Gracie said. 'Sean, you should knock on Harvey's window.'

'No way,' Sean said. 'You do it.'

He lowered his body over the side of the fence, minimising the drop to lessen the impact on his bad knee.

Jake leaned over the fence. His blond hair gleamed in the moonlight, and trouble danced in his eyes. 'I dare you.'

Sean glared up at him. 'Dares are stupid.'

'Marine nearly bit my ass off,' Jake snapped. 'And Arlo nearly got brayed in the head. You've gotta do something to make it interesting.'

'Oh, c'mon, man,' Sean groaned. He could have told them his knee was killing him, could have pulled his muddied trouser leg up to show them how hot and swollen it was, and he knew they would have let it drop. But he hated reminding the few people to whom his condition was invisible that he wasn't like them.

'Chicken shit!' Jake stood up on the bin and started flapping his arms and clucking.

'Shut up, you're gonna get us caught,' Sean hissed.

Arlo and Gracie stood up beside Jake, all three of them clucking and squawking and rocking their heads forwards and back. An upstairs light winked on in Mrs Jones's house.

'Fine, I'll do it. Just shut up, alright?'

Grinning, Arlo, Gracie and Jake knelt down on the bins again so that only the tops of their heads were visible.

Sean bit his lip, his eyes moving over Harvey Fallon's garden. Even by Dulwood's lowly standards, it was a mess. Nettles and brambles swamped the path, and snarled shrubbery separated the rear of the garden from the house. The ripped blue tarp of an old tent lay in a heap beside an upturned broken chair, half buried in the knee-high grass.

Soft *buck-buck-buck* noises drifted from the bins behind him.

'Shitheads,' Sean muttered, then started to creep towards the house.

The room that looked out onto the back garden was lit from within, a gap in the curtains providing a sliver of a view inside. Sean slowly picked his way towards it, muscles tensed to run. His usual garden-hopping routine was to employ stealth until either the sensor lights winked on or a dog made itself known, at which point he would sprint as fast as his hobbled legs would allow to the next property. The quiet and the darkness of Harvey's garden should have eased Sean's nerves, but it didn't. The shadows wavered like folds of cloth concealing something, and the silence stretched like a malignant smile.

Sean hesitated, turned back to his friends. Jake gave him a thumbs up, Arlo and Gracie shooed him on. Sean wasn't sure how well they could see him, but he flipped them off anyway.

Sean pushed through the needle-like leaves of shrubbery. His gaze fixed on the gap in the curtains, through which he could see a TV stood on a corner unit, a clock on the mantelpiece above the fireplace.

As he drew closer, he saw Harvey Fallon sat on a tatty brown sofa. He was wearing jeans, a thermal jumper and Spongebob Squarepants slippers. Sean grinned to himself, the tight ball of anxiety round his chest slackening. He fisted his hand, ready to knock on the glass, but as he inched closer he saw that Harvey was polishing something. Something metallic and sleek and black…

A gun.

Sean flinched at the sight of it, and Harvey must have caught the movement because his head suddenly snapped up. His eyes fastened on Sean, who gasped and flailed backwards.

'Shit.' He started to push his way back through the overgrown path. His outstretched palms caught on the branched thorns and he whimpered as he hopped through the tangled brambles. 'Shitshitshitshitshitshitshit.'

The others had already jumped over the fence and they stared at him in shock, no doubt wondering why he was prancing through the prickles towards them instead of tearing across the garden to the next property.

Harvey slammed the back door open and stepped outside. Backlit by the light from inside the house, he stood framed in the doorway, a towering, slope-shouldered monster of a man. Then he was walking towards them, slapping the prickles and thorns aside. All the names Sean had heard the locals call Harvey whizzed through his head as he watched the big man approach: psycho, paedophile, pervert, screwball, lunatic…

'He's got a gun!' Sean yelled as he broke free of the brambles. 'He's got a fucking g—!'

His feet tangled in the blue tarp and he staggered, almost fell. Righting himself, he pelted towards his friends, who were now desperately trying to climb back into Mrs Jones's garden. But there were no bins propped beside the fence in Harvey's garden to help them climb it, nothing they could use to lever themselves over.

'Huh-huh-who's there?'

'Here!' Jake said. 'There's a hole here!'

He managed to find a section of collapsed fence into which he slid one foot. But the wood was old and rotten, and as he started to scrabble upwards, the panelling gave way. He crashed to the ground, twisting his ankle as he landed.

He howled in pain, grasping at his foot. Gracie and Arlo dropped beside him and hooked their hands beneath his arms, but when they pulled him up, Jake yelped.

'Duh-duh-don't d-do that!' Harvey Fallon shuffled towards them. 'Huh-he's hurt.'

'Whoa whoa whoa!' Arlo flung his hands up, his eyes glued to the weapon dangling in Harvey's hand. 'We're sorry, we didn't mean no harm, don't shoot us, man!'

Harvey glanced down at his gun as though he had forgotten he was holding it, then slid it into his belt.

'I'm n-n-not g-going to shoot you.' Harvey spoke the words as though the very implication appalled him. 'Duh-do you w-want m-me to l-l-look at it?'

Jake shook his head and pulled himself to his feet. He tested his weight on his injured ankle, winced in pain. Sean watched Harvey, unsure of what to say. The guy was taller and more solidly built than any of the Dulwood Dogs, the gang that ran the neighbourhood, but he possessed none of their swaggering menace. As Harvey glanced around the garden, clearly ill at ease despite the gun in his waistband, Sean recognised a vulnerability in him, a childlike quality that was rare to see in adults, especially ones that had grown up on this estate.

'Should I c-c-call someone?' Harvey said.

Jake studied Harvey for a moment, as though trying to decide if he was really as harmless as he appeared. 'Nice slippers.'

Harvey glanced down at his feet and a small smile flickered at the edges of his lips. 'S-S-Spongebob.'

Jake took a limping step forwards. 'Is that thing real?'

Harvey stared at him blankly and Jake nodded at the gun.

'Your piece.'

Harvey's smile flattened into suspicion. 'Wuh-wuh-what were you duh-duh-doing in m-m-my g-garden?'

'Sorry, we didn't mean any trouble,' Sean said. 'It was their stupid dare.'

'Gobshite,' Gracie said, shoving him.

'Y-you weren't g-going to b-b-brick my w-windows? K-kids are always b-bricking my wuh-wuh-windows.'

'No!' Sean said. 'We're not like that, honest. The kids that do that shit are wankers. I don't blame you for having a gun.'

'The teachers at school are always telling us that guns are bad,' Gracie said. 'Talib – he's this kid in our class – well, his older brother, Dumi, he got shot outside the old community centre last week. Did you hear about that?'

'I huh-heard.'

'Do you have a license for that thing?' Gracie said. 'Because you know you really should have a license to own a gun.'

'Shut up, Grey,' Sean said. 'It's not like he's running around shooting people.'

'I'm just saying coz he could get into a lot of trouble if he doesn't have a license,' Gracie said, defensively.

'Do you have any more guns?' Jake said, his face lit up with excitement.

Harvey glanced back towards his house, his discomfort clearly building.

'You don't have to worry, we won't tell anyone if you do,' Arlo said. 'Swear we won't.'

'Yeah, we won't tell,' Sean said. 'Will we, Grey?'

Gracie shook her head.

Jake took another limping step towards Harvey, a crooked grin on his face. 'But we'd love it if you'd show us your collection.'

DAY 3

Alone in the conservatory, Sean eyes the packages of clay, his thoughts freefalling back in time to the only sculpture he'd ever made: the clay robin he had been planning to put forward towards his Future Creators exam, and which is now sat on the window ledge in his bedroom.

He rips open the packaging, trying to ignore the tremble in his hands. He has decided to sculpt a replica of Michelangelo's *Atlas Slave*, a piece from a collection of four sculptures called *The Prisoners*, so named for the way he left each of them half submerged in rock. It is an ambitious choice, considering he has so little experience, but something about the images in the book speaks to him. Looking at them gives Sean a vague feeling of claustrophobia. Their pained expressions convey the agony of their struggle to liberate themselves from the stone, and now Sean imagines himself as a sort of fifth prisoner, only instead of his body being enclosed in stone, it is his voice.

Using one of the beginner's sculpting books, Sean trims some armature wire, bends it in half, forming a loop at the top which will be the figure's head. Using a pair of pliers, he twists the stiff wire into the rough shape of his model. He works slowly, checking the book regularly to make sure he is doing everything correctly. Once he has the lines of its body shaped, he uses a hammer to bend nails over the wire feet, securing it to a plywood board.

Sean opens a packet of air-dry clay and begins to block the torso, then the arms and legs. Once he has a rudimentary shape he uses a fettling knife to cut away excess and start to add detail. As he works the peripheries of his world expand, even as his focus shrinks down to the malleable material in his hands. The trembling in his fingers fades, hesitancy and self-consciousness fall away. Concepts of time and self no longer exist, and in this state, Sean is unburdened by his past, untroubled by his future.

Only when Grandad enters the room does Sean blink back to his surroundings. The padded knees of the old man's gardening trousers are coated in mud, his gloves are tucked into his equipment belt. He looks from Sean to the sculpture on the armature and Sean swears he sees the old man flinch.

Grandad sits across from him at the table.

'Sean, I've been thinking.' His voice is filled with a hesitancy that sets Sean's nerves jangling, because he hasn't sounded nervous like this since the first day they met at Creswick Hall. 'You've been here three days now and you still haven't left the house. So much solitude isn't good for a young lad like you.' He glances at the clay figure and clears his throat. 'I can't force you to go back to school before you're ready, but Miraede and I have spoken, and there's a youth club just down the road. We both agree it would be a good idea to enrol you.'

Sean tries to keep his face a mask, but a flicker of distress must betray him, because Grandad starts talking more quickly, his voice acquiring a pleading edge.

'Now, it wouldn't be for long, lad, just a couple of hours a few times a week. You'll get to mingle with other kids your own age, play games, watch films, make friends. I really think if you just give it a chance, you'd surprise yourself. Look, I know you don't want to leave the house, but you must, lad. You simply must.'

Sean meets Grandad's eyes. Unspoken words crash around his skull like caged thunder.

Please don't make me go, Grandad. I can't go.

'Oh, Sean.' Grandad's face crumples at Sean's expression, but there is steel behind his eyes. And the worst of it is, Grandad thinks he's doing the right thing. 'It'll be alright, it'll be okay now, lad.'

Sean's gaze falls to his twisted legs. *What do you know? How can you have any idea what it's like?*

'Maybe we could enrol you in an art class?' Grandad says. Sean looks up to see the old man staring at his miniature *Atlas Slave*. The sorrow in his face is there and gone before Sean can question what it means.

Later, Sean goes into the library and reads two more of Grandad's short stories from *The Baku*. Like 'Luca', each story in the collection is named after its main character. The second one, 'Will', is about a young boy who is terrified of sharks. Whenever he is on the water, either fishing with his dad, kayaking or windsurfing, he can't help but imagine a triangular fin emerging from the water and cutting a frothy trail towards him. But however troubling his overactive imagination when he is out at sea, ironically it is when he is on dry land, safely tucked up in bed, that true terror flares.

Sleep plunges Will into cold, salty water, and then it uncages the shark. Almost worse than seeing it is the moment before when he *can't* see it, but knows that it is there, somewhere beneath him. Then a fin slides upwards, cutting through the surface of the sea, and streams towards Will with a speed almost impossible to track.

In his dreams he twists in the water, pumps his arms and legs in desperation to get away. But he never makes it far. At the last moment he always turns, sees the shark rising out of the water. Its teeth are incurved blades, its eyes fathomless black pits. Its jaws close around him and Will wakes, screaming and thrashing at his bedsheets.

Will has suffered from these nightmares for as long as he can remember, and they continue to plague his sleep until the day he comes across the Baku. He sees the statue when he is on holiday with his family, visiting a museum in Berlin. A poem etched on a plaque in front of the statue invites him to write down his worst nightmare and feed it into its mouth. Will does so, and that night he does not dream of the shark. Nor does he dream of it the next night, or the night after that. Weeks pass, and Will starts to believe he has truly cured himself of the recurring dream that has for so long disturbed his sleep.

But during the day he begins to feel watched. Tense, anxious, alert to a danger that common sense tells him does not exist. He starts to glimpse the Baku from the corner of his eye, but whenever he turns around, there is nothing there. Even the relief from his nightmares begins to trouble him. He feels a dark hole in his consciousness, as though the shark in his dream has bitten something out of him. The void scares him even more than the shark had, and he feels as he had in his dreams, aware of a danger swimming unseen beneath him, but unable to see it.

Then one night Will has the worst dream of them all. The shark attacks him, but this time when its jaws clamp around him, tearing through flesh, muscle and bone, severing arteries, cracking ribs, he does not wake up.

Will's parents hear him screaming in his bed. By the time they reach him, he is dead. His bedsheets are soaked in blood, his hair drips with seawater. Barely detectable beneath the thick tang of blood is the briny smell of the ocean. Bite marks slice his flesh to the bone. One of his arms is missing, the bloodied stump of his shoulder exposing severed arteries and shredded muscle.

The third story, 'Khaba', is set in the ancient past. Khaba is a young Egyptian boy who begins to suffer terrible nightmares after seeing his mother die in childbirth. He resents his baby brother, Nikare, blaming him for their mother's death. But in his dreams, ill-feeling turns into something darker and more sinister. Then, Nikare is a demonic entity, horned and slab-muscled, with flame-red eyes and a serpentine nose. He is a beast, who killed their mother, and who now wants to kill Khaba.

Khaba's nightmares persist until the day he is playing by the riverside and sees the Baku. The statue stands among the reeds of the Nile, its plinth sunken in a bank of black silt. Khaba reads the inscription written on a plaque in front of the statue, and the next day he returns with a roll of papyrus, on which he has written his name and his nightmare. He pushes this into the Baku's mouth, and for a while the dreams stop. But while he finds peace once more in sleep, his days become a waking nightmare.

No one else appears to see little Nikare's dark eyes flare with fire or the chitinous growths that begin to swell beneath his soft temples. They don't see the way his button nose grows slimmer, more serpentine each day, or how his soft baby nails seem to be lengthening into talons. Khaba tries to tell himself he is imagining it, because he only sees these changes in his little brother from the corner of his eye, and whenever he turns around the child looks normal. But deep down he knows something is wrong.

Khaba is playing with his best friend, Nyla, on the riverbank the day Nikare shows up. At first, Khaba is concerned to see his little brother unattended. Their sister, Akela, was supposed to be looking after him, but when he asks Nikare where she is, the small boy does not respond. Khaba starts to walk towards him, but he stops when he realises the child is changing shape.

All the subtle changes he had only glimpsed before now occur right in front of his eyes. Horns split through the boy's fleshy temples, curling beneath his jaw like those of a ram. Claws split his skin, fangs rupture his gums, his eyes ignite. His tailbone lengthens, thickens into a crocodilian tail, and his flesh hardens to ripples of bone.

Khaba screams and cries out a warning to Nyla, but she does not seem able to see the transformation in Nikare. The creature that had once been Nikare streams forward on its hands and knees. It grabs Khaba, who kicks and thumps at the beast but is unable to shake it off. The demon drags him under the water of the River Nile, which closes over his head like a tomb.

When Sean reaches the end of Khaba's story, he closes the book. Outside, the sun is sinking into the trees, the shadows are thickening. For a while, he sits there, listening to the hiss and snap of logs settling in the hearth, thinking he can almost hear Khaba's screams echo in his mind, and see the colour of Nikare's eyes in the smouldering fire.

He sets the book on the table and goes upstairs to bed.

DAY 4

The days are beginning to take on a familiar rhythm for Sean, and he finds a simple comfort in the monotony of his new life. It helps the numbing. The forgetting.

By the time he gets up in the morning, it is to find Grandad in the back garden, his fingernails black with mud as he tackles the soil with spades and forks. Sean takes him a cup of tea, whereupon – without questioning whether it is something his grandson is even vaguely interested in – the old man explains what he is doing.

Sean learns the differences between dogwood and corkscrew hazel, that primula, trailing ivy and dwarf conifers are great in winter baskets. He discovers that the humongous tree above the orchard with the bright red berries is a rowan tree and that Nanna Storm planted it when she and Grandad first bought the house.

Twice a day, Grandad sits on the patio step and scatters feed across the lawn. Almost as soon as he takes up his position, birds feather down from the sky, one after the next, until there are six, seven, eight of them, nipping seeds from the grass. In those moments, he looks to Sean like a little boy. As though the birds are peck-peck-pecking away not only at the nuts and seeds but at Grandad's gathering years.

In the afternoon, Sean sketches in the conservatory or sits in the orchard beneath the rowan tree where the subtle scents of jasmine and iris jostle with the smells of climbing plants and shrubs. Later, he gathers fresh vegetables from the greenhouse and helps Grandad cook dinner. After they have eaten they sit together in the library, where Sean either reads or sketches.

Sometimes, he wonders what his mates would say if they could see him now. They'd probably think he'd had a lobotomy. Grandad has more get-up-and-go than he does these days. Just watching him at work in the garden exhausts Sean. Pruning the climbing roses, cutting shoots from tree trunks, preparing the soil for next year, cleaning out and topping up the bird baths, digging in the compost manure, raking leaves from the lawn, weeding, sowing, pruning, planting, re-planting: he works the garden with the energy of a man half his age.

But he never goes near the shed.

Almost as though that piece of land doesn't belong to him.

Sean is sketching on the bench beneath the rowan tree. He can see Grandad through the kitchen window, his nutso hair all mussed up as he pounds dough in a blizzard of white flour. He is making lasagne for dinner, cooking the pasta from fresh, pureeing tomatoes for the sauce, chopping a bunch of vegetables from his greenhouse.

As Sean watches him, his thoughts flash back to the day he overheard Mum talking to the old man. It was three or four years ago now, and the only contact between the two of them that Sean had been around to witness. But the memory is too jagged to hold in his mind, like squeezing shards of shattered glass, so he looks at it sideways, through a filter of his own making.

He and Mum were playing Monopoly when the phone rang. Mum rose to answer it, walking backwards down the hall.

'I'm watching you, Seanie, don't you even think about cheating,' she warned, a grin in her voice.

Sean held his hands up, schooling his face into an expression of innocence as Mum, still watching him, lifted the phone to her ear.

'Hello?'

The smile in her eyes wilted.

'Dad?'

There was no warmth in the whispered word, but there was definitely *some*thing there. Something cold and hard and broken. Her body tensed and she twisted away from Sean. Her red hair fell across her face, forming a drape around her cheekbones.

'How did you get this number?'

The usual honeyed tone of her voice contained a chill that Sean did not recognise.

'Don't ever call here again.'

These words were hissed into the phone with a venom Sean had not known her capable of. She slammed the receiver back into the cradle, then wrapped her arms around her stomach, as though she had just been kicked in the gut, hard. Her eyes were glued to the phone.

'Mum?' Sean said, standing. Their game of Monopoly was forgotten. He would let her have all his pretend money, all his properties, if she would only stop holding herself like that, all hunched up and hurting.

She turned to him and Sean was shocked by the grim pallor of her face. She looked confused, as though she had forgotten he was there at all.

'Mum? What's wrong?'

She walked back down the hall, sat on the floor in front of their game, picked up the dice. Her face was white as bleached flour. Looking into her eyes, Sean felt like he was watching a storm through a fragile pane of glass.

'Was that your dad on the phone?' He spoke the words softly, as though they might bruise.

She squeezed the dice so hard that her knuckles turned white.

'You really don't like him, do you?' Sean said, too young to understand there were things she wouldn't speak of, even to him. 'I guess he must have done something really bad, huh?'

Mum looked at Sean and pain flashed across her face. She let out this shaky sigh and pulled him into a tight hug. Resting her chin on top of his head, she wrapped her arms across his chest.

Like she was his seat belt, locking him in tight for a collision with the world.

'Pay no attention to me, Seanie,' she said, tousling his hair and backhanding tears from her cheeks. 'These aren't worries for my little lad.'

They never spoke of Grandad again.

The breeze picks up, whisking Sean's hair across his brow. Through the kitchen window, Grandad's mouth is opening and closing as his blade falls over and over on the chopping board. He is singing, oblivious to his grandson watching him.

Clouds slide across the sun, the day darkens. Sean is alone in the garden, but he feels suddenly as though he is being watched. His scalp crawls. He looks around but there is no one there. His eyes track to the shed, and the curtain inside twitches. Sean's breath snatches, goosebumps skitter down his arms. The curtains hang limp, unmoving, but he was sure there had been something there a moment ago, something that had jerked away from the gaze of his eye.

Grandad sets two heaving bowls of lasagne on the table and sits down with an exhausted sigh. His clothes are dusted with flour and there is a streak of it across his cheek.

'Tuck in, lad, before it gets cold.'

Sean picks up his knife and fork, cuts a corner from the lasagne. Warm cheese dribbles from between the layers of pasta.

He thinks of the time Mum cooked homemade lasagne. It had the consistency of lino, and even though she peeled off the top layer of charred pasta, every mouthful tasted like scraped-off chunks of oven dirt.

'We really ought to think about getting you enrolled in school,' Grandad says, grating parmesan over his plate. Sean looks out of the window at the writing shed, thinking of that twitching curtain. He remembers Mum's stricken face after she had hung up on Grandad, the haunted look in her eyes. Again, he wonders what the old man did, what could have been so terrible that she refused to even talk to him on the phone.

'I know it's tough, but we can't have you sitting round the house all day. I was thinking we could take a walk down to Allerton Mills to have a word with the headmistress. Remember, I told you that I'd already met with her and enrolled you—'

Sean phases out the sound of Grandad's voice and eats another forkful of lasagne. It really is delicious. Probably the best lasagne he has ever tasted. But he'd swap it for Mum's cremated lino version in a heartbeat.

DAY 5

Rain lashes the car as Grandad drives Sean to the youth club. Wind buffets the pedestrians, the trees flail at the sky.

Grandad pulls up in the church car park. St Joseph's is gothic and imposing, its tall bell tower cutting into the dark night. The youth club is run in the hall beside the church, a smaller, less imposing brick building. There are only a few cars parked outside, but Sean knows the hall will be full of kids. His stomach churns at the thought of walking inside. Of *hobbling* inside. Everyone will turn and stare. They always do.

'Here, take this,' Grandad says, pulling a mobile from his pocket and handing it to Sean. 'So you can text me,' he explains when Sean hesitates. 'I've put my mobile number in there, just in case you're late out or I need to get hold of you.'

Sean slips it into his pocket.

'I can come in with you, if you want,' Grandad says. Sean glances at him and is surprised by the storm of worry he sees in the old man's eyes. In that moment, he looks so like Mum that a lump forms in his throat. 'If it… makes it any easier?'

Sean shakes his head, then opens the car door and climbs out. He has no intention of going into the youth club, so the last thing he needs is the old man walking him to the door. His sketching pad and pencils are in his rucksack, along with *The Baku*. Once Grandad has gone, he will find somewhere he can read and sketch alone.

He slams the door shut and waits for Grandad to drive off. The rain forms rills around his shoes and pastes his hair to his skull. The old man is bent low over the steering wheel, watching him. The smile on his lips is trying to tell Sean he is not worried, but his eyebrows, which are incapable of hiding anything, are tucked into a frown.

Oh God, he's waiting to see me walk inside.

Grinding his teeth, Sean turns away from the car and walks towards the church hall. Over the blustering wind and the hammering rain, he listens for the grumble of the car's engine, the sound of tyres rolling away. It doesn't come.

He stops on the path, turns and waves. *You can go now, Grandad. Look, I'm about to walk in. Nothing to see here. Toodles!*

The old man waves back but shows no sign of leaving. Sean huddles deeper into his coat as rain dribbles down the nape of his neck, then, inwardly cursing, starts to walk towards the church hall. Taking a deep breath, he pushes the door open.

He finds himself stood in an alcove, another set of double doors separating him from the main hall. Relief washes through him. He can hear muffled chatter from within, the faint strum of a guitar, a sharp bray of laughter. He forces himself to wait a couple of minutes before opening the door through which he entered, and when he does, Grandad's car has gone.

Feeling conspicuous, even though there is no one around, he hurries across the car park towards the church. The massive wooden doors are closed, and for a moment he worries the building has been locked up for the night. But when he twists the handle, the door swings smoothly open, as though he has been admitted by a ghostly custodian.

Sean steps into the narthex. The smell of incense and flowers and polished wood tangle on the air. Candles burn in tiered holders along the walls, flames flexing in the gust of wind that follows him inside.

He moves to one of the candle stands. Their heat warms his chilled skin. He supposes they should be beautiful, these flames that have been lit for the sick and the dying. Hopeful. But the sight of them sends anger flashing through him, and the intensity of it leaves him breathless.

He thinks of Mum, but the memories are too painful to dwell upon. He stares at the wavering flames and his anger grows, until it is so huge he feels as though it is all there is of him. He wants to cry, but he doesn't. Tears flow from him as freely as words these days. Blood from a stone. Instead, he takes a deep breath, fills his lungs, and blows. Nine of the flames wink out, smoke spiralling from their wicks. But the rest of the candles keep burning. Stupid, foolish, futile prayers. He blows again and the darkness thickens around him, the shadows inching closer until he has extinguished every single one.

It doesn't matter.

They were never going to be answered anyway.

His hands are shaking so he stuffs them into his pockets. All the pews are empty and the church is tomb silent, nothing but the sound of his feet scuffling the red carpet as he walks down the aisle. Moonlight stabs blue fingers through the stained-glass windows, draping the church in its dreamy glow.

Sean sits down, pulls *The Baku* from his bag, and starts to read the next story.

He has not been reading long when the church door opens. He pauses, lowers the book onto his chest. Exhaling the story and inhaling reality feels the same way it always does – like he has been dragged away from a crackling fire and thrown naked into an ice bath.

He hears voices, the shuffle of feet, the bang of the door slamming shut again. Worried his absence from the youth club has been noticed and that someone has been sent to find him, he scooches low to avoid being seen, then peeks over the back of the pew.

Three people are huddled in the narthex. If Sean had not blown out so many candles he would have been able to see their faces more clearly, but the darkness makes their shapes grainy and indistinct.

There is a skinny man wearing a shabby hoodie. Gaunt-faced, hollow-cheeked, there is something snakelike about him. He has the worn-in look of someone straight off Dulwood. Beside him, there is a boy of around sixteen or seventeen. He has a crew cut and is wearing a varsity jacket that makes Sean think of a jock. A new-money kid, playing at being a gangster. Behind Snake and Jock, a blinged-out skinny girl in a tracksuit hoists herself onto the table where the hymn books and Mass cards are stacked. Her hair is gelled into a ponytail tight enough to justify the scowl on her heavily made-up face. Her chunky earrings are so large they rest on her shoulders and her fingers are covered in rings. She doesn't look like Gracie, but the way she swings her legs as she examines her nails makes him think of his old friend.

Sean strains to hear the exchange between Jock and Snake, but catches only a few snatched words. Still, it doesn't take a genius to figure out Snake is dealing drugs. The faces of Jesus and Mary gaze down with sad, beneficent eyes as Jock thrusts a wodge of notes into Snake's hands. Snake counts the cash, passes a small plastic baggie to Jock. The exchange has the reverent feel of a priest handing out the Eucharist to a parishioner, except this is just so grimy.

Though these drug dealers are nothing like his best friends, for some reason Jake, Arlo and Gracie pop into Sean's mind. Perhaps because the scene he is watching play out is one he can imagine in their future if they don't escape Dulwood.

Sean had always thought Arlo had the greatest chance of escape, and that he, Sean, would end up stuck forever on

Dulwood. *But here I am. I've escaped. I can put that part of my life behind me.* The thought does not bring him the relief it should, only a dull ache in the pit of his stomach.

When the whole thing is over, Snake shoves open the church doors and the three figures disappear into the night. Sean flips his book open again and carries on reading.

Fifteen minutes before youth club finishes, Sean waits inside the alcove of the church hall, pretending to read the noticeboards until the doors open and kids start to spill out. He drops in behind them, as though he is part of the jostling throng.

Grandad is waiting in the car and Sean climbs in with a sigh of relief.

'That bad was it?' Grandad says with a wry chuckle. Then, noticing Sean shivering, he frowns. 'Your lips are blue, lad. Haven't they got heating in that place?'

He starts the car and turns the blowers on full blast.

'You did well tonight,' he says, as he drives out of the car park. 'I know it was hard, walking into a place like that when you don't know anybody, especially with… well… it was brave of you, lad.'

Grandad glances at him, and Sean sees pride in the old man's starshine eyes. He cringes from the praise, knowing he does not deserve it. He thinks of the way he hid in the church, cloaking himself in fictional stories, all because he was too nervous to walk into a room of kids his own age. It would have been alright if Gracie, Jake and Arlo were there with him. Suddenly he misses his friends so much, he feels their absence as an ache in his chest.

When Sean first arrived at Creswick Hall they had tried to visit, but he had refused to see them. He did not reply to their texts, and when they write to him he throws their letters away, unopened. He doesn't want to hear what they are doing because he already knows. Nothing has changed for them, not really. While they were playing Xbox and skipping school and hanging round the estate trying to think of new ways to prank each other, Sean's entire world had imploded. He misses them, yes, but hearing from them would only be a reminder of how things used to be. They are his old life. A life that hurts too much to think of now.

Better not to think about it at all.

Sean stares out of the window, allowing his thoughts to blur like the houses and trees outside.

When they get back to the house, Grandad makes them both a hot chocolate and they sit in the library, reading. Sean delicately traces his finger across the page, as though the sentences are gossamer strands of spun gold.

'My God, lad.' There is a crack in Grandad's voice that matches the broken look on his face. 'You're so like her when she was small.'

Sean can see Mum in Grandad's eyes, the memory of her dancing behind his face. He closes his book and stands up, then he walks out of the room. He doesn't want to be rude, but he is not ready to hear Grandad talk about her.

He goes up to his room. Despite Grandad saying he could redecorate however he wanted, Sean has left everything exactly as he found it. There are no books on the bookshelves, no posters on the walls. The only signs of his occupancy are an open suitcase at the foot of the bed that belches clothes across the floor, his knee brace that is propped against the wall, and his clay robin on the window ledge.

He moves to the window and parts the curtains. Clouds choke the moon and smother the stars. Fairy lights climb the trees, shaping their outlines against the darkness.

Sean sits at the desk and pulls his sketchpad from his bag, flips to a clean page, and begins to draw Bling, Jock and Snake. He remembers the detail of their clothing quite clearly – Bling's hoop earrings and tracksuit, Snake's scruffy hoodie, Jock's varsity jacket and buzzcut – but their faces are less distinct. Having only seen them from a distance, and only then in the shadow-cluttered church, he cannot quite remember what they looked like, but the longer he draws the easier it becomes. He forgets himself, as though the process of drawing briefly erases him from the world.

He doesn't know how long he has been sketching when the sensor lights in the garden wink on. The glare is like a finger snap in front of Sean's eyes. He blinks at the sketch, at first unsure what he is looking at, but then he recoils.

From the neck down he has drawn Jock, Bling and Snake, each of them recognisable by their distinctive clothing. But in place of their faces, he has drawn the faces of his friends. They look older in his sketch, more jaded, ravaged by addiction, but Sean can't deny it is them: Arlo's head on Snake's body, his eyes sunken, skin flaky, wrinkles beginning around a hard, flat mouth; Jake's face in place of Jock's, his blond hair snarled, filthy, hanging in clumps round his face; Gracie's face where Bling's should be, her lips chapped and peeling, the skin around her eyes oddly stretched as she glares hungrily at the bag of pills in Jake's hand.

With a strangled cry, Sean rips the sketch from the pad, scrunches it up and tosses it into the bin. He doesn't want to think about what he has drawn, pushes it from his mind. *It's just a drawing,* he tells himself. *It doesn't mean anything.*

He looks out of the window, his gaze moving over the garden, seeking distraction. He wonders what it was that caused the sensor lights to switch on. A *fox, probably. Maybe a deer?* Dulwood estate had never been a place for wildlife and he has never seen a real deer.

He pulls on his dressing gown and hurries downstairs, slides the patio door open. The sensor lights are still on when he steps outside.

Grandad is sat on the bench. Sean hadn't been able to see him from his bedroom window, and he realises it was probably Grandad who activated the sensor lights.

Sean is about to go back inside, but he hesitates, watching the old man. His gaze is riveted upon the shed, his expression is rigid. Shadows gather like pools in the hollows of his cheeks; they hang from the pockets of flesh beneath his eyes. In that moment, there is something dead-looking about his face, and if it had not been for the slow twist of his head towards Sean, he might have thought Grandad really *had* died, sitting here in the freezing cold. A shudder runs through Sean that has nothing to do with the frost-glazed night.

'I miss her, lad.'

The lights that had shone in the old man's eyes earlier that night are gone, the stars imploded into black holes. He turns back to the shed again.

Sean follows his gaze, greasy nausea slithering through him. Hulking shadows drape the building like a death shroud, and he feels as though he could wrap his fingers around them and peer beneath their folds. *What would I find under there if I could look? What's waiting beneath the dust and darkness?* He thinks of the conviction he had felt the other day that he was being watched, the way the shed's curtain had twitched when he turned around, as though someone – some*thing* – had jerked away from his gaze.

Sean looks back at Grandad. His expression is slack, cadaverous. It is as though he has forgotten his grandson is there at all. And for reasons he can't quite understand, it is this that scares Sean more than anything else.

BEFORE

Sharon Carter was having a divorce party in The Dog and Gun, and the entire estate had come out to celebrate. Sean would have preferred to hang out at Arlo's and play Xbox, but Jake had convinced Diesel Betty, the landlady, that she would need extra hands on deck for the night and that he, Sean, Gracie and Arlo would be glass collectors if she paid them a tenner each.

Of course, almost as soon as they started work, they began looking for ways to dodge it. At first they went around the pub, sneaking suds from abandoned pints to see if they could get drunk like the adults. When they grew bored of this, Gracie suggested they mix their own cocktail. Sean swiped an empty jug from behind the bar, and they coasted from table to table, pilfering half-drunk glasses of wine, bottles of Hooch, vodka tonics, even a half-full bottle of cava. Thankfully, the pub was heaving so Diesel Betty didn't notice what they were doing.

Sean and Gracie went into the back of the pub while Arlo and Jake smuggled them drinks, which they poured into the jug, making a mud-coloured cocktail they named The Puke.

'Hey, Sean,' Arlo said, joining them in the back, beer glasses clipped between his fingers. He tipped a half-drunk pint, which he had surely swiped when someone wasn't looking, into The Puke. 'Your mam's here.'

Sean's stomach dropped. Mum hadn't been well recently, and he knew Diesel Betty had told her to take some time off from working behind the bar. Sean told himself she was just exhausted, but he was worried about her. The lines on her face were more deeply carved, the circles beneath her eyes so dark they looked like bruises. And she was losing weight at an alarming rate. Looking at her made him think of Shirley Mills, who used to live a few doors down from him. He'd been a big bloke before he got sick, a bouncer in a club in town. Older women on the estate were always saying he was *so handsome*, even if he was five stone overweight, how he could be *a real ladykiller* if he'd only lay off the junk food and the booze. By the time cancer had done with him, he'd lost more than half his body weight. No one said he was handsome then.

Sean wished his mum would book an appointment at the doctor's, but knew she wouldn't. It was as though she didn't realise she was sick. It wasn't easy being a single mum, especially on Dulwood.

He poked his head round the back of the door, scanned the pub. Mum was talking to Denny, Jake's big brother. *Probably asking where Jake is, knowing I'll be with him.* Sean wondered whether he would be in trouble for working tonight, but as he watched his mum he saw her stagger, giggling as she caught herself against the table. She'd obviously been drinking.

'Don't take this the wrong way, man,' Arlo said, appearing beside him, 'but your mum isn't looking too hot.'

'Shut up, Arlo,' Gracie snapped.

'What? She looks ill, that's all I'm saying. Hey, if she's refusing to get herself checked out, maybe you should get in touch with her old man. Didn't you say he was still alive?'

'I've never spoken to him,' Sean said, which wasn't what Arlo had asked him, but he wanted to shut the conversation down. All he knew about his grandad was that Mum despised him. Sean had googled the old man a few times, so he knew he used to be an author, that he had a big fancy house on the other side of town. But there was no way he was going behind his mum's back and reaching out to him, not after seeing the efforts she had taken to cut him out of her life.

Jake moved towards them, his face simultaneously elated and terrified. He was holding a bottle of Jack Daniels.

'I swiped it from behind the bar,' he said, glancing over his shoulder as he poured the contents into the jug. 'We better do one before Diesel Betty clocks on.'

They snuck out the back door, taking their cocktail with them. The regular bar staff didn't try to stop them; the gang had already proved themselves more of a nuisance than a help.

CCTV cameras, encased in high-mounted steel cages, blinked down at them as they ran across the car park. The ground was littered with empty beer cans, cigarette stubs, slips of tin foil stained with crack. The air smelt of burning cars.

Across from the pub there was a bin shed, beyond which a grassy verge sloped up to an abandoned park. Last year they had found an old mattress propped beside the bins. It had taken all four of them to drag it up the slope and to wrestle it through the brambles. Once it was safely concealed by the trees, they had scrubbed it down with bleach to try and eradicate the stink of vomit and piss. It hadn't worked, but Jake had shown up one day with a roll of plastic sheeting and an inconsistent story about how he had come across it. They all knew he'd stolen it, but no one mentioned it, not even Gracie. With the addition of a few clean blankets that Arlo brought from home, they could detect no hint of the stench.

Their mattress beneath the trees became their safe space in the war zone of Dulwood, their magical flying carpet that could carry them away from all the shit that surrounded them. All they had to do was lie down on their bed beneath the sky, look up, and reimagine their surroundings.

Now, Sean flopped down on the mattress, Jake dive bombed beside him. Gracie, carrying the cocktail jug, lowered herself carefully onto the edge. Arlo leaned against a tree and stared into the distance. His tall frame, black glasses and floppy dark hair gave him a scholarly look that was incongruous to Dulwood. Sean could see him becoming a literary professor at some prestigious university someday, someone with his own office and his name on the door. Out of all of them, Sean saw the clearest path out of Dulwood for Arlo.

Sean tilted his face to the sky. Beyond the spindle-tipped branches, the stars swayed back and forth.

'I feel sick,' he said.

'That's The Puke, don't worry about it,' Gracie said.

'But he hardly drank any,' Jake said, holding a lighter to the tip of his cigarette. 'He can't be pissed.'

'He's pissed coz he's half your size,' Arlo said. He grabbed Sean's cheek, squeezed and shook it. 'Look at him, the cute little pudding.'

'Fuck off,' Sean said, swiping at Arlo, but he was laughing as he said it.

'I don't know how you can keep drinking that shit,' Arlo said, watching Gracie take another sip.

Gracie shrugged, lowering the jug to the ground so she could massage her scalp. 'Gets better the more you drink.'

Her cornrows had been freshly done and she had been complaining all night that they were too tight. Sean thought she needn't have bothered, her hair looked better unbraided, but when he'd told her this she'd looked just about ready to punch him in the face. That was the thing about Gracie. She couldn't take a compliment.

'It's freezing, why can't we go to yours?' Gracie asked Arlo.

'I told you, my mum's having a meeting at ours. She's hell-bent on getting this youth club in the old community centre off the ground. We could go to yours.'

Gracie gave him a pointed look. 'My dad's home.'

'Let's go to Sean's, then,' Jake said.

Sean felt suddenly cold all over. He scrabbled for something to say, some excuse that would sound plausible. His friends hadn't been to his flat for a long time, but with Arlo's house always so readily available, it had never been an issue.

'It's not that cold,' Arlo said, watching Sean. 'I think I'd rather stay here. Drink some more of The Puke, Grey, that'll warm you up.'

The back doors to the pub slammed open and angry voices rose on the night. Sean moved to the trees, peered through the branches. Karen and Lee Sneddon, Tammy's parents, were arguing in the middle of the car park.

'They're always at it, those two,' Gracie whispered, behind Sean. 'You'd think he'd just fuck off like all the other dads round here. It's not like Karen'd be sad to see him go.'

As though to emphasise Gracie's words, Lee suddenly punched Karen, a sharp jab that snapped her head back and sent her tumbling backwards. Shaking his hand, ignoring her whimpers, he crossed the car park, walking as though he was making his way across the deck of a yawing ship. He got in his car, revved the engine, and tore away, while Karen staggered to her feet and shoved her way back into the pub.

'Did you guys hear about Tammy?' Arlo said.

'No, what about her?' Jake said, perking up. He was desperately in love with Tammy, a pretty blond who lived on Dulwood and was a couple of years above them at their school.

'She's pregnant.'

'No!' Jake said, his face crumpling with despair.

'Sorry, Jakey,' Arlo said. 'Lee's proper pissed off about it.'

'No shit,' Sean muttered. 'She must be… what… fifteen?'

'Fourteen,' Gracie said, flopping down on the mattress. 'Her mum and dad want her to have an abortion but Cassie swears she's keeping the baby. Tammy reckons her dad'll put her out of the house if she keeps it, though.'

They sat in silence for a while, each of them thinking their own thoughts and comfortable enough in each other's company to let the silence grow. It was Gracie who spoke first.

'I hate this place, me. Soon as I'm old enough, I'm getting out of here.'

'Like it's that easy to leave,' Arlo said, joining them on the mattress. 'This place, it's like cement or something. If you hang round too long, it hardens round your feet, doesn't let you go.'

'Yeah, well, I'll just make sure I don't hang round too long then,' Gracie said. 'I won't give the cement time to harden.'

'Grey, you don't know what you're talking about.' Arlo's voice held an edge of bitterness that took Sean by surprise. 'You think there's anyone living on this estate that doesn't want to get out?'

Gracie shrugged. 'Maybe once they wanted out, but people give up easy. That's just the way it is. I don't mean just here, people are the same everywhere.'

Sean watched her, wondering how she knew so much about people everywhere when they had seen so little outside of Dulwood. He hoped she was wrong, though in truth it was not something he often considered. He took each day as it came; it was the only way for him to get by.

'Just the other day I overheard Gizzie talking to my mum about his last interview,' Arlo said. 'You know how hard he grafted at uni, that he came out with a first. Well, none of that mattered, it still went shit for him. Soon as those fancy bastards interviewing him heard where he lived they got all pissy. Asked him if he'd done any work experience over the summer holidays like all the other applicants. But you tell me, how's he supposed to work for free when we're all so skint? It all went downhill from there.'

'Gizzie'll find a way, he'll make it out of Dulwood,' Gracie said. She shoulder-nudged Sean. 'Just like Picasso when he does his Future Creators exam next year.'

'Nah,' Sean shook his head. 'That course costs thousands. My mum… she just doesn't have that sort of cash.'

'We'll think of something,' Gracie said, as though saving thousands of pounds was nothing but a minor inconvenience. 'We've got time to figure it out. Just remember, if you get out of Dulwood first, you take us three with you.'

'Yeah,' Jake said, staring at the glowing tip of his cigarette. 'We get out together or we don't get out at all.'

'I never realised you were so desperate to leave,' Sean said, looking at Gracie.

She frowned at him. 'What are you on about? I want to work for NASA. I can't exactly stay here and do that, can I? All the women here are prozzies or addicts.'

'Hey!' Arlo snapped, shoving Gracie. 'My mum isn't a prozzie or an addict!'

'What's a prozzie?' Sean said.

There was a beat of silence, and then Jake, Arlo and Gracie burst out laughing. Sean felt his cheeks flush, but before any of them could say anything, the door to The Dog and Gun slammed open. Jake, Arlo and Gracie smothered their giggles, huddling deeper into the shadows.

'Oi! Where d'ye little bastards bugger off to, eh?' Diesel Betty's yell was nicotine-stained and gravelly. Sean imagined her stood in the pub's doorway, hands fisted on her hips, her fuzzy beehive sloping at half-mast. 'I'm gonna bray the shit out of all four of ye, see if I don't!'

She slammed the door shut and they all collapsed into fits of laughter. Lying down on the mattress, Gracie turned to Sean. Her eyes still held a smile, but there was curiosity in them, too.

'How do you do it, Sean?'

He blinked, confused. 'Do what?'

She waved her arms expansively, pointing to nothing and everything. To the high tower blocks across the road, the bin sheds behind them, the razor wire that curlicued the top of the walls.

'How do you look around and not see the shit everywhere? It's like you just don't let the darkness in.' Her smile dimmed. 'You paint the world the way you want to see it. I wish I could do that.'

Jake took a sip of The Puke and hiccoughed, passing the drink to Arlo. 'He's just not very of-serpent.'

'*Observant*, you moron,' Gracie said. 'And he's a fucking artist, observing is what he does best.' She turned back to Sean. 'Look up at the sky, tell us what you see.'

'Huh?'

'Just do it, will you.'

'You're taking the piss,' Sean said, making to stand up. The ground lurched beneath him, the tree trunks shifted, blurred. Gracie caught his hand, her eyes on his face. Sean wondered whether she had drunk too much of The Puke, too.

'Please, Sean. I'm not taking the piss. Honest.'

He sighed and lay back down on the mattress. Overhead the stars arced back and forth, as though rocked by the hand of some faceless divinity.

'I see stars, I guess. Same as you.' He glanced at Gracie, but she was still looking upwards, and he could tell she wanted more. He looked up again, squinting, trying to skewer the stars to their fixings.

'Well, I can see Orion.' He shot an arm skywards, one pointed finger sketching the constellation, though the stars seemed to swerve away from his touch. 'And Capella and Auriga, and—'

'I showed you those ages ago,' Gracie said, impatient now. 'Everyone can see them if they know where to look.'

'Grey, what do you want him to say?' Jake said. 'He's already told you—'

'Shhhh!' she snapped.

Jake muttered something indecipherable, Arlo hid his grin in The Puke. Gracie watched Sean.

He took a deep breath and sighed it out. Looking up, he felt as though he could topple straight into the velvet darkness and spin out into the void forever. He wondered how far it stretched, if there was ever any end to it. And even though he was lying here with his three best friends, the vastness of it all suddenly made him feel a loneliness more profound than any he had ever felt before.

His vision blurred, shuffling the stars into new arrangements and shapes. Without thinking, he drew an imaginary pencil across the sky, mapping new constellations.

'I see a canvas,' he said, softly. 'Waiting to be painted.'

Arlo and Jake burst out laughing. Sean's cheeks flared hot again. He sat up, scowling at his friends. But Gracie wasn't laughing. She was still lying down, the skin around her eyes pinched, as though she was straining to see what he saw.

Sean pitched his voice low so the others wouldn't hear him. 'What do you see?'

'I just see stars,' she said, and sighed. 'And a lot of darkness.'

DAY 6

'I want you to think back to that day.'

Miraede closes the pad she has been scribbling in, places it on the table beside her.

'Think about what you did before you went home.'

No, I don't want to. I don't want to think about any of it.

He turns away from her, his thumb working small circles over the scar on his hand. He is aware of the tension in his body, the way his jaw has tightened, his arms crossed over his chest. He had forgotten Miraede was coming to see him today, and had been looking forward to starting a new sculpture straight after breakfast.

'I know it's painful, Sean, but returning to the trauma is the best way of dealing with it, processing it. It's the only way you can recover your voice.'

Who says I want to recover it?

'It was Friday, wasn't it? Your last lesson of the day was Art. You normally went to Arlo's house for takeaway on a Friday after school—'

I'm not going to think about it, you can't make me!

'—but on this particular Friday you weren't going. It was a big day for you. Straight after school you were meeting with the examiners for the Future Creators course. It was a hot day, the hottest of the year, and—'

I'm not doing this I'm not doing this I'm not doing this.

But already an image is forming, growing sharper with every detail Miraede adds to the scene, until the pixels in Sean's mind become smaller, clearer, brighter. Yes, it had been a hot day. Stifling. Sun poured through the classroom windows, turning it into a greenhouse of wilting kids. Mr Dolan's sweat patches spread from beneath his armpits to his ribs, darkening his pale purple shirt to a deep puce. Sean can see him now, slouched behind his desk, fingers laced atop his mountainous belly as he silently eyes his class, as though ruminating on what, specifically, he dislikes about them so much.

Miraede is still talking, but Sean can no longer hear her. He does not need her to paint the scene with words, because the soft lilt of her voice has been replaced by the scuff of chair legs against linoleum and the low buzz of his classmates' chatter.

Outside The Paddock, the day is grim and grey, but Sean's skin tingles with the warmth of a sun that beams through the classroom windows of 8LM. Sweat prickles his back, sticking his school shirt to his skin. There is something in his hands and he looks down, sees that he is holding—

—a clay robin. He can't wait to see Mum's face when he shows it to her. He normally feels embarrassed showing her his

sketches and sculptures, but this is different, somehow. He knows the robin is good.

Mum loves rifling through his art folder at the end of the year. She handles his work with the delicacy of a scholar admiring ancient papyrus, and displays her favourites in frames, as though they are prize pieces in the collection of a world-famous artist.

Sean turns the robin over in his hands. It looks so real, he can almost feel its warmth against his palm, feel the flutter of its caged heartbeat thrumming against his skin.

Arlo slides into the seat beside him and immediately proceeds to rub his own sculpture over Sean's face, making kissy sounds as he does so.

'Get off!' Sean snaps, shoving him away.

'Carmalita! Control yourself!' Arlo shakes a finger at his model and turns to Sean. 'Sorry, man. My girl's horny but I didn't think she'd stoop to trying it on with my best friend.'

Sean frowns at Arlo's clay sculpture. 'That's a girl?'

He supposes there is something vaguely human about the model, though to call it in any way feminine is a stretch. Its face is a square lump, its hair resembles a helmet. A thick torso merges into clunky, shapeless legs. The only indication of the model's gender is supplied by the gigantic twin boulders Arlo has moulded to its chest. Despite the slipshod effort he has made with the rest of the model, Arlo has taken particular care with the model's breasts, which are perfectly symmetrical, lovingly smoothed to a polished finish, and topped with a bullet-hard nipple.

'This isn't just any girl,' Arlo says. 'This is my girl. She makes Tammy McCarthy look like a cave troll, don't you think?'

Sean frowns at the model. 'She looks like a dude.'

'A dude? A dude? What are these, then? Man-mammaries? I don't think so. What you got there, anyway? Come on, show me. What is that? A parrot? A penguin? What?'

'Sean, that's amazing!' Megan says, stopping at his desk. She leans over to look at his clay robin more closely. Her pale hair smells of vanilla and heaven, and Sean flashes Arlo a smug grin. 'Cassie, come look at Sean's robin!'

'It's great, isn't it?' Arlo says, shoving Carmalita behind his back. He nods sagely at Sean's sculpture. 'I was just telling him how good it is. But then, I taught him everything he knows, so—'

'Are you putting this towards your Future Creators exam?' Megan says, turning to Sean. 'You totally should, it's brilliant!'

Before he can answer, the door opens and Mrs Keegan enters. She walks over to Mr Dolan, her eyes scraping the classroom. When she sees Sean, she flinches. And that small expression, that blink-and-you'll-miss-it glance, slams the wind right out of him. Because, right then, he knows.

Mrs Keegan speaks quietly to Mr Dolan and the two of them step out of the classroom. The door closes and the volume in the classroom swells. Kane stands up and pounds his crotch against his table, making high-pitched gaspy sounds. Some people laugh, others glare at him as though they want his head to implode. Sean barely notices Kane. His hand tightens around *his clay robin, squeezes until its sharp beak cuts into his palm.*

The bell rings and everyone starts packing their things away and racing out of the room. Arlo shouts something about calling later to tell him how the meeting with the examiners went, but Sean barely hears him. He stays in his seat, as though someone has pressed a pause button that works on him alone.

When Mrs Keegan comes back into the classroom, she is wearing that same heart-slam expression on her face. She asks him to follow her to her office. Her perfume, citrusy and sharp, makes his stomach twist.

Sean panics. His head is a shaken snow-globe, each snowflake a question, trapped in the glass orb of his skull, but he can't open his mouth to frame even one of them. He is too scared. By the time he reaches Mrs Keegan's office, all those snowflake-questions have amalgamated into one huge, snow-packed boulder, too big now to put into words, encompassing too much.

Mrs Keegan closes the office door, tells him to sit down. He expects her to sit across the desk from him, but she doesn't. Instead, she sits beside him. Sean stares at his shoes, unable to lift his eyes to hers and see the answer to his question in her face. He feels as though he is going to be sick.

Mrs Keegan puts her hand on his shoulder, and with a catch in her voice, she starts to talk. Her words fall on Sean's frozen heart like an anvil on a frozen block of ice, smashing it to pieces. His hand tightens around the clay robin, until its sharp beak breaks his skin and a thin runnel of blood dribbles down his palm.

DAY 7

On Saturday night, Grandad takes Sean back to the youth club, but this time, instead of watching his grandson walk inside, he drives off as soon as Sean shuts the car door.

After nearly catching frostbite sitting in the church last Wednesday, Sean is wearing a jumper and shirt beneath his coat, as well as gloves, scarf and a beanie hat. If Grandad noticed his excessive layering he didn't say anything, but then, he's had a distracted look in his eyes all day. When he made omelettes at lunchtime he cracked the eggs straight into the dustbin instead of the frying pan, and later when they were clearing up, Sean saw him put the salt and pepper in the fridge. He had barely spoken a word all day, and silence lay over the house like a thick patina of dust.

Still, Sean thinks as he pushes the heavy doors to the church open, *I'm in no position to hold something like* that *against him.*

The candles in the narthex flicker in the sudden draught. This time, Sean leaves them burning. He is hoping Jock, Bling and Snake will return so he can sketch them and he will see their faces better in the candlelight. He finds a pew a few rows closer to the narthex than last time and takes out his sketchpad and pencils, laying everything out so he's ready if they come in.

Moonlight spears the church's stained-glass windows, painting the deepening shadows in broad blue brushstrokes.

He has almost given up on them by the time the doors swing open and Snake strolls in. He hovers in the narthex, rolling himself a cigarette. When he strikes a match, the flame throws his features into sharp relief: hooded eyes set in deep pockets, a thin, downturned mouth, rough, sallow skin.

Moving quietly, Sean starts to draw. With one eye on Snake and the other inside a dream, his hand sweeps over the paper, recreating the man in shades of leaden grey. Snake turns to blow smoke towards the altar, and Sean ducks to avoid being seen. There is scorn for the church and everything it represents in the cancerous fumes the drug dealer directs towards the altar. *Perhaps God failed Snake, too,* Sean thinks.

When Jock and Bling enter the church a few minutes later, he turns the page and starts a new sketch. Snake, Jock and Bling stay for less than five minutes, but Sean falls into a sort of trance after they leave and sketches for almost two hours.

When, finally, he comes back to his surroundings, he realises with a jolt that it is almost ten past nine. He is late meeting Grandad. He shoves his sketchpad and pencils into his rucksack and hurries outside. After sitting still for so long in the cold, the sudden movement sets off detonations of pain in his bad knee.

The stars are bright pinpoints, diamonds shattered against a sky of black glass. Sean hesitates on the frost-glazed path.

The car park is empty.

Grandad is not here.

Sean checks his mobile but there are no text messages to say he is running late. To warm his aching knee he walks up and down the path, but the movement only aggravates the pain, so he sits on the wall and waits. Every approaching car has his head snapping up expectantly, but none of them are Grandad's and Sean begins to worry.

He's ditched me.

It isn't that much of a surprise, he was always going to end up back in Creswick Hall. But only now does he realise how desperately he doesn't want to go back there. He has grown accustomed to Grandad's company. Unlike Miraede who, despite her good intentions, speaks to him as though she is hoping to trick a response from him, unlike the kids in the home, who were always teasing him for his conversion disorder, unlike Mr Collins, who treated him as though he was faking his condition as part of some bid to seek attention, Grandad talks to him as though he is a normal person, as though their one-sided conversation is the most natural thing in the world.

Sean remembers his old room at Creswick Hall and wonders whether it is still empty. *Maybe some new kids have arrived. Maybe Tony won't be there anymore.*

But he knows that's wishful thinking. Almost all the kids in

Creswick Hall have violent or aggressive tendencies, and as the smallest Sean would always be easy pickings. He remembers how Tony used to hide his knee brace and trip him up when he went hobbling round the house to find it, how he would swipe the key card to his room from the office so he and his mates could enter in the night, pin him down and pull his pyjama leg over his lumpy, twisted knee for the new arrivals to ogle with disgust or fascination or, worst of all, pity.

At least I'll have a roof over my head.

He thinks of the posters that line the walls of the corridor. 'A Family Home Like Any Other!' But what family home has posters along the hallway promoting safe sex and hand-washing hygiene? What family home has a phone that rings off the hook and a warden who makes a note of what you're wearing each morning, so he can give the police your description if you decide to run away?

Twin beams of light splash across Sean, and Grandad's car pulls up beside him. He climbs in, almost weak with relief. Huddled low in his seat, he rubs his hands up and down his arms, feeling as though he is slowly defrosting.

'Sorry I'm late, lad.' Grandad's apology sounds flat, and he does not turn to look at Sean when he delivers it.

The tang of alcohol wafts from Grandad's skin, though Sean has never seen him take a drink. It is a smell that pulls him back to Dulwood, reminding him of gatherings his mum arranged at their flat, of knocking back The Puke outside The Dog and Gun.

When they get back to the house, Sean sits in the kitchen watching Grandad make them both a hot chocolate. The distractedness that had attended him earlier is more pronounced, and there is a grogginess to his movements, as though he has either just woken up or is on the brink of falling asleep.

Grandad's gaze slides to the window as he stirs chocolate into the hot milk. At first, Sean thinks he is running a critical eye over his garden, feeling guilty about allowing his strict routine to slip, but Grandad does not look worried or guilty. He looks blank. His blue eyes are glazed, like windows to an empty room. And anyway, it is not the garden that he is looking at.

Grandad is staring at the shed.

Trying to ignore his unease, Sean takes his hot chocolate into the library and lights the fire. As the room fills with the smell of smoking logs and the sound of snapping flames, he calms.

He picks up *The Baku*, but before he can find his page, he hears the patio door in the kitchen slide open. Sean sets the book down, pulls the thick curtains back to look out of the window into the garden. The sensor lights wink on as Grandad walks across the lawn.

The old man's breath churns on the air in front of his face. Wearing his slippers, a shirt and jeans, he is not dressed for the chilly night.

Grandad passes the neat rows of vegetables, the flower beds, the pond, the nest swing, the rowan tree.

He walks to the darkest corner of the garden.

And stops.

He stands motionless in front of the shed, his back to Sean. The shadows around the building are darker than the shadows everywhere else, oilier, sleeker, yet somehow more solid. Looking at the graven angels that stand by the door to the shed, Sean is sure they are grinning. And even though he knows it is impossible he could swear the shed is grinning too. He can't see its smile, but he can *feel* it, a thickening frost against his skin.

Sean watches Grandad move towards the door of the shed. Moonlight glances down something in his hand. A key. Somehow, Sean knows it is the old key that normally hangs on the rack in the hallway. Grandad reaches out and slots it into the lock.

And it is inside that moment – between Grandad sliding the key into the lock and twisting it – that Sean realises what the old building used to be.

It was his writing shed.

The knowledge is a murmur, deep in Sean's subconscious. He thinks of the twitching curtain he saw the other day, the conviction that there had been something in there, watching him, and represses a shudder.

Grandad pockets the key and tries to open the door, but it doesn't budge. He heaves his shoulder against the wood and it swings open. As it does, Sean feels everything change, as though reality has buckled somehow, leaving behind a kink where before everything was straight.

Grandad flicks a light on inside the shed, and the eyes of the stone cherubs roll towards Sean.

He gasps and staggers back, cracking his heel on the coffee table behind him. He tells himself that he is being ridiculous, that he imagined it, that the darkness is playing tricks on his eyes.

But he is lying.

The cherubs' eyes, which a moment ago had been lost in shadow, now gleam with a pearly light, as the sensor lights strike them from a different angle.

Sean catches a glimpse of dark wood floor panels inside the shed, a desk, a chair, an old computer. And then Grandad closes the door.

Sean slumps onto the sofa. Logs crackle and spit in the hearth, filling the room with a heat that no longer soothes him. He sips the hot chocolate but it tastes sickly. He tells himself there is no reason to feel alarmed or worried. He must have imagined the stone cherubs moving, he *must* have. There's no reason to be afraid.

DAY 8

Sitting across from Miraede in the library, Sean stares out into the garden. The rain has been depressingly relentless all night and the leaden sky shows no indication it is about to stop. The flowers quiver beneath the ceaseless downpour, hard pellets of rain making the pond water seethe and boil.

Miraede's voice filters through to Sean from far away, but he is tuned in to the frequency of his own thoughts and barely hears her.

Miraede stays for half an hour. She mentions school a few times, tries again to persuade him to use hypnosis as a way of rediscovering his voice. She talks about a local art class, encourages him to join, and goes on to talk in a nebulous fashion about courage and opportunities, acceptance and denial. All the usual clichés.

When she stands to leave, Sean stands too, a small courtesy that he hopes compensates in some small way for his failure to engage with her the way she wants him to.

But Miraede is not looking at him.

She is looking out of the window.

At Grandad.

Striding across the lawn, his chin tucked low, shoulders hunched against the bitter wind. No coat, despite the driving rain. Slippers, despite the sodden grass. For the first time since Sean's arrival at The Paddock, Grandad has not spent any of his morning in the garden, choosing instead to stay in the writing shed.

Sean does not like the look on Miraede's face. At first it is hard to say why, but when she moves to the window, her eyes still tracking Grandad down the garden, and says, without looking at Sean, that she will be back next Monday, he thinks he knows what he sees in her expression.

Suspicion.

It is late afternoon and Sean is sat on a chair beneath the rowan tree, sketching, when Grandad finally emerges from the writing shed.

He disappears into the house and when he comes back outside, Sean is relieved to see he has pulled on his gardening clothes, the canvas trousers with padded knees, his body-warmer and his heavy-duty boots.

He spends the next hour on top of a ladder, clearing leaves from the gutter, then pruning the hedges and rose bushes, and even though it is a far cry from the five to six hours a day he normally puts in, Sean takes it as a good sign. When Grandad passes him on his way to the greenhouse, he ruffles his grandson's hair and Sean notes, with a touch of relief, the rugged colour in the old man's cheeks, the vibrant sparkle in his eyes.

He emerges from the greenhouse ten minutes later, shaking soil from two handfuls of freshly picked onions and garlic. Sean goes to help him in the kitchen, and they spend the next hour cooking a bean and sausage hotpot for dinner. Sean cleans and chops the vegetables, grateful in ways he cannot express for the sound of Grandad's voice, which washes through the kitchen, sweeping away the stagnant silence that has elbowed its way between them during the past few days.

If Sean notices a dullness creeping into Grandad's eyes as the afternoon slides towards evening, or a tendency for him to drift into silence mid-sentence, he is quick to dismiss it. He's an old man, after all, and he's been busy. It's no wonder he's exhausted.

Consoled by the sight of Grandad working the garden, Sean goes inside. He crawls into bed and quickly falls asleep.

Luca is walking home with Phoenix, who is babbling away beside him, seemingly oblivious to the fact his friend is not listening. The sun pierces the rips in the clouds, splashing golden bars of light on the pavement. Luca jumps over the shadows so that he only lands on the sunlit paving slabs, even though he is too old for such games, and finds that he can leap almost as high as the trees before floating down to the ground. Phoenix's voice grows quieter as he soars skyward, louder as he drifts downwards again.

His feet connect with the ground and the bars of clouds overhead seal closed. Darkness rolls across the day. Luca's feet sink into the stone slabs as though they were as insubstantial as jelly, then swiftly harden, fastening him in place. He processes this with a detached acceptance: he did *land on a shadow, so it stands to reason that the ground should eat him. Phoenix keeps walking, his voice fading as he disappears round the corner.*

The stone around Luca's feet is painfully cold. He glances up at the sky and is dismayed to see the clouds are thick and dark. He might have to wait a long time before the sun breaks clear to release him.

He glances over his shoulder and freezes.

The Mirror-Eyed Man is sat in the bus shelter. His head is bent, his long fingers curl around his kneecaps. He is not looking at Luca, but the boy feels the weight of his eyes burning through him, nevertheless. With a cry, he tries to wrench his feet free of the stone, but he is held fast.

A snatched glance reveals the Mirror-Eyed Man has moved. Now, he is stood beneath the lamppost and has almost halved the distance between them. His silhouette is so dark, it is as though someone has cut his shape from a starless night sky. Cobwebby strands of hair hang down his neck and he is tall, so tall, Luca can imagine him reaching his tapered fingers to the sky and carving a gash through the clouds. He is old, oh yes, he is old, but he is strong. So strong, he could snap Luca like a twig if he wanted to. But it is his eyes that Luca is most afraid of, because it is those mirrors of black glass that will end him.

He desperately tries to liberate his feet, hooking his hands around the back of one knee, tugging until his arms ache and his shoulders feel as though they are going to pop from their sockets. The cold tightens around him and he doesn't want to look oh god he doesn't want to look, but he does and the Mirror-Eyed Man is closer to him, so close now, so close, so terribly close and Luca grinds his teeth together, wishing he had a hacksaw or a rip-blade because if he did he would cut off his own feet to get away, oh he would he would, he'd do anything anything anything to get away from the Mirror-Eyed Man.

He squeezes his eyes closed, tells himself don't look don't look *but something touches the nape of his neck, wrapping round his skin like cold, wet tendrils. He shakes his head, his breath tearing in and out as he tries to twist away, the voice in his head grows louder and faster* DON'T LOOK DON'T LOOK DON'T LOOK *but cold fingers pull at the skin around his eyes, forcing them to open. Luca starts to scream.*

Sean wakes in a darkness so thick it bears down on him, heavy as sodden furs. His heart thunders, his hands are fisted around the bedsheets. There is a foul smell in the room, and he shivers in a pool of icy sweat.

He flicks the switch on his bedside lamp and runs his hands through his hair. The dream clings to his consciousness, and for a moment his own identity is smothered by that of Luca, so that he, Sean, feels like the dream, and Luca the reality. Never before has he had a dream like it. So vivid, so terrifying, and so *convincing*. He knew everything, *every*thing about Luca. Not only the colour of his hair and eyes, his height, the location, shape and size of his birthmarks, but also his personality, his likes and dislikes, his favourite foods, his phobias, his *memories*. Where and with whom he had learnt to ride his bike, the gifts he had received for past birthdays and Christmases, his favourite teachers and the names of his best friends. So much detail awaiting the brush of his thoughts, as though it had always been there.

The chill in the air is lifting, and as the room warms Sean's fear thaws. His pillow is soaked in sweat, so he flips it over.

Something flicks from beneath it onto the floor.

He reaches over, picks up a folded piece of paper. It is coated in a bilious slime. He unfolds it, cringing at the gummy strings that stretch across its edges. The ink is smudged but legible.

Name: Luca Russell
Age: 13
Nightmare: The Mirror-Eyed Man

The note falls from Sean's numb fingers. It is impossible. It must be a trick. Grandad. He must have put the note there. There's no other explanation. *Sure, yeah. And Grandad synched your dream to the note he shoved under your pillow. Course he did.*

No, that was obviously ridiculous. And besides, writing something like that and stuffing it under Sean's pillow as he slept would be a cruel trick. Not Grandad's style at all. *But what's the alternative, Seanie? That the Baku put it there?*

As he stares at the note on the floor it begins to curl inwards, crumpling as though crushed by an invisible hand, its edges smouldering, blackening. Sean scrabbles backwards on his bed, his eyes fixed and staring.

The note is a charred, smoking ball.

It is a pile of ash.

And then it is nothing at all.

DAY 9

The first thing Sean does when he goes downstairs is put *The Baku: A Selection of Short Stories* back on the shelf in the library. He is only halfway through the fourth story, 'Matilda', but he has no inclination to read any more after last night.

He had stayed awake for hours, tossing and turning, the nightmare playing over and over in his mind. He tells himself that he dreamt the note, but he knows it was real. He can still feel the texture of that scrap of paper between his fingers and the whisper of Luca's consciousness within his own.

When Sean goes into the kitchen, he finds Grandad standing over the cooker, frying bacon.

'We're heading out after you've eaten,' Grandad says, taking the pan off the hob and tipping the bacon onto a plate. 'There's a sculpture park out near Wakefield I thought we could visit.' Grandad slides the bacon onto the table beside a plate of buttered bread. 'It was that sculpture you did the other day that made me think of it. It's quite a big park, so I imagine you'd want to take your knee brace. What do you say, lad?'

Sean, of course, says nothing.

It is over an hour's drive to the Yorkshire Sculpture Park, but Grandad could not have picked a better day for the trip. After a night of steady rainfall, the sky is a cold, hard blue, feathered by ragged white clouds. Sean feels himself relax as he watches the fields and trees roll past the window. Grandad seems to enjoy getting out of the house, too. The further he drives, the chattier he becomes, as though the miles they put between themselves and The Paddock ease some invisible burden.

Grandad talks about the sculpture park. He tells Sean that it is set in over five hundred acres of land, that the collection is a mixture of loans and gifts from the artists. There is a lake and a woodland dotted with sculptures. Grandad has looked online and seen some of the pieces, and is especially looking forward to seeing the Woodland Spirit, Diana, a bronze statue of a woman that reminded him of the sculpture Sean made. Perhaps one day, Grandad says, Sean might be the one loaning his work to the Yorkshire Sculpture Park.

When they arrive the car park is quiet and only a few people are milling about on the path that leads to the main entrance. Grandad goes to pay for parking while Sean straps his knee brace on.

He stifles a yawn as he climbs out of the car and stretches. He has never seen so much greenery. Vast fields slope down to a thick band of trees in the distance. Halfway down the field there are three vertical sculptures. Set against the fields and trees, they look striking, almost prehistoric, like ancient totem posts or pillars. Had it not been for the modern building behind him, the cars in the car park, Sean feels as though he could be looking at the fields and hills as they were thousands of years ago.

'Henry Moore,' Grandad says, coming up beside him but looking across the field at the sculptures. 'He constructed twelve of them in total. Beautiful, aren't they? There's an exhibition of his in one of the galleries on the other side of the lake. Come on, let's have a look.'

Sean walks with Grandad into the main building, where a lady checks Grandad's tickets then motions them inside.

Walls of glass overlook verdant lawns dotted with sculptures: a huge white orchid, its petals unfurled around the stamen; an cast-iron tree with leafless bronze branches; a gravity-defying tower of cubes, precariously stacked.

They reach an alcove which houses a display of paintings, sketches and prints. Sean studies each one, soaking them all up, feeding a craving he had not known he had, only for it to swell and grow inside him, to demand more.

The back of the building opens out onto beautiful vast lawns braced by hedges. More sculptures line the pathways. Beside each one there is a plaque which names the piece and its artist.

Sean wanders, captivated, from piece to piece, but it is not only the man-made sculptures that awe him. The sky is a blue canvas that shifts and changes before his eyes and the woodland carpet contains all the colours of autumn. For the first time in weeks, he feels as though he can breathe freely.

The path forks in different directions and Sean follows a muddied trail into a tunnel of trees that broadens into a sort of den. Within the dappled shade, the dew-damp leaves glitter like emerald furs. There are no sculptures within the embrace of the trees, but Sean turns on the spot, mesmerised, his head tilted to the branches and the shafts of light that stream through the tiny gaps in the canopy. The air feels dense with magic.

Grandad follows Sean through the warren of trees and out the other side, where the path splits. The ground is thick with leaves and Sean kicks his way through them, unaware of the small smile tugging at his lips, or the broader smile on his grandad's face as he watches him.

Grandad orders two steak and ale pies and a pot of tea in the canteen. He and Sean eat the food outside, on a veranda that overlooks the valley. Sean, who despite his grandad's undeniable culinary talents has struggled to eat a full meal since arriving at The Paddock, finds the fresh air has restored his appetite and shovels the food into his mouth.

'Steady on, lad,' Grandad says, laughing. 'No one's going to take it from you.'

After lunch they set off for the lake. The path winds down the hill, growing more treacherous the closer they get to the water, until it turns into nothing but a muddied track. Sean is wearing walking boots but the leaves are slippery underfoot, the rutted cow path veined with tree roots. Despite wearing his brace, his knee is beginning to ache, but he is too enchanted by his surroundings to care.

Sean and Grandad stop to read a sign that lists all the different types of birds that can be found around the lake: goldfinch, cormorants, swallows and kingfishers. Sean can hear their birdsong all around him, their harmonious music interrupted every now and then by the harsh cawing of crows. *A murder of crows*, Sean thinks, his eyes moving over the trees.

They start to walk round the lake and Grandad points out the different types of birds on the water: coots and mallards, black-headed gulls and moorhens. He seems to know everything about them, sharing details of how to tell them apart, how they differ in nature, what they eat, when they breed. But Sean is far more interested in the trees than the birds. He has never seen any like the ones that surround him now. They are colossal, seeming to stretch skywards forever, their branches as thick as ordinary tree trunks. Sean notices many of the largest have little black plaques nailed into the bark, dedications to the dead. They remind him of Nanna Storm's rowan tree in Grandad's garden.

Sean's knee is becoming increasingly sore. Grandad must notice because he keeps stopping, ostensibly to look at a sculpture or to admire the view, but only doing so when he comes to a bench or a wall on which Sean can sit down to rest. Sean is touched by the old man's consideration, but he stays on his feet, worried Grandad will take his sitting as a sign they should head home. Sean wants to see the Henry Moore exhibition across the lake, but even more than that, he does not want to go back to The Paddock.

They cross a narrow bridge on stilts, below which water bubbles over shelves of rock. A flock of birds take flight in a furious beat of wings. Sean's foot snags on a tree root and he falls. Pain drills into his knee. Grandad turns, hurries to help him up, but Sean quickly pulls himself to his feet and they carry on.

They reach some stepping-stones that cut across a narrow part of the lake and Grandad moves ahead of Sean, spritely as a man half his age. When he reaches the other side, he turns back to Sean with a broad grin. The old man's smile falls when he sees the pain-creased face of his grandson, cautiously moving across the stepping-stones.

'I think it's time we call it a day,' Grandad says, when Sean reaches him.

Sean feels heat crush his cheeks and he curses his damned knee. Grandad is barely out of breath. In fact, he has never looked better. His cheeks are ruddy, blue eyes bright as the cerulean sky. He could probably walk round this lake five times over if he was on his own. He'd get to see the Woodland Nymph then, too. *My fault, all my fault*, Sean chastises himself, thinking longingly of the Henry Moore exhibition. *My stupid fault*.

'We can come back another day, lad,' Grandad says, reading the disappointment in Sean's eyes. 'The exhibition will be here a while, you'll still get to see it.'

Sean feels deflated as they start to walk back, but he knows Grandad is right. The excitement of seeing the exhibition had dulled the pain's sharpest edges, but now that they are leaving, every second step feels like the jaws of a steel trap are closing around his knee.

They retrace their steps over the stepping-stones, across the bridge and down the narrow path bordered by a dense thicket. Despite his throbbing knee, Sean stops, noticing a piece they must have walked straight past earlier. Nestled amidst the trees, made of wood rather than the metals so many of the other sculptures are made from, it blends almost seamlessly with the surroundings.

The plaque mounted in front of it names the piece: *Six Mourners and The One Alone*. It consists of six wooden posts, positioned in an arc, with a seventh set closest to the path. Carved into the wood of the seventh post is the inscription: *The suddenness of your departure is still hard to believe*.

The cold that slams into Sean seems to come from nowhere. He turns as still as the wooden post at which he stares, unblinking, undone by something – *what is it?* – that he feels deep in his core but cannot bring to the front of his mind. It is tucked away, trembling in the darkest corner of his consciousness, shying from the touch of his thoughts.

Clouds slide across the sun, the day darkens. The sound of birdsong grows quiet as the crows grow louder. Their coarse voices swell to a cacophony that fills Sean's world, scrambling his thoughts. So loud. They are so *loud.*

He looks up. Crows – *a murder of crows!* – flutter around the trees like black confetti. They thrash at the branches, frenzied, erratic. There is something snared high up in the branches and it is this that has driven the birds to madness. At first, Sean thinks it's a bird's nest. But it isn't the right shape. *It looks like…* The thought stutters as horror pulses through him. *It looks like a baby!* A baby, swaddled in blankets and left high up in the tree branches.

Sean shakes his head. *That's ridiculous!* But now he can hear the thin, warbling cries of an infant over the raucous squawks of the crows. He squeezes his eyes shut as the memory of Khaba's dream fills his head. *It isn't real it isn't real it isn't real.* But that doesn't stop his heart from tripping faster, his hair follicles from lifting in a million icy pinpricks.

The sound of the crows is a violence, a savage tearing, ripping away the contentment that had settled inside Sean. A *murder of crows.* A *murder. Murder murder murder.* The ugly word swells in his thoughts, as though growing fat on itself, like his own horror.

The swaddled baby is knocked sideways by the crows. Sean gasps, expecting some demonic creature to thud to the ground, some beast with burning eyes and incurved horns and hard-packed muscles. But whatever it is breaks apart as it falls, a hail of snapped twigs and woodland debris. The crows shatter from the trees, their ear-splitting caws fade to silence.

Slowly, birdsong creeps back into the day. But Sean hears only the sound of Nikare's tiny wails, beneath the grating caw of the crows.

Grandad makes little small talk in the car on the way home, and Sean feels the gloom that had lifted briefly as they walked through the sculpture park settle over him again. He has no medication on him to ease the pain in his knee and his mood only sinks deeper at the thought of returning to The Paddock.

In an exact reversal of what had happened when they drove away from The Paddock earlier, Grandad's face grows darker as they near the house, tension gathers at the edges of his mouth.

Sean realises how quickly and how heavily he has come to rely on the old man's cheerful good nature and easy company. He has never met his own dad, and despite the brevity of their relationship, Grandad is the closest thing to a father-figure he has ever known.

The clouds have thickened, the day darkens towards dusk. Grandad has turned on the heating and the warmth of the car feels safe. Sean closes his eyes. Lulled by the motion of the car, reassured by Grandad's presence, he plummets into sleep.

* * *

I peer round the column, watching Mother as she rocks back and forth on her birthing bricks, keening with pain. I can smell the saffron the nurses have rubbed on her swollen belly, the emmer wheat and honey.

They sing toneless incantations as her cries grow harsher, invoking the goddesses, Taweret, Meskhenet and Amun, but I fear they will not answer. Something is not right. Mother's cries are animalistic, panicked. She didn't make such noises when she birthed Meru. There wasn't this much blood then, either. It slides down her thighs, pools around her knees and congeals on the bricks.

Nyla once told me that the birth of a child is like the rising of a sun, but watching Mother, as she cries and rocks and bleeds, is like watching the sun crash from the sky.

Her head drops to her breastbone, her back heaves upwards, her swollen belly droops. Blood flows quicker, so thick and dark it obliterates the colourful scenes painted on the birthing blocks. I start towards her, even though I'm not supposed to be here, even though if I am seen, I will be punished. But the nurses are too busy with Mother to notice me.

The tall one kneels beside her, places her hands between Mother's legs to guide the baby from her body. The other one smiles, the expression hideous inside the echo of Mother's distressed wail.

Mother sags to the floor. She is not moving, but I do not go to her. I can't. Not now that I can see. Not now that I know. The smiling nurse cuts the umbilical cord, the tall one scoops Mother's blood into her cupped palms and rubs it on the baby's skin to protect it from demons.

But it is too late for that.

Mother has not given birth to a baby. The creature that has slithered from her womb is a demon. This is Ammit, Set and Kek, all three rolled into one. The sight of it steals my breath and I press my hand to my mouth and bite down, hard, pray silently to Taweret for mercy, to Horus for protection, to Aten that he might yet shine on Mother again.

The beast's flesh is the colour of bone, ridged and hard. Its limbs are stacked with solid muscle, a thick tail curls from its lower spine. Horns split the skin at its temples, swoop down beneath its jaw, and separate into tapered points, like the branches of a tree. Its nostrils are serpentine slits, its eyes are crimson fire, its feet are claws.

As though it can hear my private prayers, its head snaps round to me. A slow grin creeps over its face – brother! – lips skinning back to reveal row upon row of black hypodermic fangs. It leaps from the nurse's arms and scrabbles towards me, leaving a skid mark of blood in its wake. Its twisted horns gouge the mud tiles, and I have time to observe the swivel of its arms and legs, the infernal heat that blazes from its eyes, before, finally, I open my mouth and scream.

Sean gasps awake, his legs kicking out, whacking the underside of the glovebox. Grandad jumps, his hands jerking on the wheel, making them swerve on the road.

'Jesus, lad,' Grandad says, flicking him a glance. 'Are you alright?'

Sean barely hears him. He is staring at the item on his lap that had not been there when he fell asleep. Grandad's eyes are on the road, oblivious. Sean does not pick up the roll of papyrus. Already knows that if he does, he will see ancient hieroglyphics etched upon it. And that is frightening, but more frightening still is the knowledge that he will understand them. Better not to look, to watch the papyrus turn dark at the edges, smoulder, burn to ashes and disappear.

After Sean has cleared the dinner plates, he finds Grandad in the library. He is stood by the window, staring at the writing shed. Outside, the pond lights illuminate the algae and lily pads, fairy lights bracelet the trees and the moon's glow traces the contours of the garden. But not one blade of light falls on the writing shed.

Grandad turns around when Sean shuts the door. His eyes are like flat buttons and his expression is slack. They sit and read together, but Sean does not notice Grandad turn the page of his book once. Every so often, the old man's gaze slides to the window and that deadened look in his eyes deepens.

Grandad's strange behaviour makes it impossible for Sean to concentrate on his book and he decides to go to bed early. Grandad does not look up when he walks out of the room.

In the hallway, Sean's gaze snags on the key. He moves towards it, thinking, *I could hide it or throw it away. If Grandad can't get into the writing shed, maybe he'll go back to the way he was.*

His hand moves towards the key, and as it does, a rime of ice coats his fingertips. The silence of the house thrums over him, at first like a soft tide, low and shushing, but quickly growing, coagulating in the air. Every breath becomes grey and stagnant, tinged with death. And even though Sean cannot hear a voice, the silent warning that screams through the house is electric.

He staggers away from the key and the instant he does, the air clears, the smell dissipates. Sean feels the malice bleed from the atmosphere, like infection from a lanced wound.

Gulping in deep breaths, he hurries upstairs. He slams his bedroom door shut behind him and climbs into bed, drawing the covers up around his neck. Sweat sheathes his skin, but he is shivering so violently he has to clamp his jaw together to stop his teeth clattering against each other.

A few minutes later he hears Grandad moving round in the hallway. He doesn't need to see him to know he is sliding the skeleton key from its peg, and when Sean looks out of his bedroom window, he sees Grandad walking across the lawn towards the shed.

BEFORE

Sean had been trick-or-treating with Arlo, Gracie and Jake for hours and now he was exhausted. They had caught a bus into Leeds, then another into the suburbs, so they could work their way around the nicer neighbourhoods where the adults welcomed children with indulgent smiles and generous sugary offerings rather than angry insults and threats.

Sean was dressed as Pennywise, Gracie was Frankenstein, Jake was Darth Maul and Arlo was Harlequin. Sean had done Jake's Darth Maul face paint for him and had made him a double-bladed lightsaber using a small PVC pipe for the centre, pipe insulation, masking tape and metallic spray paint. Jake was thrilled with the way he looked, and had been swinging the lightsaber round all evening, brandishing it at every house owner at whom they yelled, 'Happy Halloween!'

Now, each of their giant-sized pumpkin buckets was straining beneath the prodigious weight of sweets they contained. Jake's was so full his handle had snapped, and now he carried the plastic bucket close to his chest, hindering his wild lightsaber flourishes.

It was after nine o'clock and they were back in Dulwood, the last trick-or-treaters on the streets. Sean's knee throbbed from all the walking. He didn't want to complain, but he knew he couldn't walk much further.

Small kids were rarely seen on the streets of Dulwood after dinnertime. Unlike the houses they had visited in the suburbs, where almost everyone had decorations and had left a pumpkin outside their door to welcome trick-or-treaters, most of the houses and flats on Dulwood were unadorned. This was a neighbourhood that wanted to be left well alone, where children were looked upon, not with fondness, but with suspicion and wariness. They were criminals in the making, their paths clearly carved – predetermined. On Dulwood, fear was real and it was ever-present, not something that was manufactured once a year with fake blood and pantomime screams.

'Holy shit,' Arlo said. 'Diesel Betty's left a pumpkin out.'

Sean followed Arlo's pointing finger to Diesel Betty's house. Sure enough, a pumpkin was balanced on top of her dustbin. It was not one of those polystyrene ones with the little LED inside; this was a proper, hand-carved pumpkin, with a tea light burning inside it. Sean imagined Diesel Betty sat at her kitchen table, hacking at the insides of the squash with a knife, scooping out the soggy innards, a scowl on her face and a cigarette clamped between her lips. The image was oddly endearing.

'It's a trap,' Gracie said, her eyes narrowing. 'It has to be.'

'She'll be waiting behind the door,' Arlo said, 'with a knife.'

'Or an empty vodka bottle,' Gracie nodded.

'Her granddaughter just had a baby,' Jake said, his eyes on the jack-o'-lantern. 'Great-grannies don't commit murder. Everyone knows that.'

He adjusted his pumpkin bucket, hoisted his lightsaber and moved up Diesel Betty's path. Sean looked at the others, shrugged, followed him.

'Ah, shit,' Gracie muttered.

Jake knocked on the door. Sean, Gracie and Arlo hung back, ready to turn tail and run if they needed to. The door swung open and Diesel Betty glared down at them. She was wearing a grubby dressing gown and slippers that were probably once white and fluffy but were now grey and worn. Her beehive, free of its pins, hung round her shoulders in ragged grey tails. As ever, a cigarette was wedged in her lipless mouth.

'Happy Halloween!' Sean, Jake, Gracie and Arlo said in unison, though for the first time that night, their voices rose a touch, like they were asking a question. Subconsciously they huddled closer together, watching Diesel Betty as though she were a dangerous animal. They hoped for sweets, but they could just as easily get a cuff round the back of the head.

But then Sean noticed the huge plastic bowl in Diesel Betty's hands. It was full to the brim with treats. She had everything in there: Parma Violets, bubble gum, sherbet sticks, sugar skulls; there were Dracula fangs, bags of jelly brains, Black Jacks and Banana Skids. And chocolate. Chocolate bars, chocolate pumpkins, chocolate mice. Sean could feel his eyeballs swelling in their sockets.

Diesel Betty must have just replenished the bowl, or, more likely, no other trick-or-treaters had dared to knock on her door. Sean thought of the witch in Hansel and Gretel who built a house made of gingerbread, sugar and cake to tempt kids inside so she could cook them in her oven and eat them. He tried to remember how the story ended, whether the witch succeeded in cooking Hansel and Gretel or whether they escaped, then shook the thought away. Diesel Betty was an eccentric alcoholic, not a wicked witch who wanted to eat them.

'You're looking lovely this evening, Betty!' Jake said, grinning as he took a packet of jelly witches from the bowl. He dropped the bag into his bucket then reached into the bowl for more sweets, but was promptly slapped away.

'One packet, ye wee bastard,' Diesel Betty snarled.

Sean moved forwards and scooped up a packet of chocolate mice with a mumbled thanks.

'How's your ma?' Diesel Betty said, watching Sean as Gracie moved forwards. 'I 'ant seen her since her last shift in't Gun.'

'She's okay,' Sean said, wishing it were true, hoping Diesel Betty couldn't read the lie in his face.

Gracie took a packet of Skittles and Jake groaned. 'Shit, I didn't see them! Can I swap 'em, Betty?'

'Ye can shut ye trap,' Diesel Betty said, shaking the bowl at Arlo. 'Come on you, take summat, I 'ant got all day.'

Arlo swiped a Twix. 'Thanks, Betty.'

They turned to walk away, but Diesel Betty said, 'I hear ye been over to see young Harvey.'

'He lets us shoot his guns,' Jake said around a mouthful of jellies. Gracie kicked him and Jake glared at her. 'Why you always kicking me, man?'

'Bloody fuckin' guns, easier to get round here than a fuckin' house plant,' Diesel Betty muttered.

'We only shoot cans,' Sean said, feeling the need to defend Harvey. 'And he always makes sure we're careful.'

'I pop over to check on him now and again,' Diesel Betty said, her eyes moving up the street towards the sound of raised voices. 'Take his shopping and whatnot.' Her gaze fastened on them like a slap band, her face hardened. 'I hope ye weren't taking advantage of his nature, making fun like. He has it hard enough already.'

They all quickly shook their heads, watching Diesel Betty with round-eyed solemnity.

'Good, good,' she said. 'He's a big fella but he's too soft. Lonely, too, and that's the worst of it. Aye, that's just about the worst.'

Sean and his mates shuffled from foot to foot, unsure what to say.

'Ye know, yee wee fuckers are the only ones dared knock on my door tonight,' Diesel Betty said, though these words seemed to be addressed more to herself than to them. Her expression did not so much soften – hard to imagine Diesel Betty's face ever doing such a thing – as acquire a distant look of mild surprise and maybe, though it was shocking to Sean to consider Diesel Betty feeling such a human emotion, disappointment.

Suddenly, she thrust the whole bowl of sweets at them. 'I'll give you this whole lot,' she said, shaking the bowl, 'if you take 'em over to Harvey's now. Stay with him a while, share 'em out. Go on, take it. Eat that shite 'til yer teeth stick together, I don't care.'

Jake's eyes grew wider than they did when he saw Tammy walking down the street. He shoved his broken-handled bucket at Arlo and took the bowl from Diesel Betty.

'Wow, thanks Betty!' he said, grinning at her over the mountain of sweets.

'I said yer to share 'em,' Diesel Betty said, pointing a craggy finger at each of them in turn, jabbing it twice at Jake. 'I'll know about it if ye don't mind me.'

They turned to go, each of them amazed. When they were safely out of striking distance, Jake turned around and yelled, 'I love you, Betty!'

'Fuck off with ye,' she growled back. 'And I want my bowl back!' Then, muttering to herself, she kicked the door closed. But just before it shut, Sean was sure he saw a reluctant smile playing at the edges of her mouth, the twinkle of amusement in her eyes.

DAY 10

I stand outside the door to the cellar, but I don't open it. I hear Mother's voice in my head, Mattie, the cellar is OUT OF BOUNDS! *She always says it that way, making the words so BIG that I know I will suffer for any disobedience.*

I must do it, though, I must. *I've looked everywhere for Lillie and I can't find her anywhere. She* must *be down there. I'm too old to play with dolls now, but ever since Mother soaked Lillie in lavender, she insists I take her everywhere. She thinks the herb will keep the sickness away. It's why she makes me smoke, too, and she must be right, because all our household remain in good health. Mother will be so angry if I've lost her.*

I take a deep breath and open the door.

It's dark down there. The kind of dark that swallows everything. My lantern flickers, making the shadows shiver across the walls like living things. I remind myself that I may be too old to carry Lillie around, but I am not too old for a beating if I have lost her. I have to get her back.

Holding the lantern in front of me, I move down the stairs. The darkness makes me gasp and I nearly run back up the steps, but I force myself to keep going.

It smells bad down here. Fusty and damp, but also like vinegar and dried flowers. I hold my lantern up, look round for Lillie. There she is! Sat on a table in the corner of the room. I breathe her name and move towards her, but as I do, a terrible white face with a long white beak slides out of the darkness.

Him. *I didn't see him at first because he is dressed like the shadows. A waxed black cloak, black gloves, black hat. Only the mask is white, that long, hooked beak like some huge and horrible bird. The vinegary, herby smell is coming from him, along with the smell of old meat and sickness.*

I'm so scared I can't move, not even to grab Lillie from the man's gloved hands. I think myself in Hell. My heart is trying to beat its way out of my chest and I shake like a palsied old man.

The Doctor holds Lillie out to me, an invitation to take her, squeezing her body as he does so, making her limbs contort, her cloth head twist.

I realise I'm not brave, not brave at all, because I spin round and start to run back up the stairs. The Doctor lashes out with his rod, strikes me so hard in the back that I fall. He drops on top of me, his gloved hands grip my throat. Boils burst from my skin as he gives me the sickness, great humps swell beneath my armpits. The tip of his beak almost touches my face and the smells from within make my thoughts swirl. Fever bursts through me, and as I stare into the round glass eyes of his mask I realise he has killed me he has killed me he has killed me!

Sean wakes up with a small cry, his heart beating like a heavyweight boxer. In the diffuse light that filters through the curtains, he sees the cotton rag upon which Matilda had written her note for the Baku, lying on his covers. This time, he picks it up and opens it.

Name: Matilda Bell Evans
Age: 10 and a harf
Nightmare: the dokturs

Matilda. That was the fourth story in Grandad's book, the one Sean has not finished reading. He drops the note onto the floor, shoves his hands through his hair as the smell of burning cloth fills the room. Filigree threads of Matilda cling to his consciousness: he can taste the tobacco that her mother made her smoke to protect her from the plague, feel the weight of her lavender-soaked doll, Lillie, the stinging pain of the rod switching her backside when her mother or father beat her. How she had been forced to stay home to help with the chores while her little brother went to school, how her mother had helped her learn to read and write.

The plague doctors had started to visit her best friend,Tabitha's house after a red cross was painted across her front door. Matilda never saw Tabitha again. Matilda's mother had told her the doctors were there to help, but Matilda had heard dark rumours about the men with the bird faces. She knew they carried frogs and leeches in their bags, which they placed on the naked flesh of the sick to suck out their living souls.

Tabitha's house wasn't the only one the doctors visited. They stopped at each marked door, but they never cured the afflicted within. Time and again, after they had gone, Matilda saw the dead being carried from their homes, their blackened skin covered in pustules, mouths crusted in blood, their unblinking eyes fixed and unseeing.

Even now, Sean knows the terrible smell that thickened the air of London hundreds of years ago, the horror Matilda had felt every time she saw the tall, black-cloaked men in their long-beaked masks.

Sean climbs out of bed, still trembling. He pulls the gun from his bedside table, finds the box of bullets he had hidden at the back of the wardrobe. If the Baku keeps coming to him, he wants to be prepared. He slides all six bullets into the magazine then pushes the magazine back into the gun, racks the slide so the gun is loaded. Then he puts the gun back in the drawer beside his bed.

He checks his phone. It is gone two in the morning and he has slept for less than four hours, but he knows he won't be able to go back to sleep now.

Taking care to be quiet, Sean goes downstairs into the kitchen, where he makes himself a cup of tea and takes it into the library.

He sits in front of the computer, nudges the mouse so the screen blinks to life, then clicks open the internet. For a moment he stares at the search bar, sips his tea. The wind whistles through the gaps in the windowpanes, timbers shift with a soft creak and pop, but otherwise the house is silent.

Sean types *Elbert Blake* into the search bar. A few reviews of Grandad's books pop up, all of them children's adventure novels. Written when the internet was in its infancy, there is not a great deal to look through, but the ones that have been written are generally favourable. There are no interviews with the author, and Sean suspects that, though not the recluse he is becoming today, Grandad has always been a private man.

He googles *The Baku: A Selection of Short Stories*, curious to see how it was received. He can find only one review, written by a Sally Moss. She gives the book one star and a scathing review, calling Grandad's short stories the work of a 'deranged mind'. She goes on, 'Mr Blake would do well to stick to the children's stories he clearly has more experience writing, because this is crudely written, gratuitously gory and lacking any flow or synergy.'

Sean thinks Sally, who makes no mention of suffering nightmares after reading *The Baku*, or of finding saliva-damp notes beneath her pillow, doesn't know the half of it.

He returns to his search results and notices a Wikipedia entry entitled *Baku (mythology)*. He clicks on it.

The entry describes a Japanese mythological creature that eats the nightmares of children. According to legend, if a child woke from a nightmare and cried for the Baku to come and eat its dream, it would do so. The Baku was said to protect against pestilence and evil, but if it remained hungry after eating a child's nightmare it would devour their hopes and dreams too, leaving them hopeless and empty.

Sean is surprised – he had assumed Grandad had invented the Baku. He finds it strange that it is clearly considered to be a force for good. *What happened to make it turn evil? What happened to make it change?*

A sudden gust of wind batters the window, making Sean jump. Night nuzzles against the glass. Sean closes the link, rubs his gritty eyes. He types *sleep deprivation* into the search bar and reads an article that explains how the brain cycles through five phases of sleep. Rapid eye movement (REM) is the fifth of these phases, and it is in the REM cycle, around 70–90 minutes after falling asleep, that dreams occur.

Sean leans back in the chair, an idea running through his head. Perhaps there is a way to grab some sleep and avoid the nightmares and notes beneath his pillow… *If I set the timer on my mobile to go off every sixty minutes, I'll wake up before I slip into REM and I won't have any more dreams! And if I break the cycle of sleep, then maybe the nightmares will stop.*

He finishes his tea, his thoughts on the Baku. What a terrible existence it would be to never know peace, to forever be forced to feed on the terror of children. *It's no wonder Grandad's creation went mad. There's only so much horror and pain any living creature can take before it loses its mind.*

* * *

Sean snatches brief snippets of sleep through the night, setting his alarm to wake him up every sixty minutes. By the time he goes downstairs for breakfast he feels almost giddy with relief. Though it is irritating to wake up so often, he has managed to evade any nightmares and has successfully kept the Baku from his room. He knows he can't spend the rest of his life sleeping this way, but for now he is happy to have found a temporary solution to the immediate problem.

In the kitchen, he makes himself a Pot Noodle with lashes of tomato ketchup and takes it outside so he can check on the hedgehog. He freezes on the patio.

The garden has changed.

Yesterday it had been alive with the industry of animals. Squirrels scrabbled up tree trunks, birds sang from the branches, frogs croaked on the pond's slick stones. The space had been a soothing and verdant sanctuary for wildlife.

There is nothing soothing or verdant about the garden now.

Overnight, the lawn's mint-green colour has faded and swirls of darkness curl through the grass, as though beneath it, vessels and arteries pump poisoned blood through the soil. The flower stalks sag, their greying petals creep away from the stigma, like decomposing flesh peeling from a skull. There are spots of black mould on the roses, weeds between the cracks in the paving slabs, and the scent of rot mingles with the foul-sweet scent of infection.

Sean's eyes track the worst of the destruction and he is not surprised to see it is coming from the writing shed. The flowers within its immediate vicinity are withered husks, the thin branches that scale its walls grip the building with the pulsating strength of a diseased heart. A dead mouse is half buried in the crook of a dying tree root. Dark veins swirl through the dry grass. At first Sean thinks they are black, but as he stares at them he realises they are dark blue. They remind him of the bulging veins beneath the Baku's flesh.

Grandad has only neglected the garden for a few days, but the rate of deterioration Sean sees is impossible to imagine in a lifetime of abandonment. Only the rowan tree and the space around it remain untouched by the garden's sickness.

Looking at the dead mouse, Sean thinks of the hedgehog in its crate. For the first time it occurs to him that Grandad, in his recent fugue, might not have been feeding it.

The tall grass is coated in greasy slime, but Sean pushes through it, carving a path to the crate. The hedgehog is curled up in a corner, but Sean can't tell if she is breathing. He drops to the ground, ignoring the pulse of revulsion he feels as his knees press into the sick and stinking mud.

If she's dead it will be my fault, he thinks.

The hedgehog's spines shift and relief washes through Sean.

Moving carefully to avoid startling the creature, he picks up the empty food bowl and dislodges the water bottle from the side of the crate. He hurries inside, fills the bottle with boiling water, and while it cools he makes some scrambled egg, salting it the way he saw Grandad do it.

Outside, he sets the food in the crate and fastens the water bottle back onto the side. As he does this, he notices vertical claw marks on the inside of the crate. Frowning, he leans closer and absently runs his fingers over them.

She's been trying to escape.

Sean imagines the hedgehog trying to scrabble out of the crate as the grass blackened and the flowers wilted, her paws scratching and sliding uselessly against the smooth plastic.

Once a sanctuary for wildlife, now Grandad's garden is a place the living flee.

Sean's thoughts flash back to the night he, Arlo, Gracie and Jake drank The Puke in their hidden den. Gracie looking at him, her dark eyes searching his. '*How do you look around and not ever see the shit everywhere? It's like you just don't let the darkness in.*'

But I see it now, Grey, Sean thinks.

Sean wants to take the hedgehog inside, but he remembers Grandad telling him that pregnant hedgehogs can eat their own young if their environment changes. He decides to move her beneath the rowan tree, a compromise.

He tries not to jostle the cage too much, but it is heavy and awkward to carry, and his crooked legs make it even harder for him to balance. As he passes beneath the rowan tree's shade, the putrid stench of the garden lifts and everything smells green and sweet and clean again. He sets the crate down on the grass, and hopes he has done the right thing.

Sean spends the rest of the afternoon in the conservatory, attempting another of Michelangelo's *Prisoners*, this time a replica of *The Bearded Slave*. Now that he has created one Slave from the clay, he feels as though his next attempt should be easier, but he struggles to shape the wire properly and the proportions of the figure look wrong. The air dries the clay quickly and he spends so long working on the body that it has almost entirely hardened by the time he gets to the face. He adds fresh clay over the top to try and carve its features, which only makes its head look grotesquely misshapen. He leaves it to dry beside *Atlas Slave* in the corner of the room, telling himself that at least his third attempt can't be any worse.

Grandad cooks a roast dinner, and afterwards Sean goes outside to feed the fish, knowing Grandad won't remember to do it.

He scatters the pellets across the pond and the fish swim to the surface to eat. Their movements seem slower than usual. Listless. Even the motion of their mouths opening and closing seems sluggish, and they sink into the pond's murky depths after only a few bites, leaving uneaten pellets sitting on a scrim of filth.

Afterwards, Grandad asks Sean to help him make leaf lanterns. They sit together in the orchard beneath Nanna Storm's rowan tree as the garden sinks into darkness. The flames from the flickering candles illuminate the autumn cherries, making them glow like luminous snowflakes.

Sean uses a thick brush to coat the glass with PVA glue, then covers it with white tissue strips. Drowsiness blurs his vision as he works. He pierces a hole in the lid so the candle will have oxygen to burn, then begins to press dried leaves around the outside.

Sean and Grandad work in a silence that would not have existed between them a few days ago. Sean thinks of the way Grandad was in the sculpture park yesterday, as enthusiastic as a schoolboy as he described the trees and animals. He is like another person now.

The fierce intellect behind his eyes is dulled and his gaze keeps sliding to the serried gloom of the writing shed, as though the tide of his thoughts is being pulled relentlessly back again and again by the power of some voiceless entity.

I'm imagining it, Sean thinks. *I always edit what I see these days.*

Snip.

Snip.

Snip.

DAY 11

I'm stood at the back of the hall staring at the empty, spot-lit stage.

I'm already wearing my costume, the black satin gloves that reach all the way to my elbows, the pretty beaded headpiece and tasselled dress. The make-up Miss Malone put on my face itches my skin and I have to keep telling myself not to scritchy-scratch it away. I look Glam-o-Rous, that's what Miss Malone said, and she said it with a smile as she painted up my face so I know it must be a good thing.

I wonder where everyone has gone. It must be nearly time for the show to start, but the chairs facing the stage are all empty and I can't see any of my friends.

The spotlights suddenly cut out, but before I can yell one of them switches back on with a loud clack *that echoes round the room. I feel as though my breath has been punched out of me. This isn't right. None of this is right. I try to move but I can't, like someone has driven nails through my shoes. And it's then that I know what I'm going to see. My nightmare… My worst fear… It's found me again. It always finds me.*

Slowly, the circle of light tracks across the stage. It flickers over the red curtain, then begins to climb higher and higher up the wall until it comes to a stop in the corner.

It's up there, hanging upside down, watching me. Its arms and legs are spread out like a spider's, the claws of its hands and feet sunk into the wall. It's wearing a grubby hospital gown, the sort with straps for the patient's hands and feet, only the straps are loose, hanging down its body like an unravelling mummy. Down the front of the gown there are huge rainbow-coloured pompoms. The Clown's purple hair hangs around its cheeks in dirty, knotted clumps. It's grinning a dead man's grin and its eyes are all wild and staring. Its skin is so white it looks like chalk, so white it can't be real. Only I know it is real. Just like I know its dead-man grin is real and its piranha teeth are real and its crazy, staring eyes are real.

Still watching me, it lifts one long, pale finger, presses it to its mouth. It shouldn't be able to hold on like that, upside down with one hand and two feet sunk into the walls. But it does.

The spotlight cuts out.

The darkness pushes into my eyes. I try to run, but I can't move.

CLACK. *The circle of light finds The Clown, which is now halfway down the wall.*

The light goes out again, then just as quickly CLACK *and it's back on. The Clown's feet are almost on the floor.*

CLACK. *Off.*

CLACK. *On.*

It's moving towards me. CLACK. CLACK. The spotlight flashes on and off quicker and quicker and The Clown moves faster and faster towards me, the CLACK CLACK CLACK of the spotlight turning on and off matching the THUMP THUMP THUMP of my heartbeat until both seem to smash together and The Clown is racing towards me like the image in a terrifying flipbook and I see the muck on its gown isn't muck but smeared blood and I see red strings of saliva stretch between its blade-like teeth and oh no oh no I see maggots dropping like tears from its empty eyes.

I open my mouth to scream, but too late. The Clown's breath rushes over me, and its jaws fasten onto my neck.

Sean lurches awake at his desk, his heart flailing beneath his ribs. His eyes jerk to the ceiling, half-convinced he will see a deranged clown glaring back at him.

His breath fogs the air, his room is a freezer and that awful carrion stink fills his nose and mouth. Another note is lying on his desk. He picks it up and unfolds it. His hands are shaking so much, at first he cannot read the words that are written on it.

Name: Mandy Eleanor Simpson
Age: 5 and three qworters
Nightmare: pLeez make The Clown
go away mistar Baku

There was no Mandy in Grandad's selection of short stories, but this note is as real as Luca's had been, as real as Khaba's and Matilda's.

The paper curls inwards, begins to smoulder and blacken at the edges. Sean drops it as though it has bitten him and it turns to ash as it falls, dirty snowflakes that melt into nothing before they even hit the floor.

Sean goes downstairs to the library and lies on the couch. He hadn't meant to drift off, and now his neck is stiff from sitting slumped over his desk for so long. He must have been rubbing the scar on his hand in his sleep, because the skin is pink and tender.

The house is cold and quiet. He looks out of the window. Outside, the sun sits low in the sky, shooting streamers of light between the tree branches. Brief showers have left a sleek glaze of water on the garden, making it gleam in the morning light.

His eyes wander to the writing shed and straight away his skin tightens with goosebumps. Looking at it is like touching static electricity. His gaze drifts to the cherubs, and the sight of them makes his heart lurch. Their expressions have changed. Where before their eyes were turned upwards, as though attuned to the voice of some divine entity, now their gazes have lowered and hardened into cruel slits. Gone are the sweet, softly curving smiles, replaced by evil grins. Their bared teeth are covered in mould; blue capillaries, the same shade as the veins spreading beneath the writing shed, thread their stone flesh, as though they have been struck by some terrible affliction.

The vague unease Sean had felt looking at the writing shed since seeing the curtain stir turns into something more concrete. Looking at it now, fear gusts through him, he feels as though his hair is pointing to the ceiling.

As Sean watches, one of the cherubs turns its head and locks eyes with him. Its lips skin back in a grotesque grin, betraying needle-fine fangs, rimed with lichen.

With a muffled cry, Sean grabs the curtains and pulls them closed.

Sean sits at the computer in the library, googling dream interpretation. The saliva-gummed notes, written by assorted hands, tell him that his recent dreams, and the terror they evoked, were never really his own. He shrinks from that conclusion, because if the dreams are not his own, then how does he have any chance of curing himself of them? But when he reads an article that interprets dreams of being chased by clowns as representing embarrassment, *such as shame over hair loss or having cheated on a partner*, he drops his head into his arms with a groan of frustration.

After a disrupted night's sleep, he feels wrung-out and edgy. He can't stop thinking about the writing shed, and he wonders if it is somehow linked to what is happening to Grandad.

Sean imagines himself dousing the shed in petrol, striking a match, sending it sailing through an opened window – *Whoomph!*

Fire would explode from inside as he turned in slow-motion to walk away, just like a scene from a movie. On the projecting reel of his imagination, he sees Grandad running from the house towards the shed, screaming, his Albert Einstein hair aflame, his clothes burning. He hears the roar of the fire beneath Grandad's anguished cries as his flesh bubbles and spits, begins to melt over his bones.

Horrified, Sean stands up, begins to pace, as though movement can wipe the horrible images from his mind. He knows that if Grandad were here with him, he wouldn't feel anywhere near as bad. Yearning for company, Sean goes into the kitchen to fix Grandad a cup of tea and a cheese and ham toastie.

Ignoring the uptick in his heartbeat, he picks up the mug and the plate and heads outside. As soon as he slides the patio door open, the fetid stench of leaf mould and the stink of carrion overwhelms him. The paving slabs are tacky with sludge and his feet skid beneath him, causing him to slop hot tea onto his hand.

Stepping off the path, Sean walks through the long grass towards the shed. Every nerve in his body is snapped tight, his heartbeat jitterbugs in his chest. The shadows rippling over the shed's walls grow still at his approach. Watchful. Hungry. Sean keeps his gaze averted from the stone cherubs, knowing even the slightest hint of movement will undo him. This is the closest he has ever been to the writing shed and he can taste its sickness on the air.

As he nears the shed, he sees the strange dark blue veins that squirm from beneath it and spread in wavering ripples towards the house. Sean crouches down, pushes a finger beneath the wet soil and, with a repressed shudder, hooks it around the end of one of the veins. He pulls it from the ground, examining the wormy tendril. A single drop of thick, dark liquid drips from the tip, rolls over Sean's palm. He jerks back to his feet and, with a grimace, wipes his hand on his trousers.

He moves to the shed, balancing the mug on the plate so he can open the door. The handle is coated in a scrim of ice. He pushes it down, but the door does not budge. He glances over his shoulder, fighting the urge to run back to the house.

The Paddock looks impossibly far away, like a toy house floating in a sea of black. Its walls are twisted and warped, its aspect strangely crooked, as though he is looking at it through a distorting lens. Sean hears his name float on the air, a disembodied voice that crackles with malice.

He drops the mug and plate and spins back to the door. The tea that splashes his legs is ice cold, even though he only boiled the kettle a couple of minutes ago. He pounds on the wood with the side of his fist and tries to cry out, but his words thump mutely against the physical mass at the back of his throat. He pumps the handle but it does not budge. The grind of stone tells him that the cherubs have turned to look at him, and his blood grows so cold he could swear his veins will turn to frost and shatter.

He tugs with increasing desperation at the handle until, finally, it gives with a soft *snick*, swinging wide to admit him.

Sean slams the door closed behind him and stares round the shadow-cluttered room. The first thing that strikes him is the smell. He covers his nose and mouth with his sleeve, but the cankerous stench crawls down his airway, making his stomach clench with revulsion. The walls are exposed wooden beams, the floor, wide wooden planks. An oriental rug is worn to the weave, a bare dusty light bulb hangs from a chain. Malevolence swirls through the room, as though stirred by an invisible hand.

Grandad is sat at a vast oak desk with his back to Sean. Hunched over, his fingers fly across the keyboard, his head moving every now and then to the stack of handwritten notes beside him, from which he is transcribing.

Clack clack clack clack clack.

There is something forbidding about the sound, some quality that roots Sean to the spot. Anger flashes through him. Grandad must have heard him knocking. It seems impossible that he hadn't, given how violently Sean had slammed his fists against the door.

Why didn't you let me in?

He forces himself to take a step forwards. The floorboard creaks beneath his weight and Grandad spins round, as if after all Sean's banging it is this small noise that rouses him from the trance of his thoughts. The expression on his face halts Sean in his tracks. His eyes are sunken pits, plunged into shadow by the ledge of his scowling brow. His skin looks sunken and his mouth is twisted into an angry grimace.

Sean swallows, his throat making an audible click. As though sensing his grandson's fear, the old man's face softens into a smile. But there's something forced about it. Something dishonest.

'Sean, lad,' he says, pushing his hands through his hair, making it stick up in unruly clumps. As he does this, Sean sees dark blue ink stains on the side of Grandad's right hand. His eyes move to a pot of blue biros on the desk. One of them is lying on top of a sheet of paper that is filled with writing. Sean turns his own hand over, stares at the dark blue stain on his palm, the substance the vein excreted when he tugged it from the soil.

'Goodness, I didn't mean to be so long in here. Sometimes it's hard not to get lost inside your own head, you know?' The two regard each other in awkward silence until Grandad clears his throat and drops his eyes. 'Why don't you go back inside, I'll come and make us some supper in a bit. Just need five minutes to finish up this page.'

Grandad gives him another smile that does not quite reach his eyes, then he turns back to the laptop.

Clack clack clack clack clack.

Sean knows Grandad won't come back inside in five minutes. He might not come back into the house at all tonight, and each letter he punches from the keyboard feels like the violent jab of his fingertip against Sean's breastbone.

Clack clack clack.

The sound echoes through his head and he hears it as a word, repeated over and over and over.

Out out out.

Sean walks to the door. The handle moves easily in his hand, the door opens smoothly. He hesitates before stepping out, praying he won't hear that malevolent voice whisper his name again. The garden is silent, and the house no longer looks crooked and strange. The tree trunks are obscured by banks of grey fog, but Sean senses something else there, lurking in the darkness, watching him. He picks up the empty cup and plate from the ground where he dropped them and quickly heads back to the house.

DAY 12

Sean is sat in front of the computer in the library, listening to the wind batter the trees and shriek down the chimney. He is wrapped up in his dressing gown, the heating is turned on, but he is cold with exhaustion. The pain in his knee, which is always exacerbated by lack of sleep, throbs in time with his pulsing headache. He would ordinarily take a painkiller, but they make him woozy, and he can't afford to fall asleep.

Images turn over and over in his thoughts, fragments of different nightmares merging into a chaotic horror show in his mind. He types *Mirror-Eyed Man* into the search engine, wondering if Grandad was drawing on real creatures from mythology when he wrote about him, as he had with the Baku, but he can't find anything that resembles the creature he dreamt of. He types *black glass eyes* into the search engine instead. This throws up dozens of links to teddy bear eyes and human glass eyes, all of it irrelevant except for one link that catches Sean's attention, the website of a healer who is selling an obsidian scrying mirror.

Opening a separate webpage, Sean discovers that scrying is a form of divination which involves staring into a mirror to see into the future. Obsidian is a type of black glass that is said to be perfect for divination.

Sean thinks about the terror he had felt as the Mirror-Eyed Man turned to look at him, a primordial instinct telling him he shouldn't look, that he should avert his eyes at all costs from the truth reflected in that black-mirrored gaze.

I'm sinking, sinking, sinking into a blue that goes on and on forever. I look round, but I see nothing… nothing but water, dancing with little flecks. I should be drowning, because I can feel water fill my chest with every breath, but I don't. I can breathe and it's okay, I'm not scared, even though I probably should be.

I see the shadow of Dad's fishing boat high above me. I must've fallen out. That's why I don't have my diving gear on. I guess I banged my leg when I fell, because blood trickles from a tiny cut on my shin. It doesn't hurt. It's sort of pretty, the way the blood trickles out, a thin stream that unfurls like red flowers in the water.

I can't see Dad anywhere, just the blue of the ocean, a blue that swallows everything. I'm starting to get cold. Shivering now, and maybe I do feel a little *scared. Not a lot, because Dad must be close by, I can see his boat right there, a dark shadow high above. Perhaps he's in the water with me and I just can't see him. I twist round, working my hands and feet, looking for him, but there's nothing. Nothing but the blue that goes on and on forever.*

And then I see him! Unlike me, he's wearing his face mask and flippers, his wetsuit and oxygen tank. He hasn't got his speargun, though, so I guess he must've dived into the water to find me.

I start towards him but then freeze. Did I see movement in the darkness below Dad? Yes, there's something there. Something big. A shadow breaks through the gloom. At first I think maybe it's a whale, because it's so massive. But its tail does not move up and down like a whale's; this tail swishes side to side.

Shark!

My heart seizes and I cry out, spewing bubbles.

Of course, Dad can't hear me. The shape is still far away, but it moves like a dart towards him. So fast. He can't see it because his goggles block everything except what is right in front of him, and right now he is looking at me.

He must see something in my face that makes him turn in the water. His entire body tenses, then he looks back at me, gestures wildly for me to go. But I'm frozen, like the ocean's massive weight is holding me right there. Time stops. Dad's eyes are like gobstoppers behind his goggles as he kicks towards the surface of the water. I can hear my heart – thwump thwump thwump *– as the shark swims up beneath him.*

It's so fast, its tail swinging left and right. Its jaws open, then snap shut around Dad. Teeth disappear into flesh. The water drinks Dad's screams. His regulator falls out of his mouth. The shark shakes him like a dog shakes a bone, and even from so far away I see the covers slide over its terrible eyes before blood clouds everything.

I twist away, my water-clogged scream spraying bubbles around my face. I swim upwards towards the boat before I realise the boat has gone. I have nowhere to go. No place to shelter. I look around, spinning left and right, gasping for breath.

I glance over my shoulder. The shark has clocked me. It still has the upper half of Dad's body in its mouth and now it is swimming straight at me. Its tail swings back and forth. Its wide-spaced eyes are as black as a starless night. It opens its jaws, and what's left of Dad sinks to the ocean floor, painting bruises across the water. And still it comes, its mouth a terrible rip that is stuffed full of blades. Its nostrils flare, like it's sniffing me in, like it can taste me, like it's already eating me somehow.

I'm thrashing towards the surface of the water, no longer thinking, blind with panic. Muscles burning, heart banging. Nothing inside my head but my own voice screaming – you're dead you're dead you're dead you're dead! *The shark is closing the gap between us, I can feel it, feel it in the way my skin turns into electricity. I twist round and it's right there! Its spongy snout crinkles as it tugs back, its jaws open. And like a trap snapping closed, they clamp down on me.*

Sean leaps to his feet, a scream stuck to the back of his throat. The stool he had been sat on clatters to the floor and he staggers, staring around the room with wild eyes.

His confusion lifts as he realises he is in the conservatory. Overcome by exhaustion, he had fallen asleep. Now his skin is pebbled with goosebumps, his throat is tight with cold. The air feels charged and the mammalian stink of the Baku hovers in the room.

He is alone, but any relief he might have felt is quickly eradicated when he looks outside. There is nothing there to see, nothing but a swale of weeds and putrefying flowers, a dying garden illuminated by a ghostly moon. Already the temperature is lifting, the fog that plumes from his lips disappearing in the space between one breath and the next, but the warmth does not change the fact that the Baku was in here. The knowledge sends trills of terror rippling up and down his spine.

He tried so hard to stay awake, working on the third of his Prisoners, *The Young Slave*, until exhaustion blurred his vision. He managed to finish the piece, which turned out better than he expected considering he was half-asleep when he did it. He can't remember laying his head on the workbench but knows he must have done so. His sculpture seems to glare at him in silent accusation, as though Sean had opened the door for the Baku and invited it in.

His gaze drops to a scrap of paper on the floor.

Sean picks it up, fighting the revulsion that swims through him at the tacky dampness it leaves on his fingers.

Name: Will Mitchell
Age: 9
Nightmare: Sharks

Echoes of Will linger in Sean's mind. *Will gave his nightmare to the Baku, and now the Baku has given it to me. It's purging itself of all the nightmares it's been forced to eat, but doing so is transferring part of the dreamer to me, too, little slivers of their souls, pieces of memory. Because isn't that where fear begins? With a memory?*

The note begins to curl up at the edges. It turns to ash, then disappears, as though sucked back to the crease in time from which it came.

After breakfast Sean hurries down the path, a bowl of seeds for the hedgehog in one hand, a cupful of pellets for the fish in the other. The veins have crept closer to the house in the night and the garden has deteriorated even more since yesterday.

He sets the bowl of seeds inside the hedgehog's crate, then goes to feed the fish, rubbing at the stain on his palm as he walks. He had scrubbed at the marking last night until the skin was pink and raw, but has not managed to erase it completely. He thinks of the ink he saw on Grandad's hands, the pile of handwritten notes by the side of his computer. The pot of biros. *That's crazy*, he thinks. *It can't be ink, it's impossible.*

As he approaches the pond, his hand tightens around the scooper of food. The shed's poisoned arteries have tunnelled beneath the pond, buckling and cracking the stones that surround it. Some of the heavy slabs have snapped in half and dark blue sludge seeps between the fissures.

Sean's eyes move to the water.

The fish are all dead, floating atop a coating of thick slime. Bellies bloated and distended, eyes fixed and staring.

Sean frowns at the measly contents of the fridge. He does not relish the long walk to Tesco, which will aggravate the pain in his bad knee, but if he and Grandad are to survive on something other than vegetables from the greenhouse, he does not see what other choice he has.

He slams the fridge door closed and rummages in the cupboards. There's little to choose from, so he makes do with some crackers slathered with jam. He takes the pitiful meal up to his room, sits at the desk in front of his window. The garden lies sleeping beneath a star-sprayed sky, but despite the lateness of the hour, the light in the writing shed is still on.

A ripple of movement beside the pond drags Sean's gaze. He sets the cracker he had been eating back on the plate and leans closer to the window. Someone is stood outside the door to the writing shed. The figure is too tall, too broad to be Grandad. Fear slides a shard of ice through Sean's heart. He wipes his hand over the glass, clearing the fog of his breath.

The clouds slide apart, moonlight splashes across the rotting grass, and by its pale glow Sean can see the figure more clearly.

Its body is human, but its face is something else entirely. Torn elephantine ears, blade-like tusks, a trunk as thick as Sean's waist.

The Baku is stood at the point where the inky veins taper away, as though it can only walk as far as they reach. And it is looking up at his bedroom window.

It's waiting for me to fall asleep.

Sean jerks away, and the curtains fall closed. But still he can feel the Baku's gaze burning into him, can feel the promise of violence seething from its ivory pores.

The silence of the house envelops him, reminding him that he is all alone.

DAY 13

Sean sits up in bed, knuckling sleep from his eyes. He switches off his alarm, then collapses back onto his pillow. After waking every hour through the night, his thoughts feel sodden and groggy.

He goes downstairs to get some breakfast and is surprised to see Grandad sat at the kitchen table, looking through a photo album. The sight of the old man brings with it a rush of relief.

But then Grandad looks up, and Sean's heart sinks.

His skin has a greyish cast, and his eyes are shrouded in purple bruises. He looks like a man who has only just been told his wife died, not one who lost her almost twenty years ago.

Sean glances at the open album. The black-and-white photographs are of Grandad and Nanna Storm's wedding day. They must have been taken some time in the seventies, but Nanna Storm, in a simple white dress and crown of flowers, could be a bohemian bride from today. Grandad's mullet hair and flared trousers leave no doubt as to the decade, but the sparkle in his eyes is timeless.

In one photograph Nanna Storm is stood with her back to a group of people. Glancing over her shoulder, she follows the flight of her tossed posy as it arcs towards a sea of outstretched hands. In another, Grandad is stood behind Nanna Storm, guiding her hand as she cuts the bottom tier of their wedding cake.

'People got married earlier back in the seventies,' Grandad says, turning a page of the photo album. 'But we were still teenagers, young by anyone's standards. And Ocean, she had this quality about her that just drew you in and made you fall in love with her. I know it sounds corny, but I'd never met anyone like her before in my life. I knew I couldn't keep her forever. She was like a supernova, burning too brightly to last.

'It was a long time before Stella came along,' Grandad says, softly. 'When she was little she was so like her mother. You're like her, too.' He lifts his gaze to Sean. 'Every time I look at you, it's like a little Ocean is looking right back at me.' He smiles, but there is only sadness in his eyes. 'We had so many good times, but it isn't the good times that stick, is it, lad? Those last few hours when she was in the hospice… I just can't shake them.' His gaze becomes distant, haunted. 'The disinfectant smell of the place, the sound her painkillers made as they were fed through the tube, her hand in mine, so weak… so thin…

'I could hear the radio in the next room and there was an announcement… the Queen Mother had passed away. Little things like that, they get stuck in your head, don't they, lad?' Sean is surprised to see a tear trace the contours of Grandad's wrinkled cheek. 'You know what I mean. I know you do. What happened with your mum, well, it must've been terrible for you, having to deal with all that on your own. I should've been there. I know that, and I'm so sorry. I should have tried harder to get in touch, to help. I should've done more.'

His gaze drops back down to the photo album and an expression of utter desolation twists his face. He traces an arthritic finger over Ocean's red curls. 'I should've been there.'

After dinner Grandad drops Sean off at the youth club. Just as he always does, Sean hides in St Joseph's, reading books and sketching Snake, Jock and Bling. They don't show up, but Sean doesn't need to see them in the flesh to draw them. They have taken on a life of their own in his head, and he sketches them with the paintbrush of his imagination.

In the shadowy church Sean has yet to see their faces clearly, but intuition guides his hand and personalities begin to emerge from his drawings. Though he has never been close enough to see such things, somehow he knows Snake's fingernails are hardened and yellow, laced with grime, that his cheeks are pocked with acne scars and that his left arm is covered in tattoos. That Bling has a tongue piercing and a phobia of cats, that Jock has been in and out of Youth Court for most of his childhood.

Sean intuits all these details and a dozen besides. They form an imprint on his imagination, like a psychic Polaroid, and he pours all of it into his drawings.

He is about to start a new sketch when he hears something creak behind him. He hasn't heard the door open, so there can't be anyone there; anxiety twists through him as his eyes move over the shadow-draped church.

Reassured he is alone he turns back to his sketchpad, his pencil hovering over the paper. A wave of drowsiness sweeps over him and he allows his eyes to drift briefly closed. He is tired… so tired. Even when he does sleep these days, his sleep is thin, as though half of him is still awake, alert.

Now, in this soupy state of semi-consciousness, Sean begins to draw.

His thoughts drift as he sketches, but he does not chase them, merely allows himself to exist in this half-awake, half-asleep meditation. The scrape of his pencil against the paper soothes him and his heartrate slows, his breathing deepens.

His head snaps up at the sound of another creak. A quick scan of the church reveals he is still alone. Moonlight glows through the stained-glass windows, the candles in the narthex flutter. Sean tells himself all he is hearing is the settling sounds of an old building, amplified by the cavernous space.

He lowers his eyes to his sketch and the instant he sees it, he recoils. Threads of fear bolt through him. *I didn't draw this!* his thoughts scream. *I would never have drawn this!*

It is the Mirror-Eyed Man's face. There is a savagery in the drawing that is alien to Sean, as though he had been possessed by a sudden madness when he drew it.

Shadows crouch within the Mirror-Eyed Man's sunken cheekbones and eye sockets. Heavy-handed, overlapping pencil strokes frame the narrow, vulpine face, the thin, downturned mouth. Sean has darkened the entire page with harsh lines and shadow, but he has completely blackened the old man's mirrored eyes, repeating circles that have torn through the paper. Violence simmers from the page, along with a sentience that chills Sean to the marrow.

He realises he is gripping the pencil in his fist instead of between his fingers. His hand is cramped from squeezing it so hard as he slashed at the page. The pencil itself is completely blunt, and there are three other blunt pencils on the pew beside him. As though he had sketched until he had worn down each one, then snatched up another without even realising.

Sean can't bear to look at it. He flips the sketchpad closed. His hands are shaking, the small hairs down the nape of his neck are stiff.

A slow creak, this time right behind him. The sound of wood settling beneath someone's weight. Sean feels the skin around his eyes stretching, horror making his eyes bulge.

He has no choice but to look over his shoulder.

The Mirror-Eyed Man is sat on the bench right behind him. His head is lowered, as though he is deep in prayer. He is almost bald and what hair remains hangs like old cobwebs from his mottled scalp. He is so close, Sean can see the blackheads that pit his nose, can count the lines riven deep in his brow, see the spiky dark hairs of his eyebrows. So close, Sean could reach out and touch him.

Sean leaps from the pew, dizzy with terror. His fingers curl around his sketch pad as pencils clatter across the floor. *He's going to look at me! Jesus, please don't look at me!* Luca's nightmare is now Sean's, so that he no longer knows where the fictional boy's terror ends and his own begins.

He scuttles backwards, but his foot snags on the kneeling bench and he topples over. He catches his balance as the Mirror-Eyed Man begins to rise. Sean stares at the figure, tells himself he must be imagining it, it can't be real, it *can't* be. The Mirror-Eyed Man is a character from a fictional story, the nightmare of a boy who doesn't even exist beyond the pages of a book.

Breathing hard, heart clattering, Sean takes a step back. Something about the figure standing before him is different to the vision from his nightmare. It takes him a moment to realise what it is: the Mirror-Eyed Man is wearing The Clown's bloodied psychiatric gown. His mouth looks different, too, lipless and wide, stretching almost from one ear to the other. Not only that, but there are slits down each side of his neck, as though something has slashed his skin. It is only when Sean sees the flaps of flesh ripple forwards and backwards that he realises what they are: shark gills. The creature sitting in the pew a few paces away from him is not one nightmare, but three, merged into one: it has The Clown's powder-white face and rouged cheeks, the Mirror-Eyed Man's narrow bones and shiny, reflective gaze, the shark's gills and cavernous jaws. Sean knows if it opens its mouth, its widening maw would be studded with row upon row of blade-like teeth.

Sean tries to tell himself it can't be real, because the alternative – that the Baku exists beyond the pages of Grandad's story and is somehow giving form to the childrens' nightmares – makes Sean feel as though he is skidding into madness.

Terror sprays adrenaline through his blood as he lurch-runs towards the back doors of the church and the figure in the pew twists its head to follow his flight. Sean slams the doors open and bolts into the night, expecting at any moment to hear footsteps behind him, to feel the living nightmare grab him by the hair and force him to stare into the horrible truth inside its fathomless black gaze.

Grandad does not look at Sean when he picks him up. The inside of the car stinks of booze, though Sean did not see him drink anything before he dropped him off at the church. Sean wonders how much he has had, whether he should be driving. Hard to imagine Grandad as the same man who had taken Sean to the sculpture park a few days ago. Clear-eyed, energised, engaged with his surroundings, the antithesis of the man he is now. Sean remembers his promise that they would return to the park to see the Henry Moore exhibition. *Yeah, fat chance.*

When they get home, Grandad slopes off to the writing shed without a word and Sean goes into the kitchen to make himself some dinner. He opens the fridge and the stink of fish belches over him. He removes a slimy punnet of darkening mushrooms and throws them in the bin along with some mouldering fruit and vegetables, then prepares himself a Pot Noodle and takes it into the library.

He curls up on the sofa and absently stirs a fork through the steaming food. The radiators tick and hiss, the window frames rattle, but these tiny scribbles of sound do nothing to fill The Paddock's vast canvas of silence. Despite Sean's prickling nerves, he can feel sleep waiting for him behind his eyelids. He stands up, moves to the window. The writing shed squats in soaking darkness. Sean thinks of Grandad's recent mood, the way he has lost interest in his beloved garden, the bleak, hollowed-out look in his eyes.

It's the writing shed. I don't know how, but it's hurting him.

Sean sets the half-eaten Pot Noodle down on the coffee table and hurries from the room, not questioning what he is doing, sure only of one thing: he has to find a way to persuade Grandad to come back into the house.

The noxious smell crawling from the shed hits Sean sooner than it had the other day, and even by the pale moonlight he can see the blue-black veins beneath the grass have spread further towards the house.

As he nears the shed, he can't shake the feeling that he is being watched. He hesitates, shivering on the path as his eyes probe the shadows. The trees menace the sky, their branches like snapped fingers. Many of the coloured spotlights have gone out, and the ones that remain cast a sickly glow on the decaying flowers.

He hears a voice whisper through the air and glances over his shoulder, expecting to see the terrible figure he had seen in the church sliding towards him, its grubby gown flapping around its legs, hands hooked into claws, triangular teeth punching through the flesh of slavering gums. But there is nothing there.

The sound of the wind brushing against the leaves is a hiss in his ears, the darkness mocks him. He grabs the shed's door handle and the hairs along his arm frizz at the contact. For a moment, he can feel the slow *lub-dub* of the building's black heart, as though he has placed his hand over its beating pulse.

He jerks the handle down, throws his weight against the door. This time it opens without resistance and he nearly falls straight onto the floor.

Rancid air engulfs him and Sean wonders how Grandad can bear it. The old man is lying on the couch, fast asleep. One hand trails on the floor, beside an uncapped bottle of whisky. His other hand is resting on top of his belly, which lifts and lowers with each whistling breath.

Sean stares at him, uncertain what to do. Grandad's face is slack with sleep, yet somehow, even at rest, he looks haunted. He has not shaved for days, and the dark bristles on his chin and cheeks give him a worn, rumpled look. Sean is struck by a sudden memory of Grandad visiting him for the first time at Creswick Hall. He had seemed so distinguished, cultured, charismatic. Now he looks like the sort of hobo Sean used to see hanging round Dulwood.

Sean knows he should wake him, but now that he's here, curiosity brings him pause. He glances at the computer's dark screen. *What have you been writing, Grandad? What have you been doing in here all this time?*

The wind snuffles around the gaps in the windowpanes, the cold tightens against his skin.

Taking care to move quietly, Sean walks to the desk. He sinks into the chair and jiggles the mouse. The monitor lights up. Shivering, Sean scrolls to the top of the manuscript. On the first page, a title has been capitalised.

THE BAKU II.

Thinking of all the trouble Grandad's short stories about the Baku have caused him, Sean quickly closes the document down, then right-clicks on the file. The 'delete' button pops up. *Is this it? Is this how I help you? Surely it can't be this easy. I bet you've backed the story up somewhere, and even if you haven't, I can't stop you coming back in here and writing something else.*

A sudden clatter at the window makes Sean's heart vault into his throat. He spins round, exhales with relief when he sees it's just a wind-blown tree branch tapping the glass.

But the sofa is empty.

Grandad is stood behind him.

Sean jerks to his feet, scraping the tops of his knees against the underside of the table. Pain flares through the scuffed skin but he barely notices, because Grandad's face is set in a rictus of rage. Sean is suddenly aware of how very tall he is, like a vast old oak tree towering above him. And it occurs to him, then, that this furious old man before him is not Grandad. It's him… but it isn't *him*.

'Get out of here!' Grandad roars. 'Get out! *Get out!*'

He pushes his grandson. Hard. Sean staggers, jars his bad knee and falls, smacking the side of his head against the desk. His head swims. He flinches as Grandad moves towards him, holds his arms over his head in anticipation of a blow.

Grandad freezes. He stares down at his grandson cowering on the floor, and all the rage drains from his face. Confusion flickers behind his eyes, as though he is not quite sure what has just happened.

Horrified understanding follows swiftly on the heels of shock. He takes a step towards Sean, his expression softening, but Sean scrabbles to his feet and backs away. There is an imploring look on Grandad's face, but Sean turns away from him and runs back to the house, the grinning eyes of the stone cherubs following him all the way.

BEFORE

It was Mischief Night, and Jake, their natural leader when it came to all things mischievous, was proving reticent to share his plans for the evening with Sean and the others. Sean was too preoccupied with his own concerns to push him for details. His sleep had been poor over the past few weeks, and he was becoming increasingly concerned about his mum. She was barely eating anything anymore, and her appearance was enough to draw gasps from passers-by on the street.

Now, Sean shuffled from foot to foot, his eyes scanning the building site for Harvey. The moon shone through the wind-torn clouds, casting a ghostly light over the machinery. The smell of Jake's cigarette tangled on the air with the scent of diesel, clay and overturned earth. Jake had told everyone to meet here at ten o'clock, but Harvey had yet to show.

Halloween at Harvey's had been a blast. Aside from a mad collection of shoot-'em-up games, that Sean would have happily played on all night, it turned out Harvey was a collector of films, too. He had tons of them on old videotapes, their titles written in Harvey's slow and careful hand on a white sticker across the front.

Harvey used to work for a video rental store called Blockbusters; Sean had never heard of it, probably because it went bankrupt years ago. After working a shift, Harvey would take the videos home and copy them onto blank tapes, replacing the originals the next day so he never had to pay to watch any of them. That is why he owns so many of them now. The walls of his living room are stacked with videos, and he has more stashed in boxes all round his house. He could have opened his own video rental gig, had there been anyone in Yorkshire aside from him who still watched anything on videotape.

Gracie had chosen *Psycho* from Harvey's collection of horrors. Sean hadn't thought he would enjoy it, but it was actually pretty decent as far as prehistoric films went. His enjoyment had been bolstered by the mountain of sweets Diesel Betty had given them, and the fact Gracie had sat beside him on Harvey's ratty old sofa, grabbing his arm every time something on screen scared her.

Afterwards, Harvey had told them they could come over whenever they wanted to watch another film from his collection. Sean, seeing how much Harvey had enjoyed the company, felt he should repay the kindness, and had invited him to join them on Mischief Night.

At first, Harvey was reticent. Kids in the area always targeted him on Mischief Night. Sometimes it was only firecrackers or dog shit through his letterbox, other times they smashed his windows or set fire to his rubbish bins. The night took on a menacing quality in his mind and, even though he had more reason than anyone else on Dulwood to indulge in some revenge punking, he did not want any part in it.

Sean and the others had assured Harvey that all mischief would be of a harmless nature. They would not be throwing rocks at windows or stealing gateposts, posting unwanted parcels through letterboxes or spray-painting the walls of people's houses. Seeming satisfied, Harvey had agreed to accompany them.

'Maybe he changed his mind,' Gracie said, hitching herself onto the wall. She kicked her legs against the bricks, shivering in her bomber jacket.

Sean shook his head. 'He would've called.'

'It's freezing,' Arlo said. 'Come on, Jake man. Tell us what we're doing here.'

Jake, who had been leaning against the wall, suddenly straightened, his face brightening as he saw Harvey walking, slope-shouldered, towards them.

'S'up, Harv,' Arlo said.

'Hey, g-guys,' Harvey said. His eyes skated over each of their heads, not quite able to look anyone square in the face. Sean noticed when any of them made a wise-ass comment or cracked a joke, Harvey would look away, as though the small smile at the edges of his lips was shameful.

'Right,' Jake said, looping his thumbs through the shoulder straps of his rucksack, his eyes moving over each of his friends. 'So listen, right. You all know my Uncle Shifty's been working here for the past few weeks, yeah? Well, the other day he let me into the JCB cab, showed me how to drive it like. And do you know what he does every night when he finishes? He only goes and leaves the key to the JCB behind the petrol cap. I think he does it coz—'

'What are you telling us this for?' Gracie said, looking baffled.

Sean glanced across the building site at the JCB that was parked beside a huge pile of mud. 'Oh, shit,' he muttered.

There was a beat of silence.

'You want to TWOC a JCB?' Gracie said, her voice deadpan.

'Wow, Miss Melodrama,' Jake said, rolling his eyes. 'We're not *nickin'* it. We're *borrowing* it, and we won't even drive it out of the building site. Come on.' Then, before Gracie could say anything else, he turned and strode towards the JCB.

'You can't drive a JCB, you tit,' Arlo said, as he and the others hurried to catch up with Jake.

'How hard can it be?' Jake said. 'Anyway, Shifty showed me the controls when the foreman were off. And Denny's been taking me down to the car park at the back of St Nic's and teaching me how to drive. Says I'm a natural.'

'Your Denny's a headcase,' Gracie said. 'Since when do you listen to what he says?'

Sean looked at the JCB as Jake reached around the petrol cap, feeling for the key. It was one of those backhoe loaders, with a big black bucket at the front and a smaller one at the back. Its back tyres were bigger than Sean.

'Jackpot!' Jake straightened with a grin and shook the keys in front of his friends' faces. He climbed the steps of the JCB, wrenched the door open, and slid into the seat of the cab. Then he rummaged through his rucksack and pulled out a kid's plastic construction hat.

'What are you waiting for?' he yelled, clipping the hat on. It was obviously too small for him, the black strap making his cheeks bulge. Sean suddenly flashed back to when they were seven or eight years old and Jake had been big into dressing up. He'd had a yellow construction hat just like the one he was wearing now. He'd also had a high-vis jacket and a plastic tool kit that fastened round his waist, through which he could slide a plastic toy hammer, a little saw and spanner. For a horrifying moment, Sean thought he might pull those out of his bag too, but Jake just tossed it on the floor and placed his hands on the giant wheel.

'He's not really gonna do this,' Gracie muttered.

'We won't all fit!' Arlo yelled.

'Get in the bucket then!' Jake shot back.

'I'm not getting in the bucket,' Arlo said. 'If anyone gets in the bucket it should be Harv.'

'Don't even think about it,' Sean said to Harvey, who looked as though he was about to do exactly that. Meanwhile, Arlo had mounted the steps of the cab and he and Jake were examining the controls inside.

Sean looked up at Harvey, who was staring at the JCB as though it were a rocket set to blast into space.

'What you waiting for?' Sean said.

A smile broke Harvey's face wide open and he heaved himself up the steps of the JCB.

'C-c-come on, G-Gracie,' Harvey said, reaching down and offering her his hand. His face was luminous, his eyes crackled with excitement.

'Ah, shit,' Gracie mumbled, smacking her hand into Harvey's and allowing him to pull her up.

Sean scrambled in after Gracie, using the rails to pull himself up. But the cab was designed to hold only one person, and with so many people crammed inside, half his body hung out of the door.

'Suck it in!' he said.

'Suck it in?' Even Arlo's voice sounded crushed. 'Are you kidding me?'

Somehow, Gracie, Harvey and Arlo managed to nudge over and create enough space for Sean to slam the door shut, but once he had, he realised just how little space there was inside the cab. Squeezed between Gracie on one side and the cold glass door on the other, his ribs felt as though they were being crushed in a vice. He was also desperately aware of Gracie beside him, her hip bone digging into his side, her thigh squashed against his leg.

Harvey was stood on the other side of Gracie. The cramped surroundings served only to accentuate his size and he looked far from comfortable, braced in a half squat, the back of his head pushed down by the roof of the cab. The smell of diesel, dirt and the cheap aftershave Jake had started to pilfer from Denny permeated the air. Each breath felt too small, the air quickly became too warm.

'Open a window, man,' Arlo said.

Jake cranked the front window down, and cold air wafted through the cab. Behind him the others squirmed, wriggled, sniped at each other as they tried to find a position comfortable enough in which to settle, but Jake had acres of room in the front of the cab. He ran his eyes over the gears and the buttons, the levers and the dials.

Gracie said, 'Any time today would be great. And for fuck's sake, stop *pushing* me!'

Sean said, 'You sure you know what you're doing?'

Arlo said, 'He's wearing a toy hat, of course he doesn't know what he's doing.'

Harvey said, 'Hahahaha!'

Jake abandoned his scrutiny of the controls and muttered something that Sean could not quite catch, but that sounded distinctly like *wing it.* He twisted the key halfway in the ignition and a high-pitched beep emitted from the dashboard. He turned the key further and the engine chugged to life, making the cab vibrate. He flipped a lever at the side of the wheel backwards, then lowered the handbrake and twisted in his seat to reverse.

'I can't see anything,' Jake said, frowning. 'Your big heads are in the way.'

'Oh, you can't see?' Gracie said with a scowl. 'We can't fucking *breathe*!'

Jake shrugged, eased his foot off the brake and leaned out of the window to look behind him, but instead of going backwards the JCB rumbled forwards. Jake slammed on the brakes and jerked his head back into the cab.

'Oopsies,' he said.

'Oh my God, you're such an *idiot*!' Gracie snapped.

Harvey laughed, his body shaking up and down.

'Ow!' Arlo grimaced. 'Harv, you're stood on my foot, man.'

Harvey shuffled his feet, but as he manoeuvred himself his elbow knocked Gracie in the jaw and she yelped.

'Oh!' Jake smacked his palm to his forehead. 'Forgot to put my seat belt on.' He pulled the orange band across his waist, snapped it into the buckle, then glanced back at his friends and gave them an *aw-shucks* grin. 'No belt, no brains.'

The look Gracie, Arlo and Sean gave him then could have curdled milk. Harvey grinned.

Jake flipped the lever back into reverse. This time the JCB rolled backwards, emitting a loud beeping as it did. When Jake had cleared enough space in front of him, he braked, silencing the back-up beeper. He shifted the gearstick and the truck grumbled forwards. Harvey gave a whoop of joy.

'Lights, man!' Arlo said. 'You need lights!'

'Oh, yeah.' Jake pulled the handbrake up and squinted at the buttons and levers again. 'Headlights, headlights, headlights…'

Sean imagined he heard Gracie's eyeballs smacking the roof of the cab as Jake started flipping levers up and down, testing them. The windscreen wipers switched on, water sprayed the glass. Then a high-pitched whine cut through the air, like the scream of metal. Sean felt the JCB begin to pitch forwards, as though a superhero from one of Jake's comics had lifted the back wheels clean off the ground.

'That must be the stabilisers,' Jake muttered, continuing to flip levers and press buttons. The cab began to lower back to the ground, but as it did the bucket in front of the JCB shuddered to life and slowly began to lift.

'Jesus, Jake, you said you knew what you were doing!' Arlo yelled.

'I do,' Jake said, pressing another switch. The empty bucket tipped, releasing a dirty powder of dust into the night. 'Just gimme a sec,' he muttered.

The digger at the back swung forwards, then began to lower towards the ground.

'Jake, *stop*!' Gracie yelled.

'I'm trying!' Jake said between gritted teeth, swiping desperately at the controls.

'Just *drive*!' Arlo snapped.

'Okay okay!' Jake flicked another switch that made the indicators wink on and off, then the main beams lit the construction site. He grinned. 'There you go, told you I had it.'

He lowered both buckets and stepped on the accelerator. The wheels bounced over the rutted ground, jostling the cargo within.

Icy wind blew through the open windows. Jake weaved the JCB around pyramids of mud and stacks of scaffolding, he swerved skips and cones and fencing. Even though they were all squashed in the cab, Sean felt something inside him expand as Jake drove. All his worries about his mum fell away. He felt almost as though, if Jake stepped harder on the accelerator, the enormous tyres of the JCB could take off and fly.

Jake pulled up in front of a tower of mud, glanced over his shoulder at Harvey.

'Push that one there, Harv,' Jake said, pointing at the lever beside him.

Harvey leaned forwards and pushed the lever. The front loader moved forwards and scooped up a bucketful of mud. Jake reversed, drove to the mountain of excavated mud, then showed Harvey the lever which emptied the bucket. Harvey laughed as the mudslide fell and Jake reversed, drove back to the mud pile. They repeated the procedure, Jake operating the wheel and the gears, while the others took turns to shovel mud from one side of the building site to the other.

'Right, fun's over,' Gracie said. 'Let me out.'

'One more lap!' Jake said, lowering the front loader and turning the JCB round.

'One m-more l-l-lap!' Harvey said.

This time, Jake drove the truck faster, making the most of this final spin. On the far side of the building site, the hard-packed ground gave way to churned earth that recent heavy rain had turned into a mud bath. Instead of avoiding it, Jake drove the JCB straight towards it.

'What the fuck are you doing?' Gracie said, alarmed. 'We're gonna get stuck!'

'Chill out, this baby can practically swim,' Jake said.

The JCB slowed as soon as its tyres hit the mud, though Jake was standing on the accelerator. The truck sank a little, the huge wheels span, spraying mud.

'Erm, Jake?' Sean said, worriedly.

'It's fine,' Jake said, gritting his teeth as the JCB stuttered, then juddered forwards. Sean was sure he felt the cab sinking lower, imagining the slow-turning wheels being swallowed by the thick mud.

'Jake, come on, man,' Arlo said, nervously.

'We're almost there,' Jake said.

'I want to get out,' Gracie said.

'I can't stop it in the mud, Grey,' Jake said. 'Let me just get it over the slope then I can turn around.'

Sean saw that the ground ahead rose upwards out of the mud into a sharp incline.

'You're not driving up that, are you?' Gracie said. 'Tell me you're not driving up that.'

'It's fine, this thing is designed to handle this kind of ground. You guys worry a *lot*.'

The JCB's tyres slipped and skidded through the mud, and Sean realised they were suddenly sitting a lot closer to the ground.

It occurred to him that none of them had any idea how deep the mud was. Perhaps, if the truck stopped moving, it would start to sink, sucking them down like gloopy quicksand. But after a few harrowing moments the wheels bit into solid ground again, gaining traction, and the truck climbed the incline.

He sensed Gracie relax beside him. Jake was ribbing the others for freaking out as he peered over the edge of the wheel, looking for a level stretch of land where he could turn around. But as he reached the top of the slope, the ground beneath them suddenly dipped, a sharp depression that none of them had anticipated.

Jake cried out, swung the wheel round, with a squealed, '*Shiiiiiiiiiiiit!*'

But it was too late. The imbalanced truck was already tilting. Sean felt the wheel over which he was stood leave the ground as the JCB swung to the right. He tried to plant himself against the door, but he couldn't fight gravity, and he fell onto Gracie, who in turn fell on Harvey, who fell on Arlo. Everyone was yelling as Jake span the wheel, which was suddenly slack in his hands.

The JCB toppled onto its side on the grassy embankment and for a moment, except for the high-scudding clouds sailing past the moon, all was still.

Apart from Arlo, who had knocked his elbow against the door-frame when they fell, they all escaped unscathed (unless you counted Jake's pride, which bore a dent far deeper than any marking on the toppled JCB). Back on the estate, they peeled off one by one as they each took different routes home, until there was only Sean, Gracie and Harvey left.

It was after eleven, and you didn't want to linger on Dulwood at night if you could help it. The street lights glowed beneath their cages, raised voices from within one of the houses were silenced briefly by the sound of smashing glass. A stream of fireworks streaked across the road a few blocks away, far too low to have been intended to detonate in the sky. *Idiots shooting fireworks at each other*, Sean thought.

Gracie was talking beside him, but for once Sean was barely paying her any attention. He was thinking about Harvey, hoping his house hadn't been targeted tonight. He knew it was wishful thinking; Harvey's house was always targeted on Mischief Night. Sean had already decided to walk him home in case he needed help clearing up. His mum was working late in The Dog and Gun and wouldn't finish until after midnight, so there was no rush to get back. Besides, it was a Friday – he didn't have to be up early for school in the morning.

Sean glanced over his shoulder, looking for Harvey, who seemed to have fallen behind. At first he couldn't see him, but then he realised that was because he was crouched in the rubble outside Fat Gav's house. Sean doubled back, Gracie following a half-step behind.

'You alright, Harv?' Sean said.

Harvey shushed him as he stood up. He moved slowly, and in his cupped hands he held a dead bird.

'What you got, Harv?' Gracie said.

'F-found it,' he whispered.

Sean didn't know much about birds, but he thought it looked like a robin. It had that cute, plump chest, the little black beak, the red-feathered breast and face.

'Oh, no,' Gracie said, moving towards Harvey. 'Poor thing. I wonder how it died.'

'We could bury it,' Sean said. 'Before we—'

'It i-i-isn't d-dead.'

Sean glanced at Gracie. The bird was obviously dead. Its eyes were welded shut, its tiny body completely still.

'Harv,' Sean said, hating to say it, but knowing he couldn't let Harvey carry a dead bird around with him. 'Look at it, man.'

'It isn't d-dead,' Harvey said again. Speaking so softly, Sean barely heard him. Harvey, who always seemed so self-conscious, walked past Sean and Gracie with his head up, the bird cupped gently but firmly between his big hands, as though suddenly full of surety and purpose.

DAY 14

Sean sleeps poorly through the night and gets up before dawn to feed the hedgehog. When he bends over the crate, he finds a litter of five tiny hoglets, but there is no sign of their mother.

He had expected the hoglets to be cute, but they're not. They are almost bald, sprouting only the beginnings of fine white spines, and their flesh is so thin Sean can see the roadmap of capillaries beneath. A film of skin covers their eyes, making him think of some alien creature straining to tear out of its gelatinous casing. Still, something inside him twists at the sight of them. They are impossibly small, heartbreakingly fragile.

His first instinct is to take them to Grandad, but he hesitates. *Grandad couldn't even keep the fish alive, you can't trust him with this. He'd probably do his best to help the hoglets, put them in the car to take them to the vet with the best intentions in the world... but what'd happen when he came back into the house to get his wallet or his coat? He'd forget what he was doing and end up back at his desk in the writing shed. That place has got a hold on him now and it won't let him go easily.*

Sean remembers the way Harvey had picked up the injured robin, the robin Sean and Gracie had been so convinced was dead. Harvey had taken the robin home, placed it in a box lined with paper towels and covered it with his old sweatshirt, telling Sean and Gracie it was in shock, that all it needed was warmth, quiet, darkness. He had put the box holding the robin in a small cupboard, cranked up the heating and left it in there.

Early the next morning Sean had returned to Harvey's to check on the bird. It had recovered from shock, but Harvey told Sean he wanted to inspect it for injuries before releasing it. Sean watched him remove the robin from the box, and was relieved to see it wriggle in his grip, chirruping. Its head twitched, its eyes were bright and round. Harvey lifted each wing tip, feeling for fractures or dislocations, examined its head and checked its eyes. He moved slowly, his voice soft, his stutter noticeably less pronounced as he talked Sean through what he was doing. Satisfied it was healthy, Harvey had placed the bird in Sean's hands. Beneath the soft down of feathers Sean had felt hollow bones, the speeding thrum of the bird's heartbeat, the comforting warmth of life. He had taken the bird outside, and when Harvey gave him the nod, Sean opened his hands and the robin exploded into the trees.

Harvey would know what to do with the hoglets, Sean thinks.

Suddenly, he wants nothing more than to turn away and leave the hoglets out in the garden, even if it does mean they'll die. *Everything and everyone dies eventually.*

For a while he watches the blind, squirming litter.

Then he picks up the crate and takes it inside the house.

Sean puts the crate in his bedroom, then goes into the library to google how to care for the abandoned hoglets.

His anxiety increases with every article he reads. There are reams of instructions to follow, a thousand precautions to take. The hoglets need more care and attention than a newborn baby. He needs to check them for maggots and fly eggs, weigh them and chart their growth each day to make sure they are gaining enough weight. He will have to hand-feed them every two hours, and after every feed encourage them to defecate by swiping a cotton bud dipped in olive oil between their anus and—

He wrinkles his nose with distaste.

He quickly makes a list of everything he needs to buy: Abidec to add to their food, goat's milk, plastic syringes, sterilising equipment, flea powder and anti-maggot preparation. He finds the kitchen scales so he can weigh them, the room thermostat to regulate the temperature in his bedroom, olive oil, cotton buds and a box of rubber gloves to wear when he handles them, because apparently the acids in his skin could harm them. He fills a hot water bottle and covers it with a towel, then takes everything back up to his room.

Sean sets the room thermostat to 22°C, which he has just discovered is the ideal temperature for newborn hoglets. Pulling on a pair of rubber gloves, he kneels beside the crate and places the towel-covered hot water bottle inside. Aware that the tiniest indelicacy could do irreparable damage to their thin skin, he gently puts each hoglet on top of it.

Feeling sorely unprepared for what is required of him, he hurries down to the kitchen, empties out the pantry. He finds a box full of plastic syringes stashed behind an old espresso machine. Now he just needs flea powder, anti-maggot preparation, steriliser, Abidec and goat's milk. He remembers the big Tesco near the park and estimates it can only be a fifteen-minute walk away. *If I run, I can be there and back in less than twenty minutes.*

He snatches some coins from the dish where Grandad keeps loose change, and without even stopping to grab his coat or his knee brace, he pelts outside.

Leaving The Paddock feels like a small act of rebellion, even though Grandad never said that he couldn't go out if he wanted to. Sean half expects the old man to come running after him, shouting him back and berating him for trying to leave, but Sean doesn't look over his shoulder. He runs as fast as his hobbled legs allow, his off-beat footsteps crunching against the gravel.

Everything he has learned so far tells him the litter are already doomed. Sean remembers Grandad telling him, on his second day in The Paddock, that most hoglets born in winter struggle to gain enough weight to survive hibernation. Add to this the fact they have been abandoned and Sean knows it would be a miracle if he manages to keep just one of them alive long enough to release into the wild. *But that doesn't mean I shouldn't try.*

He reaches the end of the drive and turns right onto the main road. The sky is only just beginning to brighten, the street lights are still lit. His breath prints clouds on the air as he runs, his footsteps echo in the silence. He knows he is doing his knee no favours but he can't slow down. Propelled by an urgency that he does not quite understand, he grinds his teeth against the pain. The hoglets need food and they need it quickly.

He curses himself for not being more prepared to look after the hoglets, but the truth is he had not considered the possibility that the hedgehog would abandon her litter. If she had stayed, as he thought she would, she would have been the one feeding the hoglets, cleaning them, caring for them. And she would have made a far better job of it than Sean ever could. But he thinks of the dead mouse he had seen curled in the tree trunk, the fish lying on the scum-crusted water, the decaying garden, and thinks that perhaps he should have known she would abandon them.

His aching knee forces him to slow to a fast walk, fatigue washes through him. His muscles feel heavy, tremulous, as though he has a colossal weight strapped across his back.

Suddenly, he feels the hair follicles along the back of his neck lift. He stutters to a stop, glances over his shoulder. There is a figure stood beneath the trees near the turning to The Paddock. Tall, dressed in a black cloak, its head is covered with a white-beaked mask.

The wind whisks through the tree branches, but it does not touch the cloth of the draped figure, which remains utterly still. As if it is not bound by the laws of nature.

Terror turns Sean's guts to liquid, his knees to bags of water. He can't move, as though the figure's sudden presence has welded his feet to the ground. Even from this distance, the air is redolent of scented wax and spices. In his right hand the figure holds a rod; in the left, a bag. Without looking, Sean knows the bag is full of frogs and blood-swollen leeches.

Sean tries to tell himself that the figure isn't real, *can't* be real, but Matilda's terror burns through him, threatens to drive him to his knees. Before fear can overwhelm him he turns and runs, throwing himself towards the main road, praying that the plague doctor isn't following, too scared to look over his shoulder.

His imbalanced legs cause his foot to catch on the kerb, and he falls. Pain screams through the abused joint, but he swivels to look behind him.

There is nothing there, nothing but the still, silent street and the dark opening to The Paddock's long drive.

Sean finds everything he needs in Tesco, even some Abidec to add to the hoglets' feeds, but his knee slows him on the way back, and by the time he turns onto the driveway to The Paddock the street lights have been extinguished and the sun has cleared the trees.

As soon as he gets in, he warms the goat's milk in the microwave and adds a few drops of Abidec. When it has cooled to room temperature he begins the laborious task of feeding the hoglets.

He picks one up, places it on a towel on the carpet. He tests the temperature of the milk on the inside of his wrist, then carefully slides the syringe into the side of its mouth. Gently, he compresses the plunger, and the hoglet's mouth opens and closes around the tip as it guzzles the milk.

Sean soaks a cotton bud in olive oil and, with a grimace, he rubs the tip of it gently over the hoglet's anus. Almost immediately an oval globule of poo slips out. He cleans it away, then places the hoglet on the scales and scribbles its weight on a notepad. Setting it back on the heated towel, he starts to check it over for maggots and fleas. Once he is sure the hoglet is not infested, he goes to find something to mark its quills so he can tell each one apart. The articles online suggested nail varnish, but Sean is pretty sure Grandad doesn't have any of that, so he uses his acrylic paints. He selects a shade called Blueberry and paints a stripe down the hoglet's quills, a deep blue mohican.

He sets Blueberry back on the heated towel and repeats the process with the next hoglet. He paints a different coloured stripe down each one, and names them after the shade he selects. Blueberry is followed by Violet, Silver, Scarlet and Olive.

Silver is the smallest at just thirty grams. When Sean picks him up he is so light he can barely feel him in the palm of his hand, but he feels a responsibility to keep him alive, and the weight of it is crushing.

* * *

Sean naps through the day and feeds the hoglets every couple of hours. Anxiety crouches in the pit of his stomach, and even when he could be resting, he sits by the crate, watching the hoglets as though they are performing trapeze stunts when in fact they do little except squeak intermittently and sleep.

Despite the pain in his injured knee, he drags himself up and down the stairs every few hours so he can warm the goat's milk and feed them, then cleans and toilets them. He reads an article on the computer in the library that says it is often more humane to euthanise a litter of abandoned hoglets than to try and keep them alive. *Can that be true? Are the odds of them surviving really so slim? And even if they are, could I do that to them? Isn't it better to fight for life than to give up? To work the odds, even if they're stacked against you? A chance, however small, is still a chance.*

Sean goes the whole day without seeing Grandad. A few weeks ago he would have worried that something bad had happened to him, that maybe he had keeled over in the flower beds or had a heart attack in his sleep, but these long stretches of absence are becoming less alarming now.

He tries to watch TV, but nothing holds his interest. He opens his book, but the story fails to transport him. His stomach grumbles and he thinks of the steaming lasagne Grandad made a few days ago, of his sausage hotpot. The old man had taken evident joy in cooking when Sean first arrived, but now all he seems to want to do is lock himself away in the writing shed.

Sean's loneliness suddenly swells to an aching hurt inside him. He misses Grandad's voice, misses the sound of him moving around the house, clearing pots and pans, singing to himself as he chops vegetables for dinner. Sean's gloomy mood is only exacerbated by his exhaustion, which is beginning to acquire a feverish quality.

A creaking floorboard from the hallway rouses him from his thoughts. He stands up, his wide eyes fixed on the open door. He moves towards it, straining to hear if there is anyone in the hall. If Grandad had come in from the writing shed, Sean would have heard the kitchen door open before the creaking floorboard. Whoever is out there, it isn't Grandad.

The Paddock, which moments ago had seemed so quiet, is now filled with noise. Rain whispers at the window, the wind whistles through the eaves and shrieks down the chimney, logs in the hearth spit and hiss as they burn.

Sean peers round the door and instantly the tension slides from his body. Grandad is stood in the corner of the hallway somehow, looking at the photographs on the side-table. He is wearing his waxed raincoat, the hood pulled up around his face. Water drips from his clothes and puddles on the floor, and his shoulders are shaking as though he is crying.

Sean hesitates, unsure what to do. He doesn't want the old man to be embarrassed by his tears, but walking away feels cruel.

He takes a step towards him. Grandad's sobs hitch, as though he senses Sean behind him and is trying to compose himself. He lifts a hand to his face, wiping away the tears.

The shadows at the peripheries of Sean's vision flex and curl. It is colder out here in the hallway, away from the fire. Pain flares through the scar on his hand as he reaches out to touch Grandad's shoulder, the tips of his fingers trembling in the sudden chill.

Grandad jerks round and Sean lurches away in horror.

Shadowed by the hood of his coat is the face of a clown. No. Not *a* clown. *The* Clown.

It starts to laugh as Sean reels backwards, a chilling falsetto that makes his hair spring away from his skin. The raincoat splits open and drops to the floor as the body inside shifts and grows. The Clown wears the grubby psychiatric gown it wore in Mandy's dream. But Sean knows he isn't dreaming, because if he were, this, right now, would be the point at which he woke, sweat-soaked and shuddering. That moment passes, offering no such easy escape.

Wisps of white hair drop to the floor, and purple hair sprouts like weeds from The Clown's chalk-white scalp. Its skin is coarse as sandpaper, its eyes are stygian craters, and its grin is a leer, a gaping red wound, framed by rows of interlocking fangs. Rainbow bobbles pop along the hem of its gown, like perfectly rounded flower heads quickly sprouting from their buds.

Sean's eyes bulge with terror as The Clown, still laughing, slowly stands up and starts to walk towards him. Blood drips from the tips of its claws, a multitude of forked tongues slithering from its mouth to swipe at its lips, as though it is holding the head of an octopus in its mouth.

Sean turns and throws himself towards the library, expecting at any moment to feel the nape of his neck scored by sharp talons. As he slams the door closed, he catches a glimpse of The Clown careering towards him. The wood shudders as it throws its weight against it and its laughter, a terrible high-pitched hacking, shatters, like scattered ball bearings, echoing around every corner of Sean's skull before, finally, fading to silence.

BEFORE

Sean dropped his spray cans into his rucksack, peeled off his mask and gloves and collapsed on the ground beside Gracie and Arlo.

He rarely used the streets of Dulwood as his canvas, preferring to paint outside the estate, in abandoned alleys, dank tunnels, across overflowing dumpsters and dark bridges. But it had seemed necessary for him to paint this picture on his own estate.

He had left home before the sun rose to set up before anyone was awake. Gracie, Arlo and Jake had helped lug his gear through the streets and kept him company as he worked, running to the store for snacks and drinks, watching out for signs of gangs or police. They had even helped with the painting, too, spraying swipes of colour here and there, filling in Sean's letters.

Now it was almost dinnertime, and Sean had finished. His feet ached, his twisted knee throbbed, but he felt satisfied, fulfilled. As though, in some strange way, he had explained himself.

The image stretched across the side wall of the old community centre, a rectangular blaze of colour against the precast concrete. The painting was of Sean, Gracie, Jake and Arlo, though to look at it, no one would know that was who they were. Sean had drawn each of them in matching orange jumpsuits, sat behind the bars of a cell. He had pixelated their features, like the blurred images of victims on TV, but added subtle clues so that his friends could tell each other apart. A puddle of stars splattered the floor beneath Gracie's feet, black-framed glasses poked out of the top of Arlo's front pocket, Jake had a lightsaber tucked into the band of his jumpsuit, and Sean was holding a dripping paintbrush in one hand. Splodges of orange paint dripped from the bristles onto the floor of his cell.

Above the image, in huge, wild-style letters, Sean had written: *THE ESCAPISTS*.

Their blurred faces and matching jumpsuits made their individual markings all the more pronounced, as though these were their weapons, the means by which they would turn themselves from Dulwood's prisoners into its ESCAPISTS.

'Where did Jake go?' Sean said, looking around.

'Skittles run,' Gracie said, scribbling something on a piece of paper. She was surrounded by stacks of coins, crooked towers of pound coins and fifty-pences; a stash of notes was pinned beneath a heap of pennies.

'What's all this?' Sean said.

Before Gracie or Arlo could answer, Jake emerged from around the corner. He had changed his clothes and was now wearing his Jedi costume, a brown robe over a white tunic.

'Wow, you finished. It looks epic!' He dropped his rucksack and slung an arm over Sean's shoulders. In a croaky voice that Sean assumed was supposed to be Yoda, he said, 'The force is strong with this one.'

'The fuck you doing?' Gracie snapped at him. 'If anyone sees you dressed like that, they'll kick the shit out of you.'

'Relax, no one saw me,' Jake said. 'I put it on before I came round the corner.'

'We're too old for those games, man,' Arlo said.

A wounded look flickered behind Jake's face and he started rootling round in his rucksack to hide his red cheeks. 'Yeah, I know. I wasn't gonna, like, play or nothing…' He pulled out four giant bags of Skittles and tossed them on the ground. 'You're welcome.'

Sean reached for a bag, tossed a handful of Skittles into his mouth. 'So you gonna tell me what all this cash is for?'

'This,' Arlo said, gesturing expansively at the piles of coins, 'is for your Future Creators exam.'

'We've pooled everyone's money,' Gracie said, 'which gives us eighty-three pounds and twenty-two pence. Add to that the twenty quid Diesel Betty gave us for cleaning the loos, and the money Jake got for selling his pervy magazines—'

'Hey, they weren't mine,' Jake said. 'They were me dad's, and if he finds out I nicked them he'll rip my balls off.'

'—then that gives us a grand total of one hundred and thirty-nine pounds and eighty-three pence.'

Jake tossed a rolled-up wad of notes on the ground beside the rest of the cash. 'Count again,' he said, smirking.

Gracie stared at the money but did not pick it up. 'Where did you get that?'

'Denny's stash,' Jake said. 'It's okay, he won't find out. You should see how much he's hoarding.'

Arlo stared at Jake in disbelief. 'Tell me you didn't really steal from Denny.'

'Oh, shit,' Gracie said, dropping her head into her hands. 'You're so dead.'

'You need to put it back,' Arlo said. 'And do it quick before he notices it's missing.'

'Jesus, relax. He won't find out. Denny's thick as shit, he can barely count.'

'It's dirty money.' Gracie's voice was a snarl, a blaze lit her eyes. 'Sean doesn't want it.'

'Oh, come on, that's two hundred quid there. Think how many times we'd have to scrub Diesel Betty's bogs for that much cash.'

'It's drug money, Jay,' Gracie said.

'Yeah, well. Sean needs more than pocket change to get on that course. Tell her, Sean. Tell her how much it's gonna cost. It's thousands, isn't it? Do you really think you're gonna save enough by scrubbing toilets and scraping together your pennies? Get real, Grey.'

'You need to put it back, man,' Arlo said, staring at the wad of cash as though it was a ticking bomb. 'You stole from the Dogs.

It doesn't matter that Denny's your brother. The Dogs are tighter than blood.'

Jake shrugged, pretending it was nothing, but Sean could tell from the way he was chewing the inside of his cheek that he was worried.

Sean looked at the neat stacks of coins, the small bundle of notes and the rolled-up wad of cash beside them. His friends knew he had no money, knew his mum couldn't afford to pay for his course. They had done this because they believed in him. That was worth more to him than any amount of cash.

'They're right,' Sean said. 'You should put the money back. I can't take any of it anyway.'

'What are you talking about?' Gracie said. 'Of course you can.'

'Look, I'm grateful, honest I am, but—'

'Sean, you've got a real chance here,' Gracie said. 'The sort of chance kids like us don't normally get. We won't let you miss out just coz you were unlucky enough to be brought up in this shitty neighbourhood. I mean, look at that painting. No fucking way you're missing out. No way.'

'Just don't forget about us, man,' Arlo said.

'Yeah,' Jake said, nodding. 'Remember, we get out of here together, or—'

'Or we don't get out at all,' Sean said, softly.

Approaching footsteps made them all fall silent. Quietly, they moved to the corner of the community centre and peered round. Frenchie and Rigsby, two leaders of the Dulwood Dogs, were walking across the car park. It was the first time Sean had seen Frenchie since he had been released from prison for a GBH charge.

Just the sight of Frenchie terrified Sean. Hooded and slump-shouldered, he looked like so many of the other gang members on Dulwood, but there was an edge to him that the other Dogs did not have, a deadened look behind his eyes that left Sean cold. His skin was covered in tattoos but Sean's eyes were always drawn to the word SOULJAH that was inked across his neck, to the letters MASS scrawled across the knuckles of his right hand, and ACRE across the knuckles of his left.

Beside him, Rigsby was tall and lean, his sallow skin pocked with acne. He walked with the loose-limbed swagger of a teenager, but hard living had planed the softness from his face. He was only sixteen but could easily pass for thirty. Sean had seen enough drug addicts on Dulwood to recognise the hollow-eyed, sunken-cheeked look for what it was.

The two boys stopped in the middle of the car park, beside the burnt-out Skoda. They glanced around, checking they were not being watched, and then Frenchie lifted the car's hood. He slipped a bag inside then slammed the hood shut. He and Rigsby walked back the way they had come, flicking glances left and right as they went.

'Maybe it's drugs,' Gracie whispered.

'Maybe it's a body part,' Arlo said.

'Maybe it's money!' Jake said, nudging Sean.

'Shut up,' Sean hissed.

When the two boys had disappeared, Sean started towards the Skoda.

Arlo grabbed his arm. 'What the fuck you doing?'

'Don't you wanna see what they hid?'

'Nah, man,' Arlo said, shaking his head. 'I don't wanna go anywhere near it.'

'Leave it, Sean,' Gracie said. 'C'mon, we've been here all day. Let's do one.'

'You go if you want,' Sean said. 'I'm just gonna have a quick look.'

Before any of them could stop him, he started walking towards the Skoda. The others held back, arguing, but they did not hesitate for long. Sean heard them cursing him beneath their breath as they hurried to catch up with him.

He popped the car hood. The rusty metal squealed as he lifted it.

Sean peered into the car's insides. And there it was. A black bag. He picked it up, ignoring the panicky whispers of his friends behind him, telling him to *put it back for fuck's sake, just put it back and let's go, we have to get out of here now!*

He looked inside the bag, even though he already knew, by the object's weight and shape, what it was. A gun.

Sean was used to seeing guns from all the time he'd spent at Harvey's house, plinking tin cans in his back garden with BB guns and air rifles, so the sight of this one should not have come as a shock. And yet it did. Frenchie's gun looked meaner than any of the ones he had handled at Harvey's house, even the semi-automatic that was so like the gun Sean was holding now. Harvey had refused to let any of them shoot that one, but he had shown them how to take the gun apart, how to handle it and how to load it.

Harvey's guns were for shooting beer cans, but this one belonged to the Dulwood Dogs and Sean knew it would not be used for such innocent games. He felt sullied just having looked at it. He didn't want to leave it there, awaiting the day Frenchie or one of the other Dogs decided they needed it.

'Sean, let's go!' Gracie hissed beside him.

Sean had heard rumours that the Dogs sometimes stashed their weapons round the estate in case they were searched by police, but he had never found one, never seen one being hidden. Pointing the gun at the floor and keeping his finger lifted from the trigger the way Harvey had shown him, Sean pulled the slide open and checked the cylinder.

'It's loaded,' he whispered.

'Sean, now!' Gracie said.

Reluctantly, he pushed the frame closed and placed the bag beneath the hood of the car. But he had already decided he would come back and move it when his friends were not with him; he would not sleep at night, knowing the gun was there, loaded, awaiting a victim.

DAY 15

'So, Sean, how are you doing?'

Doing great, Miraede. Just great.

'Your grandad says you're settling in well. He's really pleased with your progress.'

I'm amazed he spoke to you at all.

'He says you've been going to youth club.'

Grandad hasn't got a clue what I've been doing.

'It's a big step, Sean, and a brave one to take. You should be really proud of yourself.'

You shouldn't say that, Miraede. I have nothing to be proud of.

'I can see why you'd like it here. This house is beautiful.'

Oh, yeah. It's 'groovy'.

'And the garden, well... It's magnificent, isn't it? It must be lovely to have all this space after Creswick Hall.'

You don't see it, do you? Maybe I am going crazy.

'Do you enjoy spending time with your grandad, Sean?'

You've noticed a change in him, haven't you?

'You've been through a tremendous ordeal, but it must be...

challenging... for your grandad too, taking on the care of a young boy after living alone for so long.'

You know what, Miraede, he's not keeping it together so well. I think my coming here might have been a bad idea, after all. But you already know that, don't you?

'Sean, look at me. Please. I know this has been unbearably hard for you—'

You have no idea.

'—and you'd give anything to go back to the way things used to be.'

You don't know anything about the way things used to be.

'Your grandad loves you—'

Does he?

'—but all you want is to be back on Dulwood. A bereavement like yours is incredibly hard to deal with and there's no timeline for it. And yes, it can seem incredibly cruel, the way life marches on for everyone else after someone you love dies. Carrying on without them can feel like a betrayal. But you can't stop time, no matter how hard you dig your heels in, and you can't turn the clock back. Sean, you can't bring her back.'

—

'Tell me, have you thought any more about hypnotherapy?'

No.

'It can yield incredible results—'

No.

'—in the treatment of conversion disorder.'

No.

'You're unlikely to recover your voice, Sean, until you face up to what caused you to lose it in the first place. It's perfectly safe—'

No.

'—and I think it will help you enormously to process—'

Sean bolts up from his desk, a silent scream burning the back of his throat. Fading daylight glows around the edges of the curtains and the sketches he had been working on when he fell asleep are scattered across the table. A fetid stink lingers in his bedroom and, despite setting the thermostat to 22°C, his bedroom is so cold his breath swirls on the air. He looks at the dial on the stat beside his bed and watches, incredulous, as the digital display rapidly increases, one degree at a time: 6°C, 7°C, 8°C, 9°C, 10°C...

The cold lifts, but Sean's skin remains pebbled by goose-bumps. The Baku has been in his room again. Its note, a neatly folded sheet of mustard-coloured paper, is beside one of Sean's sketches. But he doesn't need to open it to know what is written there. The nightmare clings to his consciousness, preserved like a fly in amber by the infantile terror of a boy Sean has never met.

Ivo was seven years old when the nightmares started, the year 1902. His father had taken him to Paris's Olympia Music Hall to watch a short film called *Le Voyage Dans la Lune*. Ivo had never seen a film before, but as he watched the silent movie and listened to the live orchestra which accompanied the flickering images on the giant screen, his initial excitement had quickly mutated into disquiet.

A cast of astronomers were building a space capsule to take them to the moon. One by one they piled into the capsule, which was then shot from a gigantic cannon into space. The screen panned to an image of the moon, and as the image grew larger a face appeared in its centre. Its flesh was like curdled cheese, its grin a pantomime of malice. Suddenly, the bullet-shaped capsule hit the moon square in its eye. Flesh spurted from the spot into which the metallic profusion had embedded.

Appalled, terrified, Ivo had stared transfixed by the grisly vision. He ran from the theatre when a gloop of melted flesh dribbled from the moon man's eye, as though its strange, otherworldly anatomy was collapsing beneath the trauma.

The image burned its way into Ivo's subconscious, and that night he dreamt of the moon man. It floated down from the sky to his bedroom window, pressed its face to the glass. Its flesh was doughy and turgid, its eyes were cruel. Watching Ivo all the time, it pulled the capsule from its eye socket. It came out with a wet sucking sound, white mush pumping from the opened wound, like blood blanched of its colour. The moon man tapped the metal capsule against the glass. *You did this,* its one remaining eye seemed to say. *And now I've come to do the same to you.*

The moon man would return to Ivo many times after that. The nightmares only stopped the day he saw the Baku, scribbled his nightmare on a scrap of paper, and fed it into the statue's mouth.

Sean has never seen *Le Voyage Dans la Lune* but, through Ivo, he has sat in a plush red-cushioned seat in the exalted Parisian theatre and watched one of the first screenings. He has walked through Paris's streets and alleys, the smells of coffee and croissants fragrancing the air, and he has gazed at Gustav Eiffel's bronze-coloured tower, streaking up to the sky. Sean knows he should feel a sense of wonder, of privilege, but he doesn't. The insight brings him only revulsion and horror. He imagines the Baku standing over him as he slept, its breath choking asthmatically on all the world's nightmares; imagines it opening its mouth, swallowing its hand, pulling Ivo's saliva-soaked note from its throat, then giving it to him.

With a surge of anger he snatches the note up, rips the curtains open and fumbles for the lock on the sash window, ready to throw it open and fling it outside.

The Baku is on the patio.

Stood on the tips of the spreading blue veins, its legs are obliterated by a swirling fog. It is close enough now for Sean to see the ridges in its ivory tusks, the wrinkles around its eyes, the tracery of capillaries in its torn ears.

The paving slabs beneath the Baku's feet are buckled by the ink-swollen veins that protrude from the soil, the very same veins that trace patterns beneath its flesh. Sean knows now that it is only when he is asleep that the Baku can walk where it pleases, and that every time it feeds him another nightmare, it is closing the gap that stands between them in the waking world. *Soon, it won't have to wait for me to fall asleep to come to me… Soon those veins will reach all the way to the house, and I won't be able to wake up and escape the nightmare.*

He jerks the curtains closed. His heart is thumping so hard that his vision pulses with every thud. *It's okay, it's going to be alright. I'm awake now, it can't get me when I'm awake.* He flinches as his hand grows hot and he drops the burning note, but it is already nothing but ash. Sean passes a shaky hand over his eyes, tries to stem his panic. But he can't stay awake forever, and when he falls asleep the Baku will be waiting, waiting with its nightmares and its notes. And every dream it passes him is a stepping-stone that bridges the gap between them. What will it do when, finally, it doesn't have to wait for him to fall asleep to reach him?

It's going to feed me my own nightmare.

The hoglets squeak quietly in their crate, the sound dragging Sean's attention back into the room. A glance at his phone tells him it's 19:42. He has slept for three hours straight. He wonders if he slept through his alarm or whether he simply forgot to set it at all. He moves towards the hoglets' crate to rewarm their hot water bottle, and notices that only four of the hoglets are squirming on their blanket.

Sean's heart sinks as he kneels beside the crate. He does not bother with gloves when he picks up Silver. He is so small in the palm of Sean's hand, a feather-light weight, but there is nothing small or feather-light about his grief. He tries to tell himself he shouldn't be surprised. Silver was too small, too fragile to survive.

But the heavy, black aching is there, nevertheless. Out of all proportion to his loss. He thinks of how cold his room had been when he woke up, and he knows, he *knows*, that the plunging temperature is what killed him.

This is the Baku's fault.

DAY 16

As soon as the sun has risen, Sean finds an empty shoebox, lines it with a clean tea towel, and puts Silver inside. There is no sign of Grandad when he goes downstairs and Sean wonders whether he has spent the entire night in the writing shed.

He does not want to bury Silver in Grandad's corrupted garden. He remembers the park opposite Tesco. He decides to bury Silver there. That way he can call into the supermarket on the way back to buy some food and supplies for the hoglets.

He takes £50 from the wallet in Grandad's coat pocket and grabs a trowel from the porch, stuffing it down the back of his trousers. He considers leaving Grandad a note telling him where he's gone on the off-chance that he notices his absence, but decides not to. *So what if he does notice I'm missing? Maybe my disappearance will jolt him back to reality.*

Knowing the walk will aggravate the pain in his knee, Sean straps on his knee brace and swallows four codeine tablets with a glass of water, then slides the rest of the blister pack into his back pocket.

As soon as he passes through The Paddock's gates, the tension in Sean's neck and shoulders begins to drain away. He feels lighter, as though the air itself is buoying him up, and it's so good to breathe air that doesn't feel sickly and foul, to look at trees and plants that burst with colour instead of the rotten, diseased vegetation of Grandad's garden. His lungs feel as though they are being scoured clean and his head is clearer than it has been for days.

A mizzling rain drizzles from the grey sky, but Sean maintains a steady pace and does not rush. He is in no hurry to put Silver in the ground. The thought alone feels like a callous abandonment and he walks with the care of a pallbearer at a funeral, the shoebox held level with his chest, protective of the hoglet, even now.

It takes almost an hour to reach the park, by which time the rain has stopped and a cold ivory sun burns through a hazy veil of clouds. Despite the painkillers, Sean's knee is swollen and hot. He passes through the gates and follows signposts towards the park, the weight of the box in his hands growing heavier with every step.

The path opens onto a large square lawn that is bordered by sloping flower beds. Water squirts from a small fountain, adding a silvery tinkle to the susurrus of the wind through the trees. Other than two people sat on a bench, there is no one around.

Sean had expected a scruffy park, not pristine gardens like this. He knows he can't start shovelling soil from the manicured flower beds, but he notices a ginnel in the corner of the park, wending its way into the woods. He decides to bury Silver there, beneath the dappled shade of the trees. As he approaches the couple on the bench, he senses them turn to watch him. His fingers curl more tightly around the shoebox in his hands.

'Hayley, check out the freakshow.'

Sean looks up and freezes, surprised recognition bolting through him.

The couple on the bench are Jock and Bling.

Noticing the look on Sean's face, Jock's face hardens. 'What the fuck you staring at?'

Sean knows he should keep walking but he is skewered in place, like a butterfly to a taxidermist's board. Jock takes a long drag on his cigarette, his eyes narrowing to slits as he inhales. The filter crackles and Sean catches the sweet, spicy scent of skunk.

'I said—' He flicks his tab into the bushes and stands up. '—what the *fuck* are you staring at?'

Sean sees more than defensiveness in Jock's eyes. There is a coiled rage there, too, and he knows he is in trouble. Adrenaline shotguns through his body and he bolts back the way he came, the thump of his backpack matching the beat of his feet. He knows he should drop the shoebox so he can run quicker, but he doesn't seem able to uncurl his fingers from Silver's little coffin. The hoglet's tiny body bumps against the inner walls of the box as he runs, and the indignity fills Sean with an anger so powerful he feels it as an ache in his veins.

His hitching gait makes it impossible to outrace Jock, who quickly catches up with him. He grabs Sean's rucksack and he bundles him to the ground, the shoebox buckling inwards beneath his weight.

'Nate, what're you doing?' Bling says, hurrying towards them.

'Fucking spastic didn't answer me.'

Sean staggers to his feet but Jock grabs him by the back of the neck with one hand, snares a fistful of his coat with the other.

'It's rude to stare at people, didn't you know that?'

I'm sorry! I'm sorry! I'm sorry! I'm sorry!

Sean hurls the words from his throat, but they shatter into soundless explosions inside him. His face contorts with the effort of speech, bringing an amused smile to Jock's lips.

'What's up, retard?' Jock says, laughing. 'Are you trying to say something?'

He starts to drag Sean towards the ginnel where he had been heading to bury Silver. Sean tries to twist away – *He's going to bury me there, instead!* – but he is no match for Jock. The pathway narrows to a muddy track that is obscured by bracken and trees from anyone who might enter the gardens. Briefly, Sean wonders how Jock and Bling had ever made him think of his old friends, how he could ever have drawn comparisons. His friends would never do anything like this to anyone.

Jock shoves Sean and he tumbles to the ground, dropping the shoebox when he lands. Bling stands a few paces away, smoking and watching Sean as he scrabbles to pick it up.

'What you got in there?' Jock says.

Sean scoops up the shoebox, tries to stand up, but Jock kicks him in the ribs, knocking him back down. Sean curls into the pain and Jock wrenches the shoebox from his slack fingers. Instinctively, Sean jerks upwards to grab it back. Surprised, Jock slams his fist into Sean's chin. The brutal uppercut whips his head back and smashes his teeth together. Blood fills his mouth, but before Sean can recover, Jock lifts his foot and brings it down, hard, on Sean's bad knee.

The world shatters beneath pure, blinding agony. Sean can hear Jock's voice, but his words are meaningless. A thought, lucid and calm, winds itself like a white ribbon through the haze of raw, red pain: *He's really going to kill me.*

Jock rips the lid off the shoebox.

'What the fuck…'

He picks Silver up by the fine white quills that protrude from his skin and he is laughing, as though the dead hoglet is the butt of a terrible joke. Sean blinks back tears and looks up, not at Jock, but at Silver.

His tiny legs whisk the air and he is squeaking.

He's alive!

Sean's heart soars and he smiles through the blood in his mouth. He reaches to catch the hoglet, sure Jock is going to drop him.

Watching Sean, Jock steps back. His ice blue eyes glitter with a dangerous fusion of amusement and disgust and Sean can only watch, knowing what is coming but unable to do anything to stop it.

Jock drops Silver to the ground and brings his foot down on top of him.

The scream trapped inside Sean's throat ricochets through him, unborn.

'Jesus, Nate.' Bling wrinkles her nose as Jock lifts his foot and swipes the gloopy mess beneath his shoe onto the grass. 'What's *wrong* with you?'

Sean's stomach heaves. He twists away, vomits on the ground, purging himself of what little he has eaten. Jock is tearing his rucksack from his back, but Sean barely notices.

How can I have let this happen?

It seems impossible. When he'd picked Silver out of the crate, he was dead. There had been no doubt in his mind on that score.

You made a mistake. A terrible mistake.

Sean imagines Silver scrabbling around in the dark shoebox, desperately trying to get out, to find his way back to the warmth of his littermates.

How could you have been so stupid?

But then he realises how little he has slept over the past few days. He knows he hasn't hallucinated the scraps of paper beneath his pillow, the apparitions that have spilled from sleep into the waking world, but he can see how, groggy with sleep, he might have thought the sleeping hoglet was dead.

The knowledge does nothing to assuage his guilt. Jock throws Sean's rucksack to Bling and continues to swipe his trainer against the leaves. Bling tips the bag upside down. Sean lifts his head, looks at his belongings scattered across the ground: his mobile phone, pencils, erasers, wallet.

His sketchbook.

The bottom falls out of the world and Sean is in freefall.

'Any cash?' Jock says.

Bling picks up the wallet, flicks through it.

'Fifty quid.'

She slips it into her back pocket, but Sean isn't watching her. All he can see is the sketchbook, the sketchbook that is filled with drawings of Jock, Bling, Snake. He looks away, hoping indifference will trick them into dismissing it. But Bling stoops to pick it up. She flicks it open, and instantly her face tightens.

'Nate…'

She spins the book round so he can see. The sketch she shows him is the one in which Sean has turned them all into grotesque caricatures of themselves, but even so, their identities are unmistakable.

Snake leers over Jock, the angles of his face planed to a hardness that renders him inhuman. His eyes are sunken craters and rats scrabble over the back of his coat. Jock looks up at him with crazed bloodshot eyes. He is bare chested, and a torque bracelets his upper arm. A bent spoon sticks out of his back pocket and a tab dissolves on the end of his drooling tongue. Bling is lying down on the stack of hymn books. Her eyes roll in her skull, her lips are slack, as though parted in a moan of ecstasy.

Jock snatches the sketchbook from her hands and flicks through the other drawings, the flesh around his eyes tightening.

He drops the sketchbook and pulls Sean to his feet, slams him against a tree. Then he punches him in the gut, driving all the air from his lungs. Pain howls through Sean again, obliterating all thought.

'You better start talking, retard. What is this? Did you think you could fucking *bribe* me? Is that it?'

Bling has picked up the sketchbook and is leafing through it. 'Shit, there's loads in here. Nate, if the police find out you've been dealing again they'll sling you straight back into juvie.'

'You better start explaining, you little shit, or I fucking swear I'll fuck you up so bad, your own mam won't recognise you.'

Sean opens his mouth, straining for words that used to trip off his tongue with barely a thought. Jock's eyes narrow into slits.

'*Speak* you stupid fuck!'

He punches Sean in the face. The tender swelling from his collision with Grandad's writing desk connects with the tree trunk, squirting streamers of light through his skull. Jock yanks his head up by the roots of his hair.

'*Speak!*'

Words stick to Sean's consciousness, snared like dead flies on a cobweb. He opens his mouth, but all that comes out is a dribble of blood. He squeezes his eyes shut, focuses on the words he needs to defend himself. The trowel in his back pocket digs into him but he does not reach for it. Instead, he lets his arms fall loose by his sides.

'Babes, I think he's deaf,' Bling says, looking at Sean as though he has just vomited on her face.

Jock punches him again, and his falling fist shakes the world. A scarlet spume spray-paints the air and Sean's consciousness shudders. He presses his lips together. No point trying anymore.

Hush little baby…

The golden voice speaks from the edge of his thoughts. Jock releases Sean and he slumps to the ground. His split lips seep blood.

Don't say a word.

His right eye is puffed closed. He can't quite summon the strength to lift his head but finds he doesn't want to, anyway. He only wants to fall asleep within the comforting shade of that voice.

Mama's gonna buy you a mockingbird.

Jock is stood over him and Sean senses the older boy's uncertainty.

And if that mockingbird don't sing.

'The freak *wants* me to kill him.'

Mama's gonna buy you…

The voice fades to silence and Sean strains closer to the edge of oblivion.

Mama's gonna…

Mama's gonna…

Finally, the loving darkness folds around him.

* * *

When Sean blinks back to consciousness, the quality of the light has changed. For a while he just lies there, unable to summon the energy to stand up.

It is the thought of the hoglets that finally gets him moving. He has missed at least one feed, maybe two. He needs to get back if he isn't going to miss another. As he sits up, his wounds twinge in rhythm with his heartbeat; his body is a sobbing mess of angry, hurting flesh. His left eyelid has swollen shut, his lips feel as though they encompass his entire face. And his knee... holy *shit,* his knee.

He remembers the blister pack of codeine in his back pocket and almost weeps with relief that he hadn't put it in his rucksack where Jock would have found them. He dry swallows two tablets. They lodge in his throat and he coughs, bitterness flooding his mouth. He pops one more from the packet and tucks it beneath his tongue to slowly dissolve.

He aches in places he had barely been aware of before, and every increment of movement brings with it waves of agony. Still, he removes the trowel from his back pocket and slowly begins to dig a hole in the soil beside what is left of Silver. Then, he carefully scoops his remains into it and shovels dirt on top of him.

That done, he stands up and begins to make his slow way home.

* * *

By the time Sean gets back to The Paddock he is clinging to consciousness by the frailest of threads. The painkillers make everything hazy, and his eyes slope at half-mast even as he walks. The front door is locked, so he makes his way round to the back of the house to let himself in through the kitchen door.

The house is quiet, Grandad must be in the writing shed. Sean shambles towards the sofa in the library, feeling sleep rise behind his eyes. He reaches into his pocket for his mobile so he can set his alarm, before remembering that Jock took it.

He drops onto the couch, deciding to rest, just for a minute. He needs to find an alarm clock, needs to feed the hoglets, needs to… needs to… he shakes his head to try and rid himself of the enervating fog. But the sofa is a cradle, and the warmth of the library is irresistible. He tells himself to get up, but his muscles are slack and his eyes are sliding closed. Sleep pulls him down and he drifts, insensate, into the waiting void.

DAY 17

Sean wakes up with a convulsive gasp, filling his lungs with freezing air. He struggles up from the sofa, but his aches and pains batter him back down. Something slides from his lap, cracks upon impact with the floor. A wax tablet. The words carved into it flare in his mind, and as they do, the consciousness of a girl born in the ancient past tangles with his own.

Vita. A twelve-year-old Roman girl, through whom Sean has glimpsed a past that would turn scholars and historians green with envy. While they approximate and speculate and reverently try to piece together the damaged and degrading fragments of Ancient Rome, Sean has *lived* it. As Vita, he has pushed his way through the rowdy Roman mob, has heard the colossal roar of the crowds at the Circus Maximus. He knows the faecal stink of the packed streets, the rank sacrificial stench of blood and incense and flowers. He has stood with the crowds outside the Curia Julia and glimpsed the Emperor Vespasian amid the white-robed senators, heard their booming voices through the open doors of the senate. He has watched artists paint frescoes on the walls of his home, and at his father's lavish parties, listened to musicians play the lyre and orators recite famous poems. He has sat with a Roman tutor in the garden of his father's villa and copied the words of the Aeneid onto his wax tablet, the heat of a younger sun browning the nape of his neck.

In sleep, Vita's consciousness overcame Sean's, as though her nightmare was the amber which preserved not only her deepest horror, but all her memories.

It began the day the new slaves arrived. Among them was a young girl, not much older than Vita herself. Her name was Atana, and the two girls became secret friends. Despite the discrepancy in their social stations, Vita had been careful only to treat Atana as a slave when her mother and father were around, conscious of how they would both be punished otherwise. But in Vita's mind and heart, they were as equal as sisters.

Vita was not oblivious to her mother's scathing hatred of Atana. Over and over, she would berate the girl and beat her for the tiniest mistakes. She spoke of her as though she were a deviant, and yet she was the slave Vita's father most often smiled upon and defended, the one he sent for when he was alone in his chamber. It didn't take long for Vita to understand why. After visiting her father, Atana was often reserved, sometimes almost catatonic, and while the abuses she endured at the hands of Vita's mother were played out for all the household to see, Vita suspected that the worst of her sufferings occurred behind the closed doors of her father's chamber.

The young slave tried to run away, but a local shopkeeper brought her back to the estate only a few hours after she disappeared. After that, Vita did not see Atana again until the day she flung herself from the window of her father's chamber, where she had been locked up as punishment.

Vita was outside in the courtyard when it happened. Startled from the equation she had been working on by her tutor's alarmed cry, she followed his gaze to the stone archway above them. Atana was stood there, her white-knuckled hands gripping the stone. The first thing Vita noticed was that her father had branded the letters *FUG* across her forehead, livid and swollen welts that marked her as a runaway. The fall was not a steep one, and alone it would probably not be fatal. But the rope she had wrapped around her neck would surely do the job.

Atana looked at Vita.

'Me paenitet, o amica.'

I'm sorry, friend.

Before Vita could even cry out, Atana jumped.

She seemed barely to fall at all before the rope brought her up short. Vita did not know whether she really heard the sound of her best friend's neck snapping or if she only imagined it, but either way, she *felt* it, a terrible rending inside her. Atana slowly swung above the statue of Dionysus, her soiled feet twitching, her hair swaying in the soft breeze, oblivious to Vita's screams.

After that day Atana was waiting for Vita every time, on the other side of sleep. Over and over she relived her friend's terrible last moments, and each time felt like losing her anew. The nightmares only stopped the day she fed her dream to the Baku.

The tangling of Vita's consciousness with Sean's leaves him feeling sullied. He can taste her horror, a metallic tang at the back of his throat. *I'm not surprised the Baku wants to purge.*

Outside the library windows, the sky is dark. Moving with the caution of a rheumatic old man, Sean stands up, makes his slow way into the hallway. The grandfather clock in the hall tells him it is gone two in the morning. He wonders how many of the hoglets' feeds he has missed. As fast as his abused body will allow, he drags himself up the stairs to collect the equipment he needs to prepare their milk.

Sean is sat reading at the table when Grandad enters the kitchen. At first the old man's gaze slides over his grandson, dull and glazed, but then he frowns, blinks, and looks back at him.

'Good God, Sean!' He rushes to the table, sinks into the chair beside him. 'What *happened* to you?'

Sean can hardly blame Grandad for looking so shaken. The swelling in his face has worsened overnight, his bruises darkening to black in places, spreading ripples of dark purple and russet that fade to yellow at the edges. His left eye is swollen shut, blood congeals in the cut on his lip. The throbbing reminds him of every blow dealt, every kick delivered. If he were to lift his shirt, Grandad would see more cuts and bruises across his stomach and ribs, but Sean doesn't do that; the old man already looks traumatised enough.

'Jesus Christ, Sean. I can't believe you left the house on your own.' He drags his hand down his chin, his eyes moving over Sean's face. 'Your mum might've let you go off round the estate, but you can't just come and go like that, not here, not anymore.' He leans forward, earnest and well-meaning, the pain in his eyes as raw as heartbreak. 'You have to tell me who did this to you, lad. Please… listen, why don't you… why don't you write it down.' He stands up, snatches a pen and paper from the kitchen island. Sean notices the old man's hands are trembling as he pushes them towards him. 'Come on, write it down. Please, lad. Don't ignore this. Listen to me, we *have* to report it to the police.'

Sean says nothing, but Grandad reads the boy's refusal in the sudden blankness that occludes his eyes, in the way he twists his small shoulders away from him.

Grandad books Sean an emergency appointment at the GP for later that morning.

The doctor who calls them in looks about the same age as Grandad. Her silver hair is pinned up in a neat chignon and the wrinkles of her face pleat naturally to her smile.

She introduces herself as Doctor Taylor and then listens to Grandad as he runs through Sean's medical history, interjecting now and then with questions of her own. There is a gentleness to her manner that is not affected, and Sean can tell she is a good doctor, that people would open up to her. *She probably has children of her own. Grandchildren, too.* He imagines her taking them to the park, baking with them, teaching them how to read.

Doctor Taylor gently touches his arm and tells him to slip behind a curtain to undress for his examination.

He strips to his underwear as instructed, heat climbing his cheeks. He feels naked with his legs on display. *Don't be stupid,* he scolds himself. *She's probably seen a lot worse than my legs in her lifetime.* That may be so, but when Dr Taylor slides the curtain open, Sean can't help but flinch and lower his eyes.

'Take a seat on the bed there, Sean,' she says, moving towards him. She shines a light in his eyes and listens to his chest with her stethoscope.

'You seem to be breathing without any trouble so you probably haven't cracked any ribs.' She palpates his back, then taps fingers across his ribs. 'I'm pleased to say your lungs haven't been damaged,' she says, sitting back, her gaze moving to his injured leg. 'Now let's have a look at that knee. I'm going to have to feel it, but I'll be as gentle as I can.'

Sean winces as she squeezes the flesh around the joint.

'Okay, bend it as much as you can for me.'

Sweat beads Sean's upper lip as she directs him through a series of simple manoeuvres. He tries to do as she asks, but when she tells him to relax and pushes against the inside of his knee, the pain that blazes through him is so intense, he has to fight the urge to shove her away.

'Nothing's broken and I can give you something for the swelling, but it'd be best if you keep your weight off your knee for a while. I'll bob a few stitches in your lip, too. Think you can handle that?'

She tells him to get dressed while she gathers the equipment she needs to suture his lip. Sean pulls his trousers and shirt back on as Doctor Taylor chats quietly with Grandad. Sean wonders if she can detect the sour smell of alcohol emanating from the old man, whether she will say anything about it. *Why would she?* Sean thinks. *There's no law against taking a drink.*

After a few minutes she slides the curtain back and pulls up a stool to sit in front of him on the bed. She soaks a cotton pad with iodine and gently cleans the cut on his lip. The astringent chemical brings the stab of tears to Sean's eyes.

She draws anaesthetic into her syringe.

'Sharp scratch,' she says as she injects it into his lip.

Sean barely feels it. There are too many other aches throbbing through his abused body for this small nip to register. Doctor Taylor's movements are gentle but precise. Her eyes are light brown, flecked with green, and the understanding Sean sees in them makes his throat ache. He wonders how much she knows about him. *What does she see when she looks at me? When she looks at Grandad?*

'That'll only take a few seconds to numb your lip,' she says, withdrawing the needle. She opens a small box, using forceps to remove a curved needle attached to a long, thin thread. Her eyes search his face as she taps her finger against his lip.

'Can you feel that?'

He shakes his head. No. She nods, leans towards him with the needle, and begins to stitch his wound.

'I have to say, Sean,' she says, as the thread tugs at the meat of his lip, 'you're a tough lad. I normally have to send kids your age for a general anaesthetic to get anywhere near them with a needle. But being tough doesn't mean allowing whoever did this to you to go unpunished. Sean?'

Her hands pause in their work and Sean blinks up at her. Her head is tipped to the side, her eyes peering into his, as though if she looks at him from the right angle, her words might slide through his barriers and reach him. 'Don't let them get away with it.'

Shame floods him and he looks down at his feet.

Why not? People get away with terrible things all the time.

Sean leaves the surgery with bandages round his knee, a pair of crutches and a prescription for some high-dose painkillers. Doctor Taylor had told Grandad to keep hold of the painkillers to make sure he was spacing them properly through the day, but Sean knows the old man will forget her instructions as soon as they get back to The Paddock. All Sean has to do is watch Grandad to see where he puts them.

Grandad drives to the supermarket after the doctor's surgery. He tells Sean to wait in the car, but Sean ignores him and climbs out, hopping round the side of the car to pull his crutches from the back seat, unwilling to let this opportunity pass by without taking full advantage of it.

In the supermarket, Grandad fills the trolley with so much food, anyone would think he was preparing for a nuclear war. He seems more like his old self today, so much so that Sean begins to question whether he really saw something different in his eyes. Miraede felt something was off, Sean was sure about that, but she would surely have run screaming from the house had she seen the things Sean had seen.

He knew, from his recent research, that sleep deprivation could cause hallucinations… but he had found Luca's note beneath his pillow before the sleepless nights had even started. And he had only missed out on a few hour's sleep when he woke in Grandad's car with Khaba's papyrus on his lap.

No, he was sure what was happening was real, despite the fact no one else could see it. You didn't need to be able to see something for it to exist.

Sean leaves Grandad to find goat's milk and tins of meaty cat food, putting all of it in his rucksack.

At the checkout, Grandad frowns as Sean empties everything onto the conveyor belt. The lady on the till scans the cat food, and

Sean feels the old man's eyes on him, but if he's figured out that the hedgehog has given birth to her litter, he makes no mention of it.

When they get to the house, Sean throws away all the old goat's milk and prepares a fresh feed. He takes it upstairs, moving carefully on his crutches, the warm milk stuffed into his back pocket.

He is pulling on his rubber gloves when he glances down into the crate and sees that Blueberry is not moving. *He's just sleeping,* Sean tells himself. He picks up the hoglet, hoping to feel a tremble of movement. Blueberry's mouth is parted, his paws tightly curled. Sean touches the tip of his nose. Nothing. *He'll come round*, he thinks, laying him back on the warm towel. *Just like Silver did. Just like Harvey's robin did.*

He picks up Olive and starts to feed her. Every now and again, his gaze flicks to Blueberry, looking for a twitch of movement that does not come.

Sean is in the library reading a book when Grandad comes in from the writing shed. In the few hours he has been gone, the old man looks as though he has aged ten years. His face is drawn, the skin pulled too tight across his bones. His blue eyes are rheumy, bloodshot, and there is a disconnected look about them, as if, even though he is here in the room with Sean, his mind is held captive in some other place. His clothes swamp his skeletal frame, and for the first time Sean is struck by how much weight Grandad has lost since he arrived.

'Sean, lad,' Grandad says, blinking.

It's painful, watching the struggle it takes for him to drag his consciousness into the room. Every time he goes into the writing shed he seems to lose a little more of himself. Sean feels a wave of pity for him, but then he remembers how the old man had shoved him, the coiled rage that had burned behind his eyes. His hand moves reflexively to the lump at the side of his head.

'What time is it?' Grandad says, glancing at his watch. As he does, Sean notices he is holding a book. 'Good God! That can't be right. Almost ten? You must be starving! How about I rustle up some dinner. There's pizza in the freezer, or I could make us a quick curry?'

Sean barely registers a word. He is staring at the book in Grandad's hands. *The Baku: A Selection of Short Stories.* Sean had replaced the book in the library, but he suddenly wishes he had thrown it in the bin or burned it.

He tears his eyes from the book, looks at the old man. Dark blue veins lattice his face, threads of the same colour curlicue the lighter blue of his eyes, as though his blood has been replaced with ink.

'You know, I barely remember writing these stories,' Grandad says, running a hand over the book's front cover. 'I wasn't in a good place back then and I think writing them… well, I think it was a good way of lancing some of the poison from inside me, you know? It's not good to keep all the bad stuff inside, Sean. You have to find a way to let it out.'

The old man walks out of the room and Sean hears the kitchen door slide open and closed. He doesn't need to look out of the window to know Grandad is heading back into the writing shed.

Later, when Sean returns to check on the hoglets, he finds Blueberry in the exact same spot where he left him. Leaving him with the litter any longer feels cruel, and besides, Sean knows he is dead now. He picks him up without putting his gloves on and the tiny hoglet's body is stiff and cold.

He can't find another shoebox, so instead he wraps him in a clean tea towel. Reluctant to leave the house after what happened the last time he did, Sean decides to bury Blueberry beneath Nanna Storm's rowan tree.

Outside, the sky is midnight blue and star-spangled. Sean digs a small hole in the dew-damp grass, breathing in the fresh, clean smell of the overturned soil.

He lays Blueberry in the ground, throws a handful of dirt over his tiny body, and packs the soil down tight. Tears prism his eyes, but he wipes them away angrily, scolding himself for his weakness. He climbs to his feet, dusts dirt from his hands. Then he limps back inside to warm milk for the three surviving hoglets.

DAY 18

After feeding and cleaning the hoglets, Sean goes into the kitchen and makes himself a cup of tea. The door slides open and Grandad stands framed in the doorway, his hands full of freshly picked produce.

'Sorry, lad, didn't mean to startle you,' he says, using his elbow to push the patio door closed. 'Just got some vegetables from the greenhouse, thought I'd make us a nice beef stew for tonight.'

Sean takes a step back, his eyes widening with horror.

The vegetables hanging from Grandad's hands are withered and spoiled beyond all recognition. A leprous coat of white mould furs the outside of the shrivelled food, patches of dark green dapple their surfaces. The slimy roots have tangled together, as though bound by some sick, amoeboid intelligence, and they drip oily liquid onto the floor. Even had Grandad left the vegetables beneath a relentless summer sun, they could not have degraded as much as this.

He moves to the sink and dumps everything into it.

Horrified, Sean inches closer. Hunks of soil have dropped onto the floor, slick puddles that seethe and bubble with maggots. He gags at the smell, covers his nose with his sleeve as he carefully steps over them.

Grandad picks up a knife, untangles what was once a vegetable. He runs the blade across its surface and skin sloughs away, like the greasy sliding of flesh from a decaying corpse. Beneath it, the pulp of the vegetable is riddled with maggots. A beetle scuttles over Grandad's hand, its black carapace glistening.

Sean imagines Grandad sat down in front of a steaming plate of beef stew, oblivious to its corrupted ingredients; imagines his teeth sinking into maggots, severing centipedes, biting through beetles, their insides exploding in his mouth, dribbling down his chin, wriggling mandibles protruding from his lips as he chews.

Grandad looks up and grins at Sean. Those blue-black veins Sean had seen before have multiplied, so that now they almost obliterate the true blue of his eyes. Dark threads fan from the hollows of his sockets towards his sunken cheeks.

'Grab a knife, lad, come and give me a hand.'

The stink makes Sean's stomach heave, but it is Grandad's eyes that sicken him the most.

'Sean?' Grandad drops the knife into the sink and moves towards him. 'Sean, are you alright?'

Sean stares into the old man's eyes, willing them to change back to normal.

'Why don't you go have a lie down while I fix dinner? Try and have a bit of a kip, lad, you look shattered.'

A beetle wriggles from the space where Grandad's pupil should be. It drops to the floor and scurries towards Sean. Swallowing a sob, he rushes from the room, not even bothering to grab his crutches.

Sean spends a few hours in the conservatory, sketching Vita and her tutor, sitting together in the terraced gardens of her family's courtyard, surrounded by tall pillars and statues.

The smell of cooking meat fills the house, but beneath it Sean detects the scent of rot and putrefied vegetables. When Grandad calls him for dinner, Sean ignores him. He can't bear the thought of watching the old man eat his grotesque meal, or of sitting across from him and looking into that cobweb of ink that covers his eyes.

A few minutes later, Grandad peers through the door.

'What's wrong, lad? Aren't you hungry?'

Grandad's eyes have returned to their normal shade, the dark capillaries that threaded his flesh have disappeared. Sean realises how much he has missed this, Grandad's way of asking him questions with no expectation of an answer, pulling him back into a world that feels as though it has elbowed him out of it.

'I'll leave some plated up for you in the fridge, just in case you find your appetite later,' he says, then closes the door behind him.

* * *

Sean thrashes awake at his workbench, confused panic making him feel sick and off-kilter. He is in the conservatory and the Baku's stink coats the frigid air. A note drops from his lap onto the floor, but he does not pick it up.

Woven through Sean's consciousness is the terror of a four-year-old boy. Tiernan, who every night dreamt he had been abandoned, left to wander the streets, lost. Sean can summon the feeling of the green wax crayon which Tiernan had used to carefully and painstakingly write his note, the way he had strained over each letter, asking his mum to help him with the number 4, which he always struggled with. The feel of her warm, strong hand around his own, that steady hand that, in his dreams, he would give anything to hold again.

The nightmare, simply named: *lost*. The boy's infantile terror is like an infection inside Sean, stealing his breath and making his heart beat up into his throat.

Trying to ignore the wad of paper on the floor as it smoulders, burns, disappears, Sean glances at the old-fashioned clock radio on the workbench, the one he took from the kitchen to use as an alarm since Jock took his phone. He tested it to make sure it worked, and the hacking alarm is so loud it could probably rouse an entire neighbourhood. And yet, somehow, Sean has slept through it.

He pushes back from the workbench and goes upstairs to feed the hoglets. Scarlet has not put on weight for two days, and Sean notices with a twist of unease that she is slower than usual to take to the pipette.

BEFORE

Sean was sat in Arlo's living room, playing *Star Wars: Battlefront* with Jake and Arlo, when they heard the stutter of gunshots. Arlo paused the game, and for a moment none of them moved. Sometimes it could be hard to tell if the sound of gunfire came from Arlo's PlayStation or the street outside. This time it was the latter. Panicked shouts lit the night, tyres burned with a loud squeal.

Their game forgotten, Sean, Arlo and Jake moved to the window and peered outside, just as a speeding car swung around the corner and disappeared. In the street lights' sulphurous glow, two dark-clothed teenagers propped up a semi-conscious boy as they staggered across the road. A fourth boy paced as he spoke into his mobile, one hand clutching a fistful of his own hair.

Sean stared at the injured boy. His arms were slung over his friends' shoulders and he was trying to walk, but there was no strength in his legs. His chin sloped on his breastbone and his hoodie covered his face. There were tattoos across the boy's knuckles. Sean couldn't read them from this far away, but he knew that MASS was inked across the knuckles of his right hand, ACRE across those on his left.

'Someone shot Frenchie,' Sean said.

Jake pulled his mobile from his pocket. 'I'll call an ambulance.'

'Shit, they're bringing him here,' Arlo said, paling as he watched the boys lurch towards his house. He moved towards the door, flung it open. 'Mum!'

But Mel must have heard the shots because she was already running down the stairs. Emma was in Mel's bedroom, crying. She was only nine days old, and her wails had a fragile, warbling quality.

'It's Frenchie,' Arlo said, following his mum into the kitchen. 'He's been shot.'

Hammering on the door. Instead of flinching, Mel threw it open and the Dulwood Dogs shoved their way inside. Sean recognised the other boys instantly. Taro and Rigsby. They used to call by Arlo's house to see Mel when they were younger. Arlo's mum had watched all the kids in Dulwood grow up, even helped raise many of them when their own families failed them. She was the unofficial surrogate mother for all the unwanted kids of Dulwood. Taro's and Rigsby's visits had tapered off more recently; clearly they had less need of Mel now that they were making money with the Dogs.

Sean watched them lower Frenchie to the floor with a gentleness that he had not known them capable of.

'Oh my God, Billy,' Mel said, kneeling beside him. No one called members of the Dulwood Dogs by their first names, except for their own mothers and Mel.

She turned around, her face wild with rage and grief and fear. 'Call an ambulance!'

Rigsby didn't seem to hear her. He was pacing the tiny kitchen. 'I can't believe the fuckers shot him, I can't believe they'd *dare*,' he snarled. 'They're gonna be sorry, that's it, the Dogs are gonna mess them up—'

'Call an ambulance!' Mel yelled at him.

'It's okay, Mum,' Arlo said, resting a hand on her shoulder. 'Jake called them.'

'Razor's called them, too,' Taro said. 'He's waiting for them outside.'

Where the shooting had incited Rigsby into a rage, Taro seemed quelled by it. He stood silently in the corner of the room, staring at Frenchie.

'I won't have you talking that way in my house, you hear me, Rig?' Mel said. Sean had never heard her speak like that, her voice full of razor wires, hard and unyielding. She lifted Frenchie's shirt. The bullet had punched through his stomach, and blood chugged from the hole, a spreading lake beneath him. She covered the wound again and pressed down on it. 'Arlo, get me some towels. Hurry!'

Arlo ducked around Rigsby, snatched a handful of clean tea towels from the drawer. He passed them to his mum and she pressed them over Frenchie's wound. Pain flared across his face, a brief, agonised lucidity.

Upstairs, Emma was still crying. Her tiny wails tugged at something inside Sean.

'You're hurting him,' Taro said, starting forwards.

Sean was used to seeing Taro throwing rocks through people's windows, dealing on the street corners, swaggering round the estate with his boxer, Butcher. His compassion was as jarring to Sean as the sight of Frenchie's ruptured stomach.

'We have to slow the blood flow,' Mel said. 'Billy? Billy, can you hear me? The ambulance is almost here, okay? Help is coming, sweet boy. Help is coming.' She looked at Taro, started to rise. 'Here, hold this and press down as hard as you can. I'll be back in a second, I'm just going to—'

Frenchie reached for Mel, clutching at her dressing gown with fumbling fingers. He tried to say something, but only blood gurgled from his lips.

'It's alright, I'm not going anywhere,' Mel said, sinking back down beside him. She held his hands between her own, her fingers kneaded the ugly word inked across his knuckles as though she could rub it away.

'Arlo,' she said, keeping her eyes on Frenchie. 'Go upstairs, grab me a blanket. He's in shock, we need to cover him up. Jake, I need more towels. Arlo will show you where they are.'

Jake and Arlo pushed past Sean to grab the items Mel needed. Sean stared at Frenchie. The SOULJAH tattoo on his neck stood out against his paling skin. The ferrous smell of blood thickened the air.

For as long as Sean could remember, he had been terrified of Frenchie. He had always seemed so fearless, swaggering round the estate as though it had been built just for him, taking what he wanted when he wanted it. Hard-eyed and tattoo-scrawled, violence crackled in the air around him; he looked as though he would gut you without a second thought.

Now, he looked like the kid he was. Diminished and fragile. It was as though the bullet had already killed 'Frenchie', the hard shell that encased Billy, the boy beneath. But as Sean watched the lake of blood spread out beneath him, Sean knew that it was going to kill Billy, too.

The smell of blood, the fading look in Frenchie's eyes, the desperation with which he clung to Mel… Sean couldn't bear to watch, and there was nothing he could do to help, anyway. But Emma was still crying upstairs, and he could at least help her.

He backed out of the kitchen and moved up the stairs.

She was lying in a Moses basket in Mel's bedroom. Her tiny hands were curled into fists and they pumped the air, shaking with the force of her wails. Outside, approaching sirens lacerated the night. Sean reached down and plucked Emma from the basket, held her to his chest.

He thought of Frenchie's punctured stomach, of the way the blood was throbbing out of him, but the baby's compact warmth was like a balm, calming him, fading the image in his mind. Her cries slackened as he gently rocked and shushed her, though in truth, he was no longer really sure who was comforting whom.

Sean looked down at her, wondering at her miniscule perfection. She was tiny, her body still the comma shape it had been in the womb. She had cried herself to exhaustion and now her violet eyelids were sloping down over her dark blue eyes. Sean felt his own tiredness surge, and he sank into the chair in the corner of the room.

Downstairs, paramedics rushed into the house. Sean closed his eyes, tried to shut out their voices. The past week had left him wrung out and exhausted, and he slid easily into sleep.

When he woke, Emma was asleep on his lap and Mel was stood in the doorway. He sat up, briefly disoriented. He wondered whether she would chastise him for drifting off with Emma in his arms; she could easily have rolled off his lap onto the floor as he slept.

Mel gave him a tired smile that did not reach her eyes.

'You're a natural,' she said.

Sean flicked a glance at the window, wondering how much time had passed. The edges of the curtains were still night-dark and he guessed it couldn't have been more than a few hours.

'Frenchie… Is he—'

Mel shook her head. She moved towards him, gently took Emma from his arms and sat across from him on the bed. She had changed her bloody dressing gown for a clean one, but she had not been able to entirely wash away Frenchie's blood from her hands; it encrusted her nail beds, the deep plum colour reminding Sean of cherry juice stains.

'I'm sorry,' he whispered.

She nodded, and for a while they sat in silence.

'You know,' Mel said, breaking the silence, 'I took our Holly to the RSPCA yesterday.'

Sean blinked, baffled by the swerve in conversation. Mel was not looking at him. Her gaze had settled on the corner of the room, and there was a dazed look in her eyes.

'She'd had her heart set on getting a kitten for so long, you should've seen her little face. She had one picked out in about three seconds, this wild-looking scraggly thing that looked at you like she wanted to claw your eyes out. Holly named her before we'd even signed the forms to bring her home. Mulan.

'But when I gave the RSPCA woman our address, she refused to give us the kitten. Said she was worried about the sort of environment the animal would be in. I'm not a violent person, but Christ, it was hard for me to keep my cool when she said that. I wanted to smack her. You're worried about a cat, I wanted to say. What about our kids? What about our babies? Dulwood is no place for them, either, but they don't get a choice.'

Mel took a shaky breath and looked down at the sleeping baby in her arms.

'Jesus Christ, Sean. What does that say about us, that we let children live in a neighbourhood that isn't good enough for animals?'

Sean didn't reply. He sensed this was one of those questions that didn't require an answer. Because Mel was talking about Holly and her kitten, but somehow, inside her words, Frenchie was dying on her kitchen floor. Frenchie, who she had once known as little Billy Braithwaite, the boy she had looked after when he was a baby. Sixteen years old. Another souljah of Dulwood. Dead.

DAY 19

When Sean weighs Scarlet, he discovers she has lost another three grams since yesterday. He takes longer than usual trying to encourage her to keep the pipette in her mouth, but the hoglet only manages a few swallows of her feed.

Afterwards, Sean stands by the kitchen window, watching Grandad in the garden.

He wants to help him, even though the very idea of stepping out into that dying jungle makes his guts turn to liquid. He knows he won't be too handy with his knee in the state that it's in, but he can't bear to watch the old man struggle in the garden alone. He looks more fragile than ever, his frame bent over with age, his gnarled hands clutching the handle of the rake. He doesn't see the unnatural swarm of insects bursting beneath the tread of his boots, the blighted rose bushes, the rotten grass.

Sean goes into the porch, pulls on his boots, scarf and coat. Bracing himself, he slides the patio door open.

The rotten stench slams into him like a fist. He can't cover his mouth and nose because he needs his hands to use his crutches, so he wraps his scarf round his neck, pulling it around his face to filter the smell.

The garden looks nothing like it did when he first arrived at The Paddock. The tree trunks are black, their branches crooked and bare. Everywhere he looks, Sean sees the subtle undulation of insects and arachnids. Even the sunlight that shines through the branches seems dim and sickly. In the far corner, the writing shed pumps its poisoned ink through the grass, its veins stretching closer to the house every time Sean falls asleep. Only the rowan tree remains untouched by The Paddock's affliction. The flowers that stand in pots on the ledges around the little table bloom without blemish, their colours all the more striking for the grimness that surrounds them. The brick wall that runs the length of the garden is covered in blue-black veins, but not two metres from the rowan tree, the ivy leaves are emerald green. The fruit of the rowan's tiny red buds gleam like drops of blood in the cold autumn sun, and its leaves, a dozen shades of yellow and orange and russet, cling to the branches in stubborn defiance of the evil that laps at its peripheries.

Sean forces himself to move down the garden. Paving slabs give way to grass and his crutches sink into the soil with a wet squelch.

Grandad is stood ankle-deep in a vile, writhing basin, digging up the roots of a small tree. Beetles swarm over his trouser legs, but he keeps digging as though everything is as it should be. Dark webs lattice his wrinkly hands; they creep up his neck to fan across his cheeks and brow.

He presses his boot onto the edge of his spade, pushing it deeper into the bubbling soil. There is a ripping sound and the tree lilts, poised to topple. Exposed roots glisten, slick with navy-coloured slime. The tree falls, and as it does, Sean suddenly remembers what it had looked like when he first arrived at The Paddock: a flowering cherry tree, covered in flutters of pale pink blossom. The memory brings with it a swell of sadness so overwhelming it could almost be grief.

Sean's sadness is followed by a burst of anger. He drops his crutches to the ground and picks up a pair of secateurs that Grandad has left lying on the grass. He limps to a cluster of veins in the grass, and crouches down. Beneath him, masses of larvae wriggle and squirm, worms tumble and writhe through the viscous soil. Beetles scuttle over his hands and something slithers round his ankle.

He shudders, glances at Grandad, hoping to see an echo of his own revulsion in the old man's face. But Grandad's attention is no longer on the garden. He is staring at the writing shed. His shoulders are slumped, his arms hang limp. The spade slides from his hands, lands on the ground with a wet smack. Then, with the vacant look of a sleepwalker, he starts to walk towards the shed.

Choking back a sob, Sean uses the sharp point of the secateurs to burrow into the soil. He hooks the blades beneath a thick, beating artery and pulls it from the ground. Gummous ink bubbles beneath his fingers and the gaseous stench that belches from the ground makes his stomach turn over. But the anger is still there and the anger is good. It galvanises him, forces him to act despite the palsied tremors that rattle through his body.

He squeezes the secateurs together until he can feel the thick *thwump-whump* of the writing shed's heart vibrating through his hands. The carbon steel blades are surgically sharp, but they make no dent in the muscular artery. Sean squeezes harder. The tendons on the inside of his wrists pop up, his temples thump. The stink is almost unbearable, but he does not allow himself to think of that, does not allow himself to think about all the things that are scuttling, crawling, slithering over his skin. He summons all his strength, focuses it between his hands, forcing the blades together. His hands tremble with the strain, his knees grind into the soil, sending splinters of pain through the ravaged joint.

An inhuman scream blasts through the garden as the blades close. The severed artery spews dark blue ink. Some of it squirts into his mouth, bitter and vile. Spitting in revulsion, Sean scrabbles backwards, but the artery lashes round his ankle, tugs him down. He starts to crawl away, skidding in the slippery ink, but the artery tightens around him.

Sean twists round, looking for Grandad, but there is no sign of him. He is probably already at his desk, lost in his story.

Whip-fast, thinner veins encircle Sean's legs. Ink fountains over him from the artery's two severed ends as the veins move up his body, curl round his waist, his neck. They squeeze his carotid, as though palpating the pump of his speeding heart.

More veins slide over his arms, lashing them to his sides, and Sean realises he still has the secateurs grasped in one curled fist. He flicks the blades open. His fingers are slick with ink but he manages to slide them between his skin and the tangle of veins round his chest.

Adrenaline lends him a strength he had not known himself capable of, and this time the shears cut through the veins easily. Again, that scream lacerates the air, a scream that makes Sean want to squeeze his eyes shut and clamp his hands over his ears. The severed veins droop to the ground, their spouting ink slowing to a trickle.

Sean staggers back to the house, skidding and sliding on the ink-soaked grass. As his adrenaline hit fades, pain barrels through his knee, but he keeps moving, the back of his scalp prickling with the image of another thick artery lashing out, hooking round his waist and pulling him back.

Only once he has reached the kitchen door and slammed it shut behind him does he turn around. The garden's tentacular anatomy is descending into the ground, like ancient sea monsters sinking beneath an oil-spilled ocean.

The disease is everywhere, in every atom of soil, every particle of air, and I'm the only one who can see it. Which means I'm the only one who can fix it. And I think I'm going to need more than a pair of secateurs to do it.

* * *

Sean throws his stained clothes in the bin, then soaks in a hot bath for over an hour, scrubbing at his skin until it is pink and tender. But no matter how hard he scours his flesh, it is impossible to wash the ink away completely. It is as tacky as tar, tattooing angry bruises across his skin, and though the stench of rot and infection fades, the chemically sweet tang of biro ink clings to him.

After he has dried off, he goes into the library to use the computer. As he googles sleep deprivation, his fingers stumble over the letters on the keyboard, as though someone has rearranged them the previous night. His head thumps, his eyes ache in their sockets. Now and then he finds himself staring at nothing, unaware of how much time has passed.

He reads an article that claims it is impossible to avoid REM sleep for a sustained period of time, even where methods are employed to wake the sleeper before that stage begins. The more REM sleep-deprived you become, the sooner after falling asleep you enter it. After prolonged stretches of sleep deprivation, a phenomenon called microsleep occurs: brief, unintended episodes of sleep, whereby the subject drops off for a few seconds, or drifts into a state of blankness with their eyes open. In microsleep, people fail to respond to outside information or stimulus because part of their brain is effectively asleep, even though, upon waking, they would be convinced they had been awake the entire time.

Sean needs help staying awake. He thinks of the boxed-up espresso machine he found when searching for the hoglets' supplies. *Caffeine should do the trick,* he thinks.

* * *

'Doctor Taylor was in touch with me over the weekend,' Miraede says, when the two of them are sat in their usual places in the library. 'She told me about the attack. Said you are unwilling to press charges.'

Miraede lets the words hang between them.

'You know, Sean, these conversations are entirely confidential. If there's something you want to confide in me, it won't go any further.'

There's nothing I want to confide in you, Miraede.

'You could write it down?'

I don't want to write anything down, either.

'Your grandad seems a bit distracted today.'

Distracted. Yeah, you could say that.

'People handle grief in very different ways. Sadness, depression, anger, guilt, despair, fear, all these things – they can sweep you off your feet when you least expect it.'

Grandad isn't grieving.

'The thing is, Sean, at the moment the only person in your life is your grandad, but he's trying to navigate his own grief. The two of you together, well, it can make for a very… *charged* atmosphere. It might do you good to spend time with other people… People who are, perhaps, less emotionally involved with what happened than your grandad.'

I don't need help from anyone. I'm better on my own.

'Arlo's written you another letter. Sean, he's worried about you. Gracie and Jake are worried, too. They only want to see you get better. They miss you.'

—

'Sean, listen, if I feel that you're in trouble, then I have to report it to social services.'

Social services can't help with my kind of trouble.

'You did everything you could for her, Sean.'

No. I didn't.

'I know you blame yourself, but her death was not your fault.'

You weren't there. You don't know what you're talking about.

'Sean, there was nothing you could have done—'

The sun has slid from the sky, the night is gathering, and Sean is buzzed on 'espresso'.

The instructions for the coffee machine were tucked inside the box, beside a stash of espresso sachets that are six years out of date. Sean doesn't concern himself with that; he is in no position to be fussy.

The first cup tastes like bitter soap, even with the copious amounts of sugar he adds, but he forces it past his lips anyway, following it with another. And another. Each cup leaves a sour taste in his mouth, but the shots are so small he could knock back each one in a quick, nip-nosed gulp. *Besides, it's not as though I'm drinking it for the taste.*

Sean remembers the time he, Arlo and Gracie slept over at Jake's to binge-watch the entire third season of *Stranger Things*. To help them stay awake, Jake had prepared them each an artillery-shell-sized thermos of strong coffee. Sean, who was easily the smallest of the four, had not made it halfway through his flask before he started to feel amped. His heartbeat turned to a hummingbird flutter that took his breath away. Terrified he was suffering some sort of cardiac failure, he had tipped the remains of his coffee into the nearest plant pot when his mates were not looking.

He won't tip it away this time; he would sooner risk a heart attack than fall asleep and allow the Baku to close the gap between them.

By now, he is on his fifth espresso shot and is feeling twitchy and on edge. If he looked in the mirror, he would not be surprised to see his hair pointing to the ceiling.

He hits the switch on the espresso maker. As he watches black liquid trickle through the filter, fatigue sways through him. He wonders how long he can fight off sleep. He doesn't need forever, just enough time to figure out a plan of action.

The green light on the coffee machine pings, snapping Sean back to his surroundings. He picks up the two fresh cups of espresso and turns back to the table. And it is then that he sees it. In the corner of the room, the beginnings of mould have buckled the wooden floorboards, spiderweb ink-veins spiral up the walls.

The infection has spread to the house.

DAY 20

After yet another night of broken sleep, Sean's skin itches with tiredness, his eyes burn in their sockets. He sits in the library trying to read, but the sentences sway on the page, seductive and strange. He sets his book down and goes into the conservatory, hoping that manual work will help him stay awake.

He starts to sculpt the last of Michelangelo's Prisoners, this time *The Awakening Slave.* But the movement of his hands feels clumsy, and he is barely aware of what he is doing. His eyes blur and a fuzziness clouds the edges of his thoughts. His arms slow in their work, his head slopes forwards then jerks back up.

Sean swipes the back of his hand across his eyes, feels the warmth of sleep behind his shuttered lids. Gritting his teeth, he squints at the shape emerging from the clay, telling himself to *focus focus focus* but the safety blanket of consciousness keeps sliding from his slackening grasp, as though someone is tugging at its edges. His skull tingles and the warmed clay seems to shape itself around his fingers, like a hand encasing his own, guiding him towards sleep.

His head snaps up again, his heart ratchets to a frantic rhythm. Was he asleep? No. He doesn't think so. His heavy-lidded gaze moves to the garden.

The Baku is stood in front of the window.

So close now, the tips of its ivory tusks click against the glass. Thick mist clogs its lower body like curdled milk as it watches Sean with unblinking composure. He can see the beast with perfect clarity – its porous skin, like petals of bone, the fine maze of ink-filled capillaries that fan its temples and engorge its veins, the scowling wrinkles around its obsidian eyes, the grime around its hooked talons – but then it begins to fragment and fade. The lines of its body lose their sharpness, acquiring the same quality as the tongues of dirty mist that conceal it from the waist down, and it bleeds into the night, leaving only a vague impression of where it had been.

Sean sees a haze of scratches in the glass where the Baku had been stood.

It was coming for me, he thinks. *It knew I was falling asleep and it was coming.*

Sean can feel himself shutting down. His thoughts are foggy and his entire body aches. Shapes materialise at the periphery of his vision, shifting and amorphous, but when he turns around there is no one there. He doesn't know whether he is hallucinating or if his nightmares are solidifying in the waking world. *Does it even matter? Hallucinations can't hurt me any more than nightmares.* The thought brings little consolation.

He picks up his sculpted robin from the ledge, studies it in the dim light. It looks like it could be the same bird Harvey plucked from the mud on Mischief Night, only Sean's rendering is the colour of clay. It feels like forever since Sean allowed himself to think of his old friends, but the weight of the clay bird in his hands feels oddly comforting now, like a warm hand reaching towards him from the past, anchoring him.

He looks at the alarm clock and the display flicks from 2:01 to 2:02. *How long is it since I last slept properly?* The last considerable stretch of sleep was days ago, when the Baku had passed him Vita's dream. *When was that? Two days ago? Three?* Aside from that, he has been snacking on sleep to get by, when what he really needs is to feast.

When his chin slopes towards his breastbone, dreams surge up behind his shuttered lids, like rabid dogs held back on a fraying leash. He imagines the writing shed's fingertips pummelling through the ground towards the house every time he dozes off, paving an inky path for the Baku. *How many more nightmares will I have before the Baku is at the front door? How long do I have before it can reach me when I'm awake?*

Aware that caffeine is no longer cutting it, Sean slides the robin into his pocket without thinking and goes to run himself a cold bath. As it steadily fills, he hears the kitchen door slide shut downstairs. He quickly turns the taps off and listens.

Grandad is crashing around as though he is trying to find his way through the house in the dark.

The sounds stop abruptly and silence falls over The Paddock once more. Sean creeps down the stairs as quietly as he can, wincing at the squeak of his crutches, which are like small screams in the sudden quiet. Grandad is sprawled across the sofa in the library. The smell of booze reeks from his skin, a low rumbling pours from his throat. Sean has not yet seen Grandad drink so much as a glass of wine with dinner, so the sight of him like this brings with it a new sort of fear.

If I'm really going to delete his new book, then this is my chance.

Still, Sean hesitates. The memory of the old man's anger steals his courage, the lump at the side of his head where he struck it against the desk tingles with remembered pain. There had been such blazing rage in Grandad's eyes when he shoved him. And for what? All Sean had done was glance at the title of his new story. How would he react if he discovered Sean had deleted the entire manuscript?

What other option do I have? Sit around and wait until the Baku is knocking on my bedroom door? It's coming for me, no matter what. I have to do something to try and stop it.

Sean goes up to his room for the loaded gun. He suspects he will not be able to use it against a beast as powerful and ancient as the Baku, but figures it is better to have some kind of weapon than nothing at all. Back in the hallway, he hurriedly pulls on his coat and boots. He opens the drawer in the kitchen where he knows Grandad keeps his matches, and pockets them. The stupor of indecision that has plagued him over the past few days evaporates. He moves to the hook where the key hangs. The sight of it lifts the hairs along the nape of his neck. The air tightens with tension, the temperature plummets.

Before he can change his mind, he snatches the key off the peg.

The beam of Sean's torch quivers as he takes in his surroundings.

The stone flags beneath his feet are shattered and humped by the veins that burrow beneath them, veins that climb the walls of The Paddock in a toxic embrace. The writing shed's stench infiltrates the entire garden.

Sean forces himself to keep walking, telling himself he already knew the Baku's infection had reached The Paddock. He has seen it. He knows the Baku is close now.

The wind screams through the spindly branches, as though it too senses evil. Sean sees half-formed shapes in the shadows: The Clown, the Mirror-Eyed Man, a young slave…

Don't think about it. Don't think don't think don't think just get into the shed and move fast just in and out because it's all in your head there isn't anything there it's not real.

Sean aims his torch at the ground a few feet ahead so he can see the arteries and veins beneath the grass, and he carefully steps over them. The soil is bubbling and bilious and his pyjama bottoms are slaked with slime. His crutches sink into the mud, making his progress slow and awkward.

'Hush little baby, don't say a word.'

Sean freezes. His hand moves to the gun in the waistband of his jeans. The words echo in his mind, a chorus of children, a haunting chant. His eyes whip to the stone cherubs, even though he knows it can't have been them. They stare back at him, their lichen-coated eyes hard and hateful.

'Mama's gonna buy you a mockingbird.'

The Baku's voice merges with those of all the children whose horror it has fed upon. Sean turns around.

The Baku is stood on the lawn, blocking Sean's way back to the house. Its chest moves up and down, its wrinkled trunk shifts slightly, and Sean knows it is smiling.

'And if that mockingbird don't sing.'

Its deep undertone plaits the children's voices together, like the conductor of a dark orchestra. Something crawls inside its eyes, some intimate knowing that is for Sean alone. His heart beats violently in its cage of ribs.

'Mama's gonna buy you a diamond ring.'

Sean takes a step back, unable to rip his eyes from the Baku. It lifts its trunk and tilts its head to the sky, the moonlight falling on the ragged shreds of its ears, glancing down the corded muscles of its chest and shoulders. Engorged veins distend the flesh of its neck, and Sean knows if he could feel its pulse, it would beat in time with the expanding vascular system beneath the garden. Because everything – the Baku, the veins, the corruption, all of it – is coming from the writing shed. *That's where its heart is,* he thinks. *Inside that fucking building. Because that's where it started.* The Baku's eyes roll upwards, the dark cave of its mouth opens, impossibly wide, shaping a scream from which thousands of blowflies pour, as though they have been gestating in its stomach only to be vomited up now in a buzzing stream of black bile.

Sean runs through the garden, his only thought to put as much distance as he can between himself and his pursuer. Rain pours down the back of his neck, his torch slices the blackness as he pumps his arms, a rapid seesawing blade of light. He fights a path through the bracken, heedless of the way it scratches and tears at his skin, gritting his teeth against the pain in his swollen knee.

He slams into the door of the shed as he hears an abrasive grating. Without looking, he knows the stone cherubs have turned to watch him. He tries to slide the key into the lock, but his hand is shaking too much.

Snatching a glance over his shoulder, he sees the figure coast towards him, not twenty paces away now. It glides as smoothly as if it were moving on runners. Though the rain-thrashed garden is otherwise clear of mist, the figure rides upon a thick bank of fog that obscures it from the waist down.

With a sob Sean turns back to the door and uses both hands to guide the key home. The lock clicks open and he is inside. He slams the door behind him, locks it, then grabs the chair and wedges it beneath the door handle, before backing away.

He strains to hear over the muffled thump of his own heartbeat, his ragged breath, the rain drumming on the corrugated roof of the shed, the wind whisking the trees. He is trapped. Trapped by the thing waiting for him on the other side of the door.

Knock.

Knock.

Knock.

Sean's horror swells. He jumps back and bangs his hip against the edge of the desk, knocking the pages of Grandad's manuscript to the floor. His legs crumble like dry sand. Huddled on the ground in a puddle of scattered papers, he points the muzzle of his gun at the door.

He is soaked in sweat.

Shuddering.

He shakes his head slowly from side to side. This can't be happening. This can't be real.

A sudden burst of static erupts from the old radio on the desk. It fades, as though tuned by an invisible hand, to the voice of a male broadcaster.

'Has died in her 102nd year. Buckingham Palace said the end was peaceful, and the Queen was at her side. Members of the royal family—'

Sean's eyes trace the length of the cord, which lies on the floor like a dead snake. Plug pins pointing upwards towards the ceiling. Drawing electricity only from the air's malignant energy.

Knock.

Knock.

Knock.

Chills ripple over his skin. Breathing hard, he tightens his finger on the trigger, ignoring the sly whisper in his thoughts that says there is nothing he can do to protect himself.

'"She was," he said, "admired by all people, of all ages and backgrounds, revered within our borders and beyond." Parliament is to be recalled for MPs to pay their tributes next week. The Queen Mother's body will be—'

The broadcaster's voice sounds old-fashioned, laced with the elegance of a bygone era.

Knock.

Knock.

Knock.

'...who, at times, had seemed so indestructible, but whose life finally ebbed away at a quarter past three this afternoon. She died at her home close to the castle, where she'd been since the funeral of her younger daughter, Princess Margaret—'

The key pops out of the lock, lands with a dull *thunk* on the floor. Blowflies stream through the gap in the keyhole, the low drone of their beating wings accompanying the basal chord of Sean's own horror. They darken every surface, an undulating mass that makes the room pulse like a living thing.

The door handle begins to turn.

Sean's heart slams into his sternum. He wants to press his eyes closed and pretend he is somewhere else, somewhere bright and loud and warm, or just somewhere – *anywhere* – far away from here.

But he can't look away.

Can't move.

A tear tracks a path down his cheek, like the tip of an ice-cold finger. He stares at the door handle as it twists, knowing what stands on the other side, knowing what has come for him.

The handle snaps back up, the mounting tension dissipates. Sean feels the Baku's departure in the lengthening space between his heartbeats and in the slackening of his muscles. The room is still cold, but it has lost its glacial chill, and the nauseating intensity of the smell fades. He looks around, but there is no sign of the blowflies that moments ago had coated every surface.

Sean climbs to his feet. His limbs feel shaky, weak. He can feel the adrenaline slide from his blood, and in its absence fatigue rushes in. He grabs onto the edge of the desk to stay upright, then lowers himself into Grandad's chair.

He eyes the door, judging the distance between himself and it. Wondering if that is how close the Baku can come to him now. If it is, then it will probably only need to feed him a few more nightmares before it can close the gap completely.

There is a bottle of whisky on the table. With trembling hands, Sean uncaps the lid and drinks in convulsive gulps, the glass clattering against his teeth. The liquid is like paint stripper, far stronger than anything he ever sampled on Dulwood. Spluttering, he presses the back of his hand to his lips. The alcohol burns his chest and throat, but after a moment the scalding fades and a tingling warmth spreads through him.

He sinks back in the chair and allows his gaze to slide over the room. Only now that the immediate danger has passed does he notice how much the shed has degenerated since the last time he was in here. The floor has warped atop the swell of veins that push up from the ground; they track the walls, splintering the wooden panels. And it would seem writing is not the only thing Grandad has been doing in here: empty bottles of whisky are stacked in the corner of the room. There are two beside the sofa. Another beneath the desk.

The computer's low hum reminds Sean what he came here for. He shakes the mouse and the screen lights up. Grandad's manuscript is open on page 309 of 312. Sean closes it down without reading anything.

He clicks on the file entitled *The Baku II* and instantly the temperature in the room plummets. Sean's eyes snap to the window, expecting to see the Baku's face pressed against the glass. His quickened breath wisps on the frigid air, but there is nothing there.

He swallows, turning his attention back to the screen.

Focus. No point getting your bollocks in a twist now. This is what you came here to do.

From the drop-down menu, he clicks *delete*.

His fingertips are oily with sweat, his heartbeat feels tachycardic.

A box pings open: *Are you sure you want to delete* The Baku II?

Wind screams through the eaves like a warning, the darkness snuffles at the window.

He clicks: *Yes*.

Something slithers through the shadows, more felt than seen, and Sean gasps, spins round. Sweat beads in the hollows of his temples; it dribbles down his sides. He turns back to the computer, finds the file for *The Baku II* in the recycle bin and deletes it from there, too.

He grabs the handwritten notes from which Grandad has been transcribing and throws them in the bin. Then he pulls the matchbox from his pocket. He lights one match, holds it to the corner of a sheet of paper. The edges curl and blacken as the flames eat the page. The fire spreads but Sean strikes another match anyway and lights another page, eager now to see them all burn.

He backs away, watching the flames consume Grandad's work. He sags in the chair, relieved but far from at ease, all too aware of the flimsy barrier that stands between him and the beast outside.

After the flames have burned themselves out in the bin, Sean moves to the window and startles at his own reflection. His eyes bulge from their shadowed sockets and terror crouches behind his battered features.

His gaze shifts to The Paddock. Only a few of the lights are on, windows gleaming against the darkness. Sean wonders how he had ever thought he was safe in the old house, because looking at it now, he knows that he isn't. Dark energy crackles around the building, and that strange distorting effect is more pronounced than ever.

Still, he knows he would be safer inside The Paddock than out here. But the thought of opening the door and crossing the garden in darkness is unthinkable. The Baku might still be out there, waiting for him.

He thinks of the unease he felt the first time he saw the writing shed, the iciness that coated his fingers when he reached for the key, the growing certainty that there was something malevolent within its walls. But his unease had been tempered by the conviction that whatever danger he sensed was contained within its walls. Even Grandad had seemed to understand this on some level, shown by the way he had avoided it for so long, allowed the grass to grow wild around its door and the weeds to climb its walls.

So what happened to make him reopen it?

Sean casts his mind back to how Grandad had been when he had visited him at Creswick Hall. Vibrant, charismatic, chatty. With sunshine in his eyes, garden dirt beneath his nails and the scent of the outdoors on his skin. Sean can't imagine that man of yesterday sitting in the writing shed alone for hours on end. He only started to do that after… after… after what?

After I arrived here.

Sean frowns, unable to see how the two things connect. Could his presence really have been the trigger for Grandad's breakdown? He doesn't see how. Yes, assuming responsibility for his care was a huge undertaking, but Sean was hardly a little kid who needed constant care and attention.

'You're so like her when she was small.'

Grandad's words catch in his thoughts like barbs. There had been such sadness in his voice when he had spoken them, such pain in his face. Such… *grief.*

Sean's gaze snags on the radio, the newscaster's words echoing in his mind. He remembers Grandad sat at the kitchen table with his wedding album in front of him. Broken, lost… like a man recently bereaved.

Sean recalls Grandad talking about Nanna Storm's last few hours, how, as he held her hand and her breath guttered to stillness, there had been an announcement on the radio that the Queen Mother had died. Sean wonders if that was what he had heard. Could it have been some sort of auditory haunting, the very same words that are burned into Grandad's mind? The plug doesn't need to be connected to the socket for the radio to turn on; there is already enough dark energy in the shed to power it. Sean can feel it crackling against his skin like static.

The Baku was the book Grandad wrote shortly after Nanna Storm died. Perhaps he started writing *The Baku II* in the hope the beast would take away dreams about his daughter.

Perhaps Grandad is haunted by the Baku as much as I am.

Sean feels as though he has touched upon part of the answer, but half the mystery still eludes him. He starts opening desk drawers, unsure what he is searching for, but hoping if he stumbles across it, he will know. But all he finds are more biro pens, pencils, sheaves of A4 paper, a folder full of old receipts and bills.

He moves to the cupboard beneath the window and opens it. Dusty books and files, stationery and unlabelled boxes. One of the boxes catches his eye. Silver clasps grip the lid, like gilded fingertips clutching secrets close.

Sean pulls it out. He pops the clasps open, lifts the lid.

Inside, there are countless loose photographs of Nanna Storm and Grandad. Mum is in some of them, and Sean feels the familiar heart-clutch when he sees her face, even though she is only a small girl in the pictures. There are dozens of letters, too, all written in the same handwriting. Sean opens one of them, pulls the letter out. He does not read it, wants only to see who it is from. It is signed *Ocean*, and dated July 10th, 1971. Working from the date on the rowan tree placard, she must have been sixteen years old when she wrote it. The envelopes bear postmarks from India, and the sheer volume of them leads Sean to wonder if she went travelling for a while. He does not open any more of them or read what she wrote; he is already snooping, but reading his grandparents' love letters feels a step too far.

His hands hesitate on an envelope addressed to Stella Blake. Sean recognises Grandad's spidery handwriting. It is unsealed and Sean's resolve not to read any private letters wavers. *I'm here to find answers, aren't I? Besides, this isn't a love letter, so it isn't really that intrusive at all.* He pulls the letter out and unfolds it.

Dearest Stella,

I know you dont want to hear from me, and after everything Ive done, I cant say I blame you. But I also know it would break your mums heart to see us as we are now.

I let you down after she died, I know that. You were broken by her death as much as I was, but I didnt see it. I wouldnt see it. All that existed for me was my own pain, my own rage, my own grief. I had no space left for yours. When you needed me the most I failed you, and for that I will always be sorry. Because however bad things were for me, they were worse for you. I see that now. You didnt just lose your mother. You lost your father, too. I should have been there for you, fought harder to keep you when social services took you away.

I want you to know that Im still attending those meetings I told you about in my last letter. Ive been sober for six months now. I know I dont deserve it, but if you think theres any chance we could meet, you would make me the happiest man in the world.

Know that I am always here for you, and if you need anything, anything at all, you need only ask.

Dad

There is no stamp on the envelope. Sean wonders what stopped Grandad from posting it. He knows Mum would have forgiven him for whatever passed between them. How different things could have been if only she had seen this letter.

But he mentions other letters that he did *send,* a voice in his head whispers. *Maybe Mum wasn't as forgiving as you give her credit for.*

Sean drops the envelope back in the box, then closes the silver clasps on the lid. There are no secrets for him to uncover here. Tiredness sways through him and he can feel the last dregs of his energy seep from his bones. He slumps to the floor, presses the heels of his hands into his eyes. He will wait until morning before opening the door and heading back to the house. Daylight might not armour him against the Baku, but it will give him the courage he needs to walk through the garden. All he must do now is stay awake.

DAY 21

He wakes up curled on the floor of the writing shed, numb with cold. Gauzy light filters through the grimy windows. His neck is stiff, his back aches and his pulse is a hammer, striking his knee over and over, reminding him of his adrenaline-fuelled flight through the garden. But all these agonies slide from his consciousness as the Baku's gamey reek fills his nostrils.

He is surrounded by a litter of notes. He bats them away and scrambles crab-like across the floor, horrified, as though he has woken up in a nest of snakes. Tracks of the Baku's saliva glisten across the back of his hand, slug-like trails of it cover his coat.

The nightmares started as soon as his eyes closed, as though sleep were a baited hook upon which they clamoured to feed. When one ended another began, dreams that were indiscriminate to time or place, a world of fear clutched like a metastasising cancer in his thoughts.

Now, as he stares at the notes on the floor, the names of the children who wrote them flare in his mind. Their intimate terrors, scored on tanned leather or parchment, papyrus or paper, are his now.

He presses his hands over his eyes, as though this might obliterate the memory of those dreams, but behind his shuttered lids they rise up. He is Maggie, trapped in a room of dolls that watch him with eyes that are toppled Xs; he is Ted, trapped and mummified in a giant spiderweb that vibrates as a thousand black-eyed arachnids creep towards him; he is Noah, running as gristle-nosed zombies with suppurating flesh chase him through streets and alleys; he is Ambrose, locked in his father's prosthetics shop, half-finished limbs trailing leather straps as they scrabble towards him; he is Daisy, trembling and terrified, unable to escape the monster that would pass as her father, even in sleep.

When Sean looks up again, the notes have disappeared. He glances at the door. It is still closed, the chair wedged beneath the handle. *But the Baku was here. I know it was here.*

He pulls himself to his feet, hobbles across the room. His hand trembles as he moves the chair from the door. Slowly, he turns the handle and peers outside. The dying garden looks bleak and grim in dawn's grey light, but the rowan tree splashes colour across its small corner, thumbing the darkness, like an errant child with a paintbrush, a pallet and all the shades of autumn.

The Baku has gone, but Sean knows that when he looks out of the window tonight, it will have moved closer to him.

He steps outside, his eyes scouring the garden as he limps across it, braced to run, a voice in his thoughts whispering he can't run forever.

Despite his growling stomach, the first thing Sean does when he gets inside is feed the hoglets. They chirp and squeak in their crate, which he takes as a good sign. He feeds Scarlet first, and is relieved when she takes to the pipette and manages to drink two millilitres of the goat's milk. He notices that her white spines are beginning to thicken, her body beginning to curl. A fine spray of whiskers has sprouted around her nose.

After Sean has attended to the hoglets, he fixes himself a sandwich and takes it into the conservatory. As soon as he opens the door, he recoils and flings an arm over his nose.

The room smells sour and sulphurous. Yesterday, aside from a few drooping flowers and a starburst of veins creeping across the brickwork in the corner of the room, nothing had looked untoward. Now, all four walls are coated in veins, every single flower is shrivelled and broken-necked. The pretty white buds that climbed the brick walls are dust beneath his feet and the creepers have turned from vivid green to black. There is fungus between the bricks, black mould spreading across the ceiling. The stone lion is covered in mildew and instead of fresh water, sludge-thick ink drools from its mouth into the basin below.

Sean looks at his four clay Prisoners, thinking of the stone cherubs outside the writing shed. A fine web of small black threads have started to creep through the plaster, as though they too have been contaminated by the Baku's spreading sickness. He knows it isn't logical, but he can all too easily imagine his miniature creations turning on him if he leaves them in here. Just the thought of them twisting their heads towards him makes his skin creep over his bones. He snatches them up and hurries out of the room, locking the door behind him.

Sean is reading in the library when the doorbell rings. Miraede isn't due to come over today, but Sean knows it's her. It's not like anyone else has ever come to visit.

The doorbell rings again, and with a sigh Sean gets up to answer it.

In the hallway the air is foul with decay, the wallpaper peeling from the walls, revealing rotting plaster beneath. The carpet is slaked in wet mould that sucks hungrily at his slippers as he walks across it.

Sean leaves the chain on the door and peers through the crack.

'Hello, Sean.' Miraede gives him a warm smile.

She isn't wearing make-up today and her hair is tied up in a ballerina topknot. The wind flicks stray strands across her face. Sean stares at her, the words he wants to say burning behind his eyes. *This is a bad place. You shouldn't be anywhere near here. It isn't safe! Go away!*

Miraede's smile wavers, concern creases her brow. She tilts her head as she considers him through the narrow gap in the door. 'Can I come in?'

He slides the chain from the lock and opens the door. Miraede steps inside and Sean watches her face, waiting for her to wince at the smell or grimace at The Paddock's deterioration. But when she turns back to Sean, her eyes are clear and her smile ready.

Sean feels his shoulders sink. He starts towards the kitchen to put the kettle on.

'No coffee for me today, Sean,' Miraede says, moving towards the library. 'Shall we just get started? I was hoping to have a word with your grandad, actually. Last time I was over he said he was going to take you down to the local school to have a look round. I'd love to hear what you both thought of it.'

Her voice is gentle and kind, laced with an awkwardness that must come from knowing she may as well be talking to a cardboard boy.

'I saw his car out front,' Miraede says, her gaze flicking to the window as she sits down. 'Could you go and get him?'

Her tone is light, but Sean hears the implication behind her words. That suspicion Sean had noticed in her expression a few weeks ago has had time to flourish and grow into something harder, something certain. Still, he can't go and get Grandad, not when he is in the writing shed. So he sits across from Miraede, hoping only to hurry their meeting along so she will leave.

'Listen, I know you don't want me here, Sean,' she says, leaning forward. 'But this therapy is part of the conditions for you leaving Creswick Hall. If I don't think you're making good progress...' Her voice drifts off and she looks out of the window, biting her lower lip. Sean realises she is genuinely worried, and he knows then that even though Miraede can't see or smell the house's affliction, instinct is telling her something is very wrong.

'You know, any information you disclose to me is strictly confidential,' she says, looking at him again. 'Whatever you tell me, Sean, it won't go any further. You don't have to speak, you could just write it down.'

Sean doesn't want to tell her anything, but memories are gathering in his mind. His hands itch to pick up a pencil, to steer the course of his thoughts towards safer territory, to escape into daydreams and create something that won't hurt him. But he has no pencil to hand, no sheet of paper. So he begins to draw Mum's face in his mind.

'Last time I was here, I said that next time I saw you we would try the regression therapy I've talked about before.'

Sean is no longer listening to Miraede. He focuses on the unfolding image in his thoughts, can almost hear the scrape his pencil makes as it glances across the internal canvas of his mind.

'...don't need to talk or even listen with your conscious mind...'

Sean sketches Mum's nose, the arch of her dark brows, slowly, cautiously revealing her gentle face to himself alone.

'…to notice the way it just naturally starts to become slower…'

He draws the starburst of freckles across Mum's nose, the dimple in her left cheek.

Miraede's voice has taken on a hypnotic, insistent quality, but Sean doesn't stay with her to the end of a sentence. His bones feel as though they have been coated in lead.

'…as you relax a little bit more…'

Warmth spreads through him, his eyelids droop.

'…to imagine you are somewhere else…'

Her voice is inside Sean's skull, a soft shushing against his thoughts.

'…and I won't know where that place is…'

Sean tries to move but his arms and legs are dead weights, as though the connections between his mind and body have been severed. He blinks and it takes forever for his eyelids to lift and lower.

'…but you will know because it is somewhere in your own imagination…'

He scrawls a corkscrew curl.

'…when you feel ready, and then allow yourself to journey back to that hot summer day…'

Sean freezes, horror throbbing through him. His head snaps up and the face he has pieced together in his mind scatters, like ash in the wind. His cheeks are damp with tears and his bitten-down nails are jammed into the scar on his hand, as though he is trying to reopen the old wound.

Miraede is leaning towards him, her eyes wide and startled. She opens her mouth to say something but Sean jerks to his feet and hurries out of the room, brushing angrily at his wet face.

DAY 22

Survive or die. There's a poetic simplicity to it, really.

Still.

Sean never used to think in such linear terms. When he lived on Dulwood, there was light and shade, tone and colours. Now everything is black and white.

The night is thinning into dawn when Sean discovers Scarlet has died. Olive and Violet wriggle on the cooling blanket, but Scarlet is tellingly still. Sean scoops her up, hoping to hear a squeak of protest or feel a twitch of limbs. But there is nothing. Nothing but her cold, unmoving weight.

In the nine days since they were born, the hoglets' spines have sprouted and grown into fine white quills. But Scarlet's quills will not grow any longer. The chart above Sean's bed that displays her weight from yesterday morning will never be updated, the film of skin that still covers her eyes will never split apart to let the light in. Born into the world blind and deaf, she has left it the same way.

The hand cradling the tiny hoglet trembles. *I did everything I was supposed to do, didn't I? I changed their bedding regularly, charted their weight, sterilised their feeding equipment after every feed. I did everything I could!*

But it wasn't enough.

Sean gently wraps Scarlet in a tea towel and takes her outside to bury her beside Blueberry. He hurries through the garden, warily stepping over the veins beneath the soil, and crouches in the grass at the base of the rowan tree. He places Scarlet down, then starts to dig.

The garden's silence has a physical weight and texture to it. The quiet pall coats everything, making the sound of Sean's breath and the scrape of his trowel through the dirt painfully loud by comparison.

Sean lays the hoglet in the ground and packs the earth over her body. For a while he sits there, breathing the clean air, reluctant to go back inside.

I should have taken them to Grandad as soon as I found them. What was I thinking? It won't be long until I'll be burying Olive and Violet here, too. I could never keep them alive on my own, it's all my fault.

Sean stands up, slides the trowel into his back pocket. He is suddenly so tired he sways where he stands. He is staring at the disturbed earth of Scarlet's grave when he hears a slow *creeeeak* that lifts the hairs along the back of his neck. Slowly, terrified to look and yet compelled to do so, he turns around.

A girl hangs from the tree that curves over the writing shed. The rope above her creaks as she slowly spins, like a withered chrysalis. Her flesh is the colour of clay, her dark hair falls in hanks around her face. There is an iron collar round her neck and her forehead has been branded with the letters *FUG*.

Sean is rooted to the spot. His skin crackles and he feels his eyes swelling in their sockets. The rope grows still, so that Atana is facing him when her eyes suddenly pop open. Her gaze is black, her sockets empty. Her mouth cracks open with a gristly crunch and the voice that issues from her dead throat is a glacial blast of air.

'Baccos in te veniat.'

The ancient Latin words hover between them, and for a moment Sean doesn't understand. He has to reach for Vita, who is lost within the folds of his subconscious, in order to make sense of them.

The Baku is coming for you.

The rope around the tree branch unravels, and Atana drops to the floor in a heap of brittle bones. She begins to rise, the dark chasms of her eyes pinning Sean as her body straightens in rapid jerks.

Atana takes her first step towards him and finally Sean staggers backwards. He runs towards the house without looking back, convinced that if he does Atana will be at his shoulder, her neck canted to the side, her noose no longer wrapped round her head but in her hands, ready to loop over his head, and the end of her rope trailing behind her like the train of a demonic bride.

Exhaustion is constantly pecking at the fabric of Sean's thoughts, rendering even the simplest of tasks impossible. His movements are muzzy, stunted. When it is time to feed the hoglets, he catches himself looking for milk in the cupboards instead of the fridge, then forgetting what order to punch the buttons on the microwave. When he tries to watch TV, the images on the screen slide out of focus.

He makes more espresso and sits at the table, pinching the skin behind his knees, nipping his arms. His fatigue is denser than that which he felt upon waking from any of his operations, the anaesthetic drugs still thick in his blood.

The espresso has gone cold, and the surface of the drink has hardened to a crust. Three blowflies are congealed in the thick scrim.

Sean goes into the kitchen to continue the sketch he had abandoned when his eyelids had begun to slide closed. But the peace of mind he ordinarily finds in his art has become a dangerous indulgence, behind which lurks a slumber that could prove fatal.

He tosses the pencil down, moves to the sink to make himself a cup of tea. He turns the tap on and grey water sprays the basin, hits the bowl hard and squirts back up onto his T-shirt. The sulphurous stink of it makes him grimace. He peels his shirt off, tosses it on the counter. He realises he is swaying on his feet, and struggles to remember what he was just doing.

A rush of anger for Grandad washes through him, and the anger is good, because it burns away the edges of his exhaustion. *If the old man had really cared for Mum, he'd have helped her out instead of letting her struggle alone. She worked so hard, and even then she could barely make ends meet. And while she was putting in fourteen-hour shifts at work, Grandad was here, in this huge house in his posh neighbourhood. Pulling weeds out of his precious garden, watering his stupid flowers. Pretending Mum didn't even exist.*

Sean slumps at the kitchen table, too tired to even stay angry. His chin dips towards his breastbone. Sleep is everywhere, waiting for him. He knows it won't have to wait much longer.

Sean is watching TV in the kitchen when Grandad comes in from the writing shed. Sean tenses, expecting the old man to ask him if he has been in the shed, or accuse him of deleting his work. But Grandad doesn't say anything.

Without a word to Sean and with the measured dullness of a sleepwalker, he moves to the kitchen sink and fills the kettle. The water that spurts from the tap is the colour of sewage, but Grandad does not notice. He turns the tap off, flicks the kettle on. A gloopy strand of dark blue slime hangs from the tap to the basin.

Sean flicks the TV off, waiting for Grandad to look at him. On some level the old man must register his grandson's presence, because he has set two mugs on the counter and placed a teabag in each. Sean finds himself hoping Grandad *will* accuse him of deleting his book and burning his paperwork, because even anger would be better than this dead-faced indifference. *He probably had the manuscript backed up on a memory stick or something*, Sean thinks. *Or maybe he just doesn't care that the work's gone. Maybe he's happy to start from the beginning again.* Sean imagines the old man sitting in front of the computer in the writing shed, his eyes glazed, his mind not really there as he retypes his story.

Grandad stands in front of the window by the sink, staring out at the garden until the kettle clicks off, then without shifting his gaze he pours water into both mugs. His aim is off and boiling liquid splashes over the worktop, but still, Grandad does not tear his gaze from the garden. He reaches for the milk and adds a splash to both mugs, but misses again, and when he tries to add sugar to his cup it scatters across the counter. Sean watches him in growing terror. He can't imagine Grandad snapping out of this strange fugue state, even if he poured the freshly boiled water over his own skin.

He stirs the drink absently, sets the teaspoon down and turns around.

Sean reels backwards in horror.

Grandad's eyes are now entirely lost beneath a network of thin, ink-filled veins. They feather across his cheekbones and temples, stretch across his mouth. Sean can see them softly pulse, pumping their poison through his body.

Grandad moves to the kitchen door, slides it open and steps out into the cold night. Sean watches him through the glass as he walks towards the writing shed, opens the door, and disappears inside.

DAY 23

Sean stands in the hallway, staring at the calendar on the wall. Working backwards, using Miraede's visits as an indication of the passing weeks, he thinks it is 11th November. In today's box, Grandad has scribbled, '*Sean's birthday*'. Fourteen today. But Grandad never looks at the calendar anymore.

Sean hears the espresso machine in the kitchen as it hisses and spits out two shots of hot black coffee. His thoughts slide back in time, to the day he talked to Mum about his plans for today. The memory hurts, and so Sean looks at it askant, his imagination shaving away the harsh edges of truth.

She had planned to take him to the seaside to celebrate. His vision blurs as an image forms in his mind. It crystallises, erasing his surroundings, replacing them with the cramped walls of his old flat.

'What do you want to do for your birthday this year, Seanie?' Mum says, dropping into the chair across from him at the kitchen table.

Sean shrugs, trying to stifle the excitement that pulses through him at the thought of his birthday. Because he knows they can't afford to do anything special. Just a few months ago Mel had taken Arlo, Sean, Jake and Gracie to The Gaming Arcade for Arlo's fourteenth birthday. Afterwards, she had paid for them to all eat in a swanky restaurant, the sort of place where the table is laid with three different sized forks, and the waiting staff actually smile at you instead of glaring at you while they snap their gum. It had been brilliant, but Sean knows there's no chance Mum can afford anything like that.

'I dunno, Mum. It's not a big deal, maybe I'll just hang out with Arlo and the others.'

'Not a big deal?' Mum was watching him, her expression sceptical. 'We have to do something. God knows, soon you'll be too cool to hang out with your old mum.'

Sean doesn't say anything, but he knows it isn't true; he will never be too cool to hang out with his mum. With her shock of wild red hair, easy smile and bohemian clothes, she is the cool one, not him.

'I know what we should do,' she says, brightening. 'We'll go to the seaside. It'll be brilliant! We'll eat candyfloss and sticks of rock until our teeth ache! We'll play on the arcades and walk down the beachfront and swim in the ocean… Oh, the ocean, Sean! You have to see the ocean!'

Mum's girlish enthusiasm makes Sean smile, despite himself. 'But we're skint, Mum. I heard you on the phone to the landlord earlier. We're behind on rent again, aren't we?'

A shadow crosses Mum's face. 'Oh Sean, I didn't know you were listening.' Her shoulders droop and she looks away from him, studying the water stains tracking down the plasterwork.

'Are we gonna be alright?' Sean hears the worry in his voice, the fragile desperation. He hates himself for it, but he can't hide it; he can't keep anything from his mum.

She looks at him again, and at the sight of his worried face her shoulders lift and she fixes her smile back on.

'We're going to be fine, I've sorted it all out.' The earnestness in her green eyes borders on ferocity, and Sean almost believes her. 'And anyway, I'm your mum, worrying about these things is *my* job, not yours.'

Sean blinks back to his surroundings, swallows around the pain in his throat. He wonders whether he will ever feel normal again, able to take a breath that doesn't hurt.

He doesn't want to fight anymore, and hasn't the strength to, anyway. He goes to his room, climbs into bed, and draws the covers over his head, feeling as though he is drawing the lid over his own coffin. He edges towards sleep, as though testing the depth of a river. But as soon as he does, it tugs him down, and he realises too late that sleep is fathomless, made of a water in which he cannot swim. He lets himself drown.

Sean is torn from sleep by the desperate need to breathe.

Something is wedged in his throat.

Panic rips through him. He rolls over the side of the bed, his eyes bulging as his hands scrabble at his neck. He tries to cough but his airway is completely blocked, so he pushes his fingers down his throat to pull out whatever is lodged there. No good. It is wedged too deeply to reach.

His pulse is thick and strained. His lungs burn. His chest heaves.

I'm going to die!

His fingers bracelet his neck as he slams his back against the wall, hoping to dislodge the sudden occlusion. His body is closing down. He can feel it happen, like shutters dropping, one after the next, severing the feeling first from his toes, feet, fingers, arms, a numbness creeping steadily inwards. Greyness feathers his vision. He has seconds to save himself.

He tries to nip the blockage between his fingers, manages only to knock it a little to the side. Air rushes down the sudden space he has created, bringing with it the taste of blood. A certainty slams through him, the cold knowledge that the Baku has shoved Sean's own nightmare into his mouth and that he is going to choke and die on it. Terror barrels through him and he shoves his hand down his throat. This time he manages to pinch his fingers around the edge of the paper and wrenches it out, flings it across the room.

Heaving air into his lungs, he scrabbles backwards, his eyes riveted upon the balled-up note on the floor. He can smell his own fear-sweat, taste blood at the back of his throat. Anger sweeps through him and he staggers to the window, rips the curtains aside.

There is a figure stood in the middle of the lawn.

But it is not the Baku.

Sean's heart seizes in his chest.

And then starts to pound.

Because the figure looking up at his bedroom window is Mum.

Her auburn hair is gilded by the moon's dream-glow and her eyes shine with tears. At the sight of Sean, a smile touches her lips. She is wearing her wool coat, the one that scratches Sean's skin and always smells of her perfume.

She takes a step towards him.

Sean knows he must be dreaming, that any moment now this perfect moment will be shattered by cruel reality. Because Mum *can't* be in the garden. It's impossible. But the knowledge does not stem the swelling ache in his heart, or the tears that suddenly fill his eyes.

Movement near the pond catches Sean's eye. The Baku is gliding towards Mum.

Mum!

Sean slams his fist against the window, his breath fogs the glass. Mum frowns at the fear in his eyes, takes another hesitant step towards him, as though *he* is the ghost, not she, an apparition she fears to startle.

No, Mum! Run!

Sean slams his door open, rushes down the hall. He is not wearing his knee brace, nor is he using his crutches, but he barely registers any pain.

He swings his body round the banister at the bottom of the stairs, and as he lurches towards the door his hip knocks against the wooden cabinet. His four Prisoners, which he had placed there after removing them from the conservatory, topple over, and one of them drops to the floor.

Time seems to slow as Sean watches it fall. The *Awakening Slave* cracks into three pieces, but the statue's clay face remains intact. Its agonised expression is turned towards Sean, but it is not the anonymous face of Michelangelo's prisoner he sees carved there.

It is his own face.

Sean, perfectly rendered in miniature. A clay-carved replica so exquisite in its precision, Sean feels as though he is gazing at himself through some sort of mirror that shrinks his reflection. An expression of pure agony is carved into the statue's face, a torture so complete that just looking at it makes Sean gasp. Because the pain he sees there so perfectly encapsulates how he feels inside.

Knock.

Knock.

Knock.

Sean feels as though he has been plunged underwater. His eyes move to the other three statues lying on their sides, and sees himself in each one, the proportions of his face crafted with uncompromised fidelity. *He* is the prisoner trapped inside the clay. Even the *Atlas Slave*, whose face is buried in the slab on his shoulders, has Sean's buckled legs and twisted knee.

Knock.

Knock.

Knock.

The sound is coming from the kitchen, but Sean can't move. His thoughts reel. How can his face have appeared in all his sculptures like that? *I would know if I had carved myself in them… wouldn't I?* He tries to recall making them, but draws a blank. Sculpting for Sean is a sort of self-hypnosis, much like a state of extended microsleep, in which he often remains unaware of what he is doing, what he is creating.

Knock.

Knock.

Knock.

The rap of knuckles is like the beat of a metronome. Mechanical. Inhuman. Sean tears his eyes from the statues and moves towards the kitchen. Mum is stood on the other side of the glass door and her eyes brighten when she sees him. Sean wonders why she circled round to the back of the house instead of using the front door, but the question is erased by his fear for her. He reaches for the key in the lock, but as he does, instinct screams at him to stop.

Something is wrong.

'Sean, sweetheart.' Mum's voice is muffled by the glass between them.

His heart melts at the sound of her voice, fond memories fizz in his thoughts. The Baku is gliding towards her, so close now. Sean twists the key in the lock and the catch opens with a soft *snick*. He reaches for the bolt at the top of the door.

Again, he hesitates.

That sense of wrongness jars through him, so strong it is like a blow. His mind scrabbles to understand his hesitation, because it makes no sense. He turns Mum's words over in his mind and one word screams out at him: *sweetheart*. An off-key note in an otherwise perfect symphony. His hands fall to his sides, his eyes grow glazed. He takes a step away from the door.

I was never my mother's 'sweetheart'.

Mum is frowning now, her hand pressed to the glass. Sean keeps walking backwards until his heel strikes the back wall of the kitchen. He stands there, his eyes fixed wide, as that crookedness, that *wrongness* aligns itself with a different version of reality.

'Sean, love, it's me.'

Her voice is full of all the tenderness a mother should hold for her son, but there is something too saccharine inside it, a terrible sweetness that makes Sean think of the foul smell of infection in the writing shed. And that word, 'love', is a savage uppercut that sends splinters of darkness shattering through him, allowing the Baku's infection to finally claim him.

I was never my mother's 'sweetheart'.

Never my mother's 'love'.

He sinks to the floor as the jaws of reality close around him. Mum stares at him from the other side of the glass. The Baku is stood beside her now, but it does not attack her.

Mum tilts her head at the same time as the Baku does. She grins and the Baku grins. Her smile is twisted, sneering, calculated. Her flowing curls lose their lustre, become brittle and lank. Her face loses its healthy plumpness, sinks in upon itself, grows sallow and pinched. The wrinkles around her eyes deepen as they spread, cracking lines across her brow, splitting crevasses around her mouth. Her gums shrink from her greying teeth as her pupils dilate and her eyes acquire a crazed, thousand-yard stare. All the telltale signs of her addiction reveal themselves, erasing the fantasy, asserting the reality.

Sean stares in appalled horror at the woman on the other side of the glass and the truth clicks into place.

'Sean? Sean, open the door.'

Shaking his head from side to side, Sean tries to replace Real Mum with Imaginary Mum. A kind face shimmers in his thoughts, but he knows it now for the mirage it was. Instead, a vision of his old flat fills his mind. Mice in the sagging sofa. Walls covered in yellow water stains, the rooms always so cold. Bodies crammed in tight, a tinned can of tangling limbs, writhing to a tuneless beat that shook the thin walls. Mum's unwashed clothes scattered around her bedroom. Empty kitchen cupboards, a constant gnawing hunger in the pit of his stomach. And always, always the smell of filth and grime beneath the sweet, pungent smell of skunk.

Memories fall on Sean like blows, pulverising the life he had tried to superimpose over the ugly truth. Sliding a needle from Mum's arm as she slept. Turning her face so if she vomited in her sleep, she would not choke. On his hands and knees, using neat bleach to clean the floor when he knew social services would be visiting, hiding needles and tabs and limping down to the glass bottle bank to get rid of all the empties while Mum slept off the worst of the night before.

In perfect symmetry, Mum and the Baku hammer their fists against the glass.

'Open up, Sean,' they say.

Only in his imagination had Mum been anything other than what she truly was: a violent, abusive addict. Her addiction as an expectant mother was the reason his growth was stunted, why he was so small; her addiction, the cause of his arthrogryposis. He had done enough research on the subject to know it was true. She loved nothing more than her fix and even pregnancy had not stopped her getting it. Sean can see her clearly now, malnourished and sickly, leaning awkwardly over her baby-swollen belly to inject between her toes.

The image untethers something inside him. He thinks of the candles he lit every day in St Paul's, and the gears of his memory stick. He recalls the incense smell of the church, the feel of the thin wax candles in his hands. But he hadn't been praying for Mum to get better. No, those candles had been for someone else.

He can't breathe.

A baby sister.

His responsibility.

His failing.

Mum had named her Sapphire, but Sean had never called her that. She was not made for that place, and there was already a Sapphire on the Dulwood estate. So he had called her Emma; there were no other Emmas on Dulwood.

Time folds in on itself and Sean is back in Arlo's house, stood in Mel's bedroom, staring down at Emma, his baby sister, crying in the Moses basket. Arlo has invited him to sleep over and Mel has taken Emma into her own bedroom to see to her through the night when she wakes. But Mel is busy looking after Frenchie, who has been shot and is bleeding out on her kitchen floor, and Emma is crying, crying as though she is the one that has been shot.

Now, in his mind's eye, Sean lifts his baby sister from her Moses basket, cradles her in the crook of his arm. Unlike him, she was born unscathed by Mum's drug abuse. A shock of dark hair, big blue eyes darkening towards a similar colour to his own. A snub nose dotted with milk spots. Dimples in her elbows. The memory solidifies until Sean can feel her weight in his arms, smell her warm baby-smell. She looks up at him, her tears taper into silence and her clenched fist moves to her mouth, to the comfort of that hard, gummy smile.

'Hush little baby, don't say a word.'

Mum's voice merges with the Baku's on the other side of the door, speaking the words of the song Sean used to sing to Emma. But Sean barely hears. He is staring at the baby in his arms, the baby he had cared for since the day Mum brought her home from hospital and every day after, until… until…

He had been late home from school because he'd had to stay behind for the Future Creators meeting, where he showed the examiners his clay robin, his final contribution to his exam. He had told Mum he would be late home, told himself that everything would be alright. Sean normally went to Arlo's after school on a Friday for fish and chips, stopping home first so he could take Emma with him. Mel liked to give him a break, taking Emma up to her room so Sean could enjoy some time with his mates, just like she had done the night Frenchie got shot. But this was a special day. Exceptions had to be made.

'Mama's gonna buy you a mockingbird.'

Sean smiles down at Emma, gently pulls her hand from her mouth. He has to remember, has to face up to the truth, but he can't do it without her. Her damp fist fastens round his finger with limpet strength.

The meeting had gone well, and the examiners told him he had secured a place. Sean had felt so happy then. He had found people who would invest in him, contribute to his studies. People who *believed* in him.

When he arrived back at the flat it had been unusually quiet. The familiar stink of skunk in the air. Mum passed out on the sofa, her bony arms tangled round some guy. Used needles on the table. Cigarettes stubbed out on the floor.

'And if that mockingbird don't sing.'

Lost inside the memory, he moves through the flat, stepping over the rubbish on the floor, taking care to be quiet in case Emma is sleeping. He wonders if Mum remembered to feed her. Will she have left her sitting in a soiled nappy for hours?

Mum rarely changes Emma's nappy herself, leaving it for Sean to do as soon as he gets in from school, even though she knows it gives her nappy rash. Had Mum held her, comforted her when she cried? Emma rarely quiets in Mum's arms. It is always Sean she responds to, Sean who can elicit a giggle when she is cranky or a burp when she is colicky. It is Sean who buys her formula and the Calpol she needs when she is running a fever, Sean who feeds her when she wakes through the night, Sean who sings her back to sleep when Mum's parties grow out of hand, Sean who changes her nappies and takes her for walks so she can breathe clean air into her tiny lungs instead of the stale, drug-laced kind.

'Mama's gonna buy you a diamond ring.'

He swings the door to her room open, and somehow, in that moment, he knows. Between the bars of the cot, Emma is motionless. The clay robin that has secured Sean's place in Future Creators falls from his nerveless fingers as he moves to the cot.

Lying on the rumpled sheets, Emma looks like a wax doll. Her arms are flung over her head, small hands balled into fists. Her violet eyelids are closed, rosebud mouth parted. Sean tries to say her name but no sound escapes his lips.

He lifts her from the cot. Her tiny body is cold. Limp. The weight of her in his arms shatters him. He holds her to his chest, as though the thud of his own breaking heart can reignite her own. He thinks of Harvey, of the little robin that Sean had thought was dead, but which Harvey had insisted was alive. He had helped the bird to heal and then he had set it free. That little robin had flown away, far away from Dulwood. If he takes Emma to Harvey, maybe he could save her, too. Maybe she can fly far, far away from here.

He moves towards the door, Emma clutched to his chest, but Mum is standing in the doorway, blocking him. And now the memories are swirling through him, each one pushing him closer to the widening chasm of grief. The way Emma grew still when he put his mouth to the seashell of her ear and sang her to sleep; how her eyelids drooped and her tiny body sagged in his arms after a milk feed; the warm, compact heaviness of her; the way her hair curled against her forehead when she was hot. She couldn't be gone. She couldn't she couldn't *she couldn't.*

The scene fragments, reforms around him. Whirling blue lights. Strings of blue and white police tape. A paramedic is sat beside him, her arm wrapped round his shoulder. Another paramedic holds Mum back as she screams and claws at him with her nails, her wild eyes full of hate fixed on Sean's face.

'Where were you, you bastard? You were supposed to look after her! I'll kill you! I'll fucking kill *you!'*

Now, Sean's memory of Mrs Keegan telling him his mum is dead flickers in his thoughts, but he recognises the fake memory for what it is: a small lie superimposed over an unimaginable truth, too horrible to accept. There was no Mrs Keegan at his school. There was only the paramedic, a stranger with sorrowful eyes, telling him how sorry she is. Telling him Emma is gone.

Gone.

Not 'dead'. That word is too ugly. Brutal. 'Gone' is a much gentler word, one that leaves open the possibility of return. But Sean knows what she means and DEAD is the word that screams through his head. DEAD, the word that falls on his frozen heart like a hammer on a frozen block of ice, smashing it to pieces.

'You killed her!' Mum is still high, her pupils dilated. She twists free of the paramedic, snatches a hypodermic from the table and lunges at Sean. *'You fucking killed her!'*

Sean curls away from her, lifts his arm over his face. The needle punctures his hand. Mum pulls it out, goes to stab him again, her face twisted with rage, a rage that is not born from the tragic death of her baby daughter, but from the drugs that lace her blood. The paramedic grabs her, tackles her to the floor.

'Sean, you murdering little bastard,' Mum says now from the other side of the door. The Baku's trunk shifts as it frames the same words, their voices entwined. It presses its forehead to the glass, and Mum does the same. 'You're going to pay for what you did. Now open up, you bent-legged little spastic. Open the door for your mother.'

That isn't Mum. It sounds like her, it looks like her, but it isn't *her. You don't ever have to see her again. Whatever's on the other side of that door, it's using your own fear against you.*

As soon as this thought forms, Mum begins to fade, until there is nothing left of her but a twist of mist curling into the night. But the Baku is still there. It pounds on the door and spiderweb cracks craze the glass.

Sean pulls himself to his feet and lurches back down the hallway, up the stairs. The air feels as though it has solidified around him, so that every step takes a monumental effort. Behind him he hears the warning scream of shattered glass.

Don't look! Don't stop!

But of course, he has to look, he has to see.

He glances back.

The Baku is stood at the foot of the stairs. Ink-distended veins bulge beneath its corded muscles, a swarm of blowflies swirl around its lower body. Its scabrous trunk is wrinkled in a snarl and its eyes are black holes.

'You killed her, you useless cripple.' The Baku's voice resonates through the house, vibrates beneath the rotten floorboards, through the crumbling walls.

Sean throws himself up the last few steps, races down the hall towards his bedroom. He slams the door shut behind him, twists the key in the lock, backs away.

He moves to his desk, wrenches the drawers open, searching.

The gun is exactly where he left it. Sean snatches it up, his hands shaking as he tucks it into the top of his jeans.

He tries to slide the window open, but it won't budge. The paint looks as though it has congealed in the space between the sash and the frame.

'Seeeeeaaaan.'

He swings round at the sound of the Baku's voice. A dark shadow blocks the light beneath the door.

'Let me in, Sean!'

Sean spins back to the window. Teeth bared in a rictus grin, he pulls again at the metal hooks, straining until his shoulders burn in their sockets and his feet feel like they are driving moulds into the floor.

The window grates in the frame, and with a protesting shriek it slides open.

Sean leans outside. There is a ladder propped against the wall from when Grandad cleaned the gutters a few weeks ago. Sean eases himself out of the window, his stomach swooping as he looks down. He grinds his teeth together and starts to scrabble down the ladder.

'You were supposed to look after her, Sean.'

He looks up, his nerves sparking. The Baku is leaning out of the window. Backlit by the bedroom light, the ragged fringes of its elephantine ears are almost translucent, muscles shift beneath its chest and shoulders.

Sean's quivering fingers slip on the rungs, his feet lose their purchase, and he falls backwards onto the diseased soil. His body howls at the jarring impact, but he shuffles backwards on hands and knees, staring up at the Baku as it heaves itself out of the window and descends the ladder on a cloud of blowflies. Its talons scrape the aluminium rails with a thin screech.

Sean pulls himself to his feet and runs. The Baku's voice vibrates through his skull; it burbles through the slick soil, seems to shiver down on him from the cold stars.

'You murdered your baby sister. I'll kill you! I'll fucking kill *you!'*

The sodden grass sucks at his heels, his crippled knee screams with every slam of his foot against the ground. He senses the Baku closing the distance between them but he doesn't stop, doesn't slow. The light is on in the writing shed and he throws himself towards it, his scream for help smashed to silence by the blockage in his throat.

The low drone of the blowflies swells, the Baku's malodorous scent intensifies. Tears stream down Sean's face. His heart is a blackened bruise, each contraction bringing more pain than the last, and Emma pulses in his thoughts between each beat.

The tips of the Baku's claws graze his skin, trailing fire down the nape of his neck. He falls, tries to crawl away as he pulls the gun from his waistband, but thousands of blowflies pour over him, a foul and buzzing blanket. The noisome smell of them makes his guts churn. The Baku hovers above him as the blowflies crawl towards his face.

'You killed her!'

Sean lifts the gun, aims the nuzzle at the Baku, pulls the trigger. But the bullet passes straight through its face, as though it is made of mist. A terrible smile darkles within its black eyes. Sean tries to twist away but the Baku's thick trunk slithers over his forehead, pinning him down. Its mouth gapes, revealing row upon row of incurved teeth. The bestial stench of its breath makes him gag. The Baku grabs Sean's hand, the one holding the gun. It twists the barrel round, presses it against Sean's temple.

'You killed her, you sick little fuck. You murdered your baby sister. You killed her! Mur-der-reeeeeer!

Sean glimpses nightmares swirling like dark stars in the Baku's mouth, a universe of strange and terrible galaxies.

'You knew your mum couldn't care for her, but you left her anyway. You wanted to escape Dulwood and you let Emma die so you could leave.'

The Baku has its hand on his and it compresses his finger on the trigger.

'Mur-der-reeeeeer!'

Sean knows what the Baku wants him to do, and suddenly he wonders why he is fighting it. He was supposed to look after Emma and he failed. She died because he wasn't there for her, so he should be punished.

This is why he brought the gun.

He should die, too.

The Baku's grip slackens as his own finger tightens on the trigger.

It all comes down to this.

His finger pulls back towards his thumb.

Numbness creeps through him, erasing fear and anger and grief. This is the right thing to do. Finally, he will put an end to his pain. Silence falls over the garden, as though it is watching with bated breath, waiting for him to pull the trigger.

The silence is ruptured by a small, warbling cry.

Emma's cry.

It emanates from the edges of his consciousness, and Sean strains towards it, following the sound. It is a blade of light that cleaves the darkness and cuts a glowing path to the truth.

And Sean remembers.

All the times he fell asleep in class because he'd been up all night trying to settle Emma; how he would skip school to take her to the doctor when she couldn't keep her bottle down; pushing her pram through the streets in the middle of the night when she wouldn't sleep, terrified of running into any of the Dogs, but even more afraid that her cries might prompt Mum into rubbing heroin on her gums to make her sleep; skipping invites to his mates' houses so he could go home and look after her; holding her in his arms as Frenchie died on Mel's kitchen floor, wishing for nothing more than to take her far away from Dulwood.

The constant worry he felt when he wasn't with her, a griping in the pit of his stomach that only eased when he came home and saw that she was okay.

Hush little baby, don't say a word.

The laughter that bubbled behind her eyes when she smiled. The way she stilled when he sang to her.

Mama's gonna buy you a mockingbird.

The dark fringe of her lashes, shadowing the plump curve of her cheek.

And if that mockingbird don't sing.

The feel of her fingers curling around his own, the baby softness of her tiny nails.

Mama's gonna buy you a diamond ring.

And the pain, the awful, heart-shattering pain of That Day.

'It wasn't my fault!'

Sean's voice pulverises the blockage in his throat. The Baku's face twists away, as though the words are blows. But now his silence has been shattered there seem to be no other words but these, nothing else to say but this. Four burning words, screamed over and over and over.

'*It wasn't my fault it wasn't my fault it wasn't my fault it wasn't my fault!*'

The rage that fills the Baku's eyes is swiftly replaced by fear. Its grip on Sean slackens and it staggers away from him, muscled chest heaving. The blowflies lift their weight from Sean's chest, a dark swirl on the air that arcs one way and then the other, as though in dazed confusion.

Sean turns the gun on the Baku, but he does not pull the trigger. An exquisite agony fills the beast's face and it roars at the sky, a bellow of rage and pain so intense it seems to fill every corner of the world. Sean feels the ground vibrate as the ink-filled veins beneath the soil retreat, narrowing as they stream back towards the writing shed. The Baku's ivory skin begins to peel away, shedding itself to the night, like cinders from a fire.

Sean is unaware he is still shouting until he tastes blood at the back of his throat. His voice is ragged and hoarse.

'…my fault it wasn't my fault it wasn't my fault…'

'Easy, lad, easy, easy…' Grandad sounds like he is a thousand miles away, but he is kneeling beside Sean on the grass, his white hair aglow in the moon's silvery light, an elderly angel. He places his hands over Sean's, prises the gun from his hands. And still Sean frames those words, his voice a tremulous, tear-soaked whisper.

'…wasn't my fault it wasn't my fault it wasn't my fault…'

'Easy, now. I got you,' Grandad says, rocking him. 'You're alright, lad, you're alright.'

Sean twists round, searching for the Baku. There is no sign of it. And by the moon's thin light, he can see the garden is changing. The withered flowers are lifting their heads, the petals are unfurling, filling with colour. The Baku's prowling stink has been replaced by the autumn smell of freshly fallen rain and clean soil. He looks up into Grandad's face. There is nothing covering his eyes, no creeping veins of ink beneath his skin.

'It wasn't my fault.'

'No, lad.' Tears stand in Grandad's starshine eyes and he pulls his grandson close, embracing him as the garden around them heals. 'Of course it wasn't your fault. None of it was your fault. You're alright now, lad. Your mother can't hurt you anymore.'

AFTER

Grandad has had the writing shed knocked down and a bank of flowers now occupies the space where it once stood. Though the cherubs resumed their benign expressions as soon as the Baku disappeared, Sean had slung them in the skip that Grandad hired for disposing of the shed.

Now, the garden lies beneath a light touching of frost, bearing no hint of its previous malady. Sean knows the sickness will not return. The grief he feels for Emma is still there, but the guilt is not, and it was this that the Baku had drawn strength from.

He knows too, after talking with Grandad, that the old man has long been haunted by demons of his own. His breakdown and subsequent alcoholism following the death of his wife was the reason his daughter was taken from him and put into care. Though neither Sean nor his grandad can ever know what happened to Stella during those turbulent years, they scarred her in ways so irrevocable that she emerged from their shadow a completely different person.

Sean feels bad for the girl his mum had been when she had lost her own mother and watched her dad slide into depression and alcoholism, but he cannot bring himself to feel bad for the woman she became. Too vividly, he remembers the cruel taunts she slung his way, mocking him for his twisted legs, openly admitting when she was pregnant with Emma – even as she drew heroin into a syringe – that she was going to avoid 'cotton candy', her nickname for crystal meth, because she was sure that was what had caused Sean's deformity. She said it openly, without shame, the glance at her son's twisted legs enough to convey who out of the two of them was the most flawed.

For years Grandad had tried to make amends with his daughter, and for a long time, she refused all contact with him. A few days after Sean's moonlit flight from the Baku, the old man had removed the box with the silver clasps from the writing shed, and together with Sean had gone through some of the unposted letters he had written to his daughter. Put together they formed a sort of desperate journal, cataloguing his desire to reconcile and put the past behind them.

It was only when Grandad had offered to help Stella out financially that she had agreed to meet with him, but when Grandad discovered she was using his money to fund her drug habit he confronted her, told her he wouldn't give her any more handouts until she was clean and sober. He offered to pay for rehab, but Stella had no interest in beating her addiction, nor did she have any interest in fostering a relationship with her father without his weekly cash deposits. Whatever flimsy relationship Grandad had managed to build with her quickly disintegrated from there, and Stella severed all contact.

As soon as Grandad heard about his granddaughter's death, he had fought for custody of Sean. He wanted to make amends, to do right by his grandson. What he had not anticipated was how much the boy's arrival would affect him. Every time he looked into Sean's eyes, he saw his daughter looking back at him. The boy's presence served as a daily reminder of his failings as a father, and the spiralling darkness of his thoughts reawakened the unhealed grief of his wife's death. Sean's arthrogryposis and conversion disorder, the death of his granddaughter: all of it could be followed back to the point at which Stella was taken from him and put into care.

Guilt and grief were The Paddock's afflictions, these the diseases Sean saw in Grandad's eyes.

Now, Grandad gently lowers the crate containing Violet and Olive onto the grass beneath the rowan tree. They have grown a lot over the past few weeks, their bellies rounding, their furred coats of quills making them look like smaller versions of their mother. In a few weeks, Sean will release them back into the wild.

'Do you think they'll be alright out here?' Sean says.

'Aye, they'll be grand. They've gotten used to you though, lad, I don't know whether they'll be going anywhere, not when they've got it made so good here.'

Sean watches the hoglets lift their noses and sniff at the air. He wonders if they sense the danger that surrounds them in this new environment, the myriad ways their tiny lives can be snuffed out. Instead of panic, Sean feels a resigned acceptance. He has done, and will continue to do, all he can for them, but he knows he can't control everything.

Tomorrow Grandad is taking him back to the sculpture park to see the Henry Moore exhibition. He has signed up for a local sculpture class and has a meeting with his old headteacher to discuss returning to school. He never thought it could be possible, but he is almost looking forward to getting back to class.

The doorbell rings and Sean looks over his shoulder towards the house. Noticing the sudden tension in the boy, Grandad lays a hand on his shoulder.

'Do you want me to answer that?'

Sean shakes his head and goes inside. At the door, he hesitates, gripping the door handle. Fear knots his throat and he wonders whether his conversion disorder is returning. He still has bad days, occasions where words scream to a stop, as though someone has pulled a handbrake on his voice. With help from Miraede, he has learned how to handle such episodes, but they can leave him wallowing in mute despair for hours.

He thinks of Gracie, Arlo and Jake, waiting for him on the other side of the door. He has finally mustered the courage to invite them over, but he can feel the old trepidations creeping over him, slowly turning him to stone.

Will they be angry with me? Should I apologise straight away for the way I've ignored them all this time? For never reading their letters and refusing to see them when they came to find me at Creswick Hall? What if I lose my voice again? What will they think of me then? So much has changed. What do I say to them? I'm not the same person I was back when we used to knock about on Dulwood.

But then he remembers something Jake had said the day Sean painted the four of them as Escapists across the side of the old community centre.

We get out together or we don't get out at all.

It had always been the four of them, dragging each other up, watching each other's backs. They had planned to get out of Dulwood together, but after Emma, Sean had forgotten them. He had left them on Dulwood and forgotten their pact.

We get out together or we don't get out at all.

Sean lost Emma, but now he knows he has not lost everything.

He opens the door.

THE END

ABOUT THE AUTHOR

Rosanna Boyle studied Classical Civilisation at the University of Leeds, after which she worked in a variety of jobs – none of which had anything to do with her degree. *The Book of the Baku* is her debut novel. Rosanna lives in Leeds with her husband and three sons.

ACKNOWLEDGEMENTS

I would like to say a huge thank you to Laura West, who picked this book up and changed my life as a writer. Thank you for your unfaltering belief in this story, for your clear-sighted guidance and your support throughout. I could not have done it without you! Many thanks to my wonderful agent, Veronique Baxter, to Sara Langham, and everyone at David Higham who has worked on this book to make it a success.

My endless appreciation goes out to my brilliant editor, George Sandison. This book deals with some fairly contentious issues and it really needed someone willing to take a chance on it. I am hugely grateful to you for taking that chance. Additional thanks to Natasha Qureshi, whose feedback and ideas helped strengthen the book, to Sarah Mather and all of the publicity and marketing teams at Titan. *The Book of The Baku* could not have found a more fitting home.

I'd like to thank Julia Lloyd for the stunning cover, which blew away any expectations I had dared to have, and also for the beautiful typesetting. Thanks also to Dan Coxon for the super sharp copy edit.

Thank you to Helen and Riley at Helicon Designs for all your help putting together my website – I could not have come up with anything near as good! Thanks to Philip Womack for the early read, and all the team at Jericho Writers.

Beth, for so so many things, not least the surprise lockdown coffee/cookie delivery. You are a wonder! Alison, for all those book chats over coffee and for being so pleased when I told you the one I was writing was really going to be a proper book! Marion, who knows all the reasons why, I love you! Nicole, for reading my short stories long ago, for encouraging me with this book, and further inspiring the next.

My incredible parents, Maria and Alan, for bringing me up around books and pretending not to know when I was reading them in the middle of the night by torchlight. To the O'Neills, Aldo, Richard, Daniel, Ruth, Vicky. Nanna Vera, who fostered my love of stories and who told all the best ones. She would have loved this so much. Thank you Madge and Frankie, the greatest in-laws I could have hoped for, and Dec, Gemma, Frankie, for all your support.

And now the big guns! A giant thank you to my boys, Barney, Milo and Eric. You three inspire me every single day and your excitement for this book has blown my mind! And Owen. Thank you. For telling me to keep at it on the bad days, for celebrating with me on the good. For reading and re-reading every draft of this book. For your endless encouragement. For everything, always.

ALSO AVAILABLE FROM TITAN BOOKS

NEAR THE BONE

BY CHRISTINA HENRY

A woman trapped on a mountain attempts to survive more than one kind of monster, in a dread-inducing horror novel from the national bestselling author Christina Henry.

Mattie can't remember a time before she and William lived alone on a mountain together. She must never make him upset. But when Mattie discovers the mutilated body of a fox in the woods, she realizes that they're not alone after all. There's something in the woods that wasn't there before, something that makes strange cries in the night, something with sharp teeth and claws. When three strangers appear on the mountaintop looking for the creature in the woods, Mattie knows their presence will anger William. Terrible things happen when William is angry.

"A true page-turner."
PAUL TREMBLAY, Bram Stoker and British Fantasy Award-winning author of *A Head Full of Ghosts*, *The Cabin at the End of the World*, *Survivor Song* and more

"Henry's storytelling is her own sort of witchcraft."
CHRISTOPHER GOLDEN, *New York Times* bestselling author of *Ararat*

ALSO AVAILABLE FROM TITAN BOOKS

DRACULA'S CHILD

BY J. S. BARNES

Evil never truly dies . . . and some legends live forever. In *Dracula's Child*, the dark heart of Bram Stoker's classic is reborn. Capturing the voice, tone, style and characters of the original yet with a modern sensibility this novel is perfect for fans of *Dracula* and contemporary horror.

It has been some years since Jonathan and Mina Harker survived their ordeal in Transylvania and, vanquishing Count Dracula, returned to England to try and live ordinary lives. But shadows linger long and, the older their son Quincey gets, the deeper the shadows at the heart of the Harker family. Whilst, on the Continent, the vestiges of something forgotten long is finally beginning to stir.

"Inventive and spooky."
MARK GATISS, co-creator of the hit BBC series *Dracula* and *Sherlock*

"A patchwork of dark thrills, woven skilfully from new and familiar voices – *Dracula's Child* is a macabre delight."
ALIYA WHITELEY, author of *The Beauty*

"It's a monumental achievement. The tale is engrossing, the tone is spot-on."
STEPHEN GALLAGHER, author of *The Authentic William James*, and TV writer for *Doctor Who*